CO
JUSTICE

Vish Dhamija is the bestselling author of eleven works of crime fiction, including *Unlawful Justice*, *Bhendi Bazaar*, *The Mogul*, *The Heist Artist, Doosra* and *Prisoner's Dilemma*. He is frequently referred to in the Indian press as the 'master of crime and courtroom drama'. In August 2015, after the release of his first legal thriller, *Déjà Karma*, *Glimpse* magazine called him 'India's John Grisham' for stimulating the genre of legal fiction in India. Vish lives in London with his wife, Nidhi.

COLD JUSTICE

VISH DHAMIJA

PAN

First published 2022 by Pan
an imprint of Pan Macmillan Publishing India Private Limited
707 Kailash Building
26 K. G. Marg, New Delhi 110001
www.panmacmillan.co.in

Pan Macmillan, 6 Briset St, Farringdon, London EC1M 5NR
Associated companies throughout the world
www.panmacmillan.com

ISBN 978-93-90742-48-6

1 3 5 7 9 8 6 4 2

Typeset in Adobe Garamond Pro by R. Ajith Kumar, New Delhi
Printed and bound in India by Replika Press Pvt. Ltd.

THE BATTLE OF JHELUM

326 BC

The Battle of Jhelum was fought between King Porus of the Paurva kingdom (in the north-west Indian subcontinent) and King Alexander on the banks of the river Jhelum. The Greek emperor defeated Porus and made him a prisoner.

Legend has it that when Alexander asked Porus how he wished to be treated, the captive king proudly replied, 'Treat me as a king would treat another king.' Impressed, Alexander indeed treated him like a king, letting him retain his land.

PART 1

THE CRIME

'There are crimes of passion, and there are crimes of logic. The boundary between them is not defined.'

– ALBERT CAMUS (1913–1960)

ONE

1

SEVEN MISSED CALLS?

Akash Hingorani was awakened by a hard jolt as the aircraft wheels thudded on the tarmac. Still groggy, he glanced at his watch. British Airways flight BA256 was bang on time. It had taken off after a slight delay from New Delhi's Indira Gandhi International Airport at 1105 hours and was now taxiing towards Heathrow's Terminal Five at 1520 hours. He pursed his lips, stretched his arms and rubbed his eyes before gazing out the window. London in January was exactly as per the textbook. The weather outside was wet and cold. And it was already getting dark. The UK had never been his chosen destination for a vacation at this time of the year, but he had been invited to speak at a college in Cambridge. For whatever reason he had accepted the invite back in October, he failed to recollect. But that was then, and he was here now.

The air hostess announced that the passengers could switch on their mobile phones but Akash wasn't expecting any calls, so he decided to keep his phone switched off. Who'd call him? It had been barely nine hours since he had left Delhi, and it was well past office hours in India. His hosts, here in the United Kingdom, had told him they'd arrange for his pick-up and the commute from London to Cambridge. One Mr Brown would be waiting for Akash Hingorani when he exited Security.

T5 was an exclusive British Airways terminal, and a shuttle service connected it to the immigration concourse. It was on the bus that he switched on his mobile phone.

There were missed calls. Seven. Missed. Calls.

All of them were from the same person – Judge Shilpa Singh.

Akash immediately checked his voicemail and heard her last message first: '*Where are you? I've been calling you non-stop … it's really urgent. Call me back as soon as you get my message; I need you.*'

He listened to all seven of the voicemails she had left on his phone. Each an encore of the other. *I need to speak to you.* Shilpa Singh wouldn't have called him if it weren't something grave. And she didn't sound like she *needed* him to attend a black-tie event with her. If anything, her voice was shriller than usual, as if she was in some kind of trouble. Anxious? Scared? Angry? Akash couldn't decipher, but it had to be something crucial if she'd called him seven times in the span of an hour.

What could have been so pressing?

He wanted to call back immediately, but he reckoned the background noise in the shuttle would not allow any comprehensible conversation. And anyway, it had been more than a few hours since the last call. Whatever emergency there might have been, Shilpa must have settled it if she hadn't called after 16:30, India time.

The business class queue at immigration was shorter. And the board in front of him clearly stated that passengers should refrain from using mobile phones while talking to officers at the desk, so he spent another fifteen minutes worrying himself sick. Once he got to the other side, he pressed call to return the last missed call. It went straight to her voicemail.

'Hello Judge, this is Akash returning your calls … Apologies for missing your calls. I was on a flight and couldn't call back earlier, but give me a call whenever you have a moment, please?'

Akash looked at his watch again. It was ten minutes past four in London, which meant it was 08:40 at night in Delhi. She couldn't have gone to sleep. Then it occurred to him that her phone hadn't rung at all, which indicated it might have been switched off. She wasn't the sort of person who switched off their mobile phone. Who switched off their phone these days anyway? And she had a child who stayed in a hostel – parents with children in boarding schools never switch off their phones. It could be out of juice, and maybe she had forgotten to recharge it? That could be a plausible explanation, but Akash wasn't convinced. She wouldn't just let her phone battery run dry and not bother to charge it. For her to be desperate enough to call him – *him of all people* – seven times.

No, something didn't sit right.

He called again as he waited at the carousel for his bag. Same result. Was there any sense in leaving yet another message for her? She would get the first voicemail and would see his missed calls whenever she switched on her phone. She'd know he'd called. He tried his luck once more as he eventually picked up his bag after a twenty-minute wait. It went straight to voicemail, yet again.

Hmm. Think, Akash!

Was she okay? Maybe she'd had an accident and had been taken into some hospital for surgery? But why would she call him? She'd have called an ambulance instead. He failed to work out what could have been so serious, as he walked out of the exit. There, he spotted the driver, Mr Brown, holding a sign with his name on it. A rotund English gentleman in his fifties, Mr Brown was clean-shaven and wearing a dark suit. His red face revealed that he enjoyed beer more than he should. Akash waved at him, and he smiled back in acknowledgement.

'Good afternoon, and welcome to England, Mr Hingorani,' he said as he took the bag from Akash.

'Good afternoon, Mr Brown,' Akash responded. 'And please call me Akash. Mr Hingorani makes me feel old.'

'You're a young lad, Akash,' Mr Brown chuckled. 'I'm Jim, by the way.'

'Jim, I need to make an urgent call before we leave. If it's okay with you, will you please pick up coffee for us both while I make this call. And then we can be on our way.'

'It's fine by me. It's a two-hour drive, give or take. Even if we leave here by five, we should be fine. Anyway, it can't get any darker.' He chuckled again and walked towards a Costa concession within the terminal.

Akash followed him as he put on his earphones and called Shilpa again. No response. It was getting late in Delhi – maybe he would hear from her tomorrow morning?

Should he be worried?

Well, there was only one way to find out.

He scrolled through his contacts and called his friend Vansh back in Delhi. Vansh Diwan, like Akash, was a defence lawyer.

Vansh was pedigreed – he was a third-generation lawyer and headed a large legal firm called Diwan-e-Khaas. The two had been classmates in law school, along with Vansh's wife, Priti, who had found her calling in corporate law, unlike the two men.

'Hey Akash,' Vansh didn't sound sleepy. 'How was your flight?'

'Good, and on time. You, okay?'

'I'm fine, thanks. What about you – are you missing us already?' teased Vansh. On not hearing his friend hit back with a retort, he suddenly became serious. 'Is something wrong?' Maybe something in Akash's voice had given away the anxiety that had been building inside him for the past hour or so.

'Why would you think something's wrong?'

'You didn't react to my wisecrack like your normal self, that's why.'

'Well, now that you ask, something doesn't seem right. I received seven missed calls from Judge Shilpa Singh – seven, can you believe it – asking me to call back urgently. I've been trying to reach her ever since I landed here, but her phone seems to be switched off. Any idea why she'd be calling me?'

'For old time's sake?' Vansh jested. He was one of the few people in legal circles who knew Akash had dated the judge a while back. Not an ideal scenario, but there you go.

'Touché! But, my dear friend, we haven't spoken to each other for about nine months now.'

'Maybe she'd called to tell you that you're the father of the child she's just delivered. The timing seems correct, if it's been nine months, a tiny little Hingorani—'

'Vansh, I'm serious.'

'Oh, okay. I haven't heard anything, but to be honest I haven't stepped out of my office since the afternoon. I'm still at my desk working on the big case I mentioned to you last week, so if something *has* actually happened, I would have missed it. Tell you what, why don't you give me ten minutes, I'll make some calls and get back to you – how does that sound?'

'Yeah, call me as soon as you can with whatever you can find out or could you send someone to her house, please?'

'Will do. Give me ten minutes.'

Akash was paying for coffee when Vansh called back. It had taken Vansh under five minutes and a single call to find out what had happened.

'Hold on a minute,' Akash said and walked away from the till, leaving Jim to collect their order.

'She's been arrested.'

'Who's been arrested?'

'Judge Shilpa Singh, who else would I be talking about?'

'You're shitting me. She's a sitting judge; how could she be arrested?'

'For your information, there is no statute in India that prevents a judge from being arrested—'

'Vansh … please focus! What's happened to Shilpa?'

'She was arrested on a murder charge this afternoon. First-degree homicide.'

'What the fuck—' Akash realized his voice had gone up a few decibels, and the use of unparliamentary language at the crowded airport terminal was earning him unwanted attention.

'Vansh, please leave everything you're doing, right now, and find out more. Please.'

'I'm sure there must've been some kind of mix-up—'

'Vansh, no one arrests a sitting judge on a murder charge because of a misunderstanding. It's got to be something grave. I'm coming back. I'll call you again as soon as I get a ticket for a return flight. Please get her out, post bail, call in all your chips, whatever it takes … Could you do that for me, please?' The anxiety was building up.

'Calm down, Akash. I've texted a few of my staff. I'll find out where she is, and we'll get her out in no time. Don't worry. I'm here and I shall take care of this.'

'Thanks, buddy. I owe you one.'

'Thank me later. Just stay cool, okay?'

'Okay, my friend.'

2

'SHOULD WE LEAVE NOW?' Jim Brown walked up to Akash with two deep red Costa cups in his hands. Costa claimed that all their cups were recycled. Really? What about the cups that weren't disposed of correctly? *Everybody lies*, thought Akash, but let it go. There were other important things on his mind.

'There's been an emergency back home.' Akash took a sip. 'I need to return immediately.'

'You mean go back to Delhi?'

'Unfortunately, yes.'

'I'm so sorry to hear this. Please let me know if I can help in any way.'

'Where's Departures?'

'Come, follow me.'

Jim took Akash to the elevator to the Departure lounge.

'May I help you?' the lady behind the counter asked.

'I'd like to leave for New Delhi today, right now, as soon as possible, please.'

'Do you have a ticket?'

'Yes, but it's for Friday evening.'

'And it's only Monday today. Let me check.'

Akash passed the printout to her. She looked at it, typed something into her computer. After a brief pause, she said: 'There are business-class seats on a flight that leaves at 1855 hours today. It will reach New Delhi at 0850—'

Red flipping eye!

'But you have to leave for Security right away—'

'Please book a seat for me. It's an emergency.'

'It will cost you ...'

Akash took out his American Express and handed it to her. 'Will that be all, Akash?' asked Jim.

'I'm sorry to have troubled you—'

'It's no trouble, no trouble at all. I live in London, and my company will charge the clients who sent me, so no worries. And thanks for the coffee.'

Akash pulled out his wallet and handed a tenner to Jim, who thanked him and left.

3

AKASH HAD CLEARED SECURITY check at 17:40. He was among the first to board the flight at 18:25. He was also the first one to finish the welcome champagne before the doors closed. He tried calling Vansh a few times, but his friend's phone was busy. He must be making calls, Akash reckoned. He called his contact at Cambridge and explained that he'd had to return due to an emergency. The host sounded sympathetic to his circumstances and wished him luck. 'Hope all goes well. Keep us updated,' he said.

At 18:55, BA 257 had started taxiing on the runway. There was traffic, and their aircraft was third in the queue.

The flight was finally airborne at 19:22.

So much for a round trip to London, Akash winced.

There are over thirty-one million seconds in a single year. If the angels of death or shocking news, like this one, could come by any second, there were over thirty-one million occasions for either to happen in any given year. It was simple math. But just when Shilpa needed him, he had to be entombed on a long flight, disconnected from the rest of the world.

C'est la vie!

TWO

1

'WHAT CAN I GET you, Mr Hingorani?'

Peace of mind? How about some reflexology to unwind my jangling nerves? Or anything else that could put me to sleep?

'Which single malts do you have?' he asked.

'We only have Glenfiddich and Glenlivet, sir.'

'Glenlivet, please.'

'Water or soda?'

'Just ice.'

'Okay, sir.'

A minute later a stewardess handed him a glass filled with ice cubes and two miniature bottles of Glenlivet. *Amusing*, he thought. In the economy class most airlines only ever give the passengers one bottle at a time. But if you could afford business class, it was taken as confirmation that you could handle more alcohol. Funny, right? As he upended his second drink, his thoughts segued back to Shilpa and whatever might have happened to her. How could she have been arrested? What kind of screw-up could make the police arrest a district court judge on a homicide charge? And who had she supposedly murdered?

He rang for assistance, and asked the flight attendant for another drink. Two more Glenlivet miniatures arrived along with another glass of ice.

'Thank you,' he said. 'Could I have some water too, please?'

'Yes, of course. I'm sorry, I thought you didn't ask for it the last time around so … I'll be back in a minute.'

The attendant returned with the water, along with the menu for dinner. 'Anything else?' she asked.

Akash figured that if he kept drinking whisky on the rocks, it would go straight to his head. He wanted to be clear-headed when his flight landed in New Delhi in the morning.

'That will be all, thank you.'

She switched off the call button and retreated behind the curtain.

They had broken up nine months ago. He hadn't even caught a glimpse of Shilpa in the courts for the past three or four months. Did she miss him? A better question, and one which he didn't wish to answer, was: did he miss *her*?

Memories could be a blessing and a curse. They kissed like an angel, they punched like a heavyweight champion; they could be a sweetheart or they could be a bitch. As the whisky calmed his nerves, the sweet reminiscences of yesterdays spent with Shilpa overwhelmed him. Faint recollections turned technicolour and grew into CinemaScope visions in his mind.

2

AKASH HAD NEVER SEEN Judge Shilpa Singh before he had walked into her court to defend his friend's employee on a false murder charge. After winning the trial, he had asked his friend Vansh Diwan, whether a lawyer dating a judge was a violation of the law the forefathers of the nation had put together. Of course not, not legally, at least, but there were bound to be repercussions if the media caught scent of such a relationship. And the media invariably sniffs out – like a pig trained to hunt truffle – anything that might work to their advantage. It would be the newsflash that the tabloids live and breathe for: *a criminal defence lawyer dating a judge*. So, although there were no rules that prevented the two legal brains courting, it was an unwritten no-no. Anyway, it was just a thought – a wicked one at that – and nothing would ever come out of it, Akash knew for sure.

But life is anything but simple.

When you spot a new word and look it up, the said word tends to appear more often than before in any text you read thereafter in the following days and weeks. Baader-Meinhof phenomenon, it's called. Likewise, if you see or meet a new person, there is always a high probability of just bumping into them again soon after. And again … and then again.

Right after Akash Hingorani's spectacular win in the court of Judge Shilpa Singh, there was a get-together at the Gymkhana Club of the who's who from Delhi's legal world. Both Vansh and Akash attended the event, as did Shilpa Singh.

'She's pretty,' Akash whispered to his friend.

'She's also a judge, and not some random judge in some alien town; she is one of the judges in whose court you will be regularly representing clients. She's an umpire in your playing field, Akash.' Vansh sounded serious. He was six-foot tall, trim with salt-and-pepper hair. His disposition was generally unsmiling unless he was inebriated, but on this occasion, he was sterner than usual, like a headmaster admonishing a recalcitrant student.

'And your point is?'

'Are you crazy – I mean, of course she's dazzling, but don't be stupid.' Vansh's words were an indication that it was something Akash shouldn't pursue.

But, Akash was smitten.

Shilpa was glowing in her deep grey saree with a pink border. Chiffon. It clung to her body like a second skin. She was shapely, wore subdued make-up, a light pink lipstick that seemed to be a compliment from whoever had woven the saree border. Her espresso hair fell straight down to her shoulders. Salon-dried, of course. She had definitely made an effort to exude that casual-glam look. Casual never just happened, Akash thought to himself. He couldn't figure out if she wore vertiginous heels under the saree, since she appeared a lot taller than he had imagined – almost as tall as him. She had been mostly seated during all their previous interactions. But whatever she did, Shilpa Singh always wore her trademark Usha Uthup-style big, round bindi. And yes, it was a matching pink, just like the lipstick, this time around.

Ignoring his friend's advice and throwing all caution to the wind, Akash walked up behind her.

'Hello, Judge.'

'Oh, hello Mr Hingorani,' she returned his smile.

'Nice to see you again.'

'Better here than in the courtroom, wouldn't you agree?' she retorted.

Oh, so she has a sense of humour too!

Then some apparently significant son-of-stupid came by and she turned to converse with him. Akash turned back to see Vansh shrug. *Told you so.*

But Akash was equally resolute. He pulled out his phone and called his driver, Mandeep. Driving was just one of the chores Mandeep carried out for his employer. Loyal like a Saint Bernard, Mandeep was more like Akash's major-domo; he carried out all routine tasks, and some not-so-routine ones too.

'*Jee,* sir?'

'Mandeep, I need a packet of India Kings. Could you get me one quickly, please?'

If Mandeep thought it was weird, he kept it to himself. Akash Hingorani wasn't a smoker. In fact, he had never smoked – except for a few careless drags at some party or a casual cigar at some get-together with old-time friends. But Mandeep wasn't one to question Akash's simple request. Maybe his boss wanted the smokes for someone else.

Five minutes later, Mandeep came to the party hall to deliver the cigarettes.

'Thank you, Mandeep, I have another small job for you,' Akash whispered, putting his arm around his driver as he walked him out of the party and into the garden. Mandeep had been Akash's driver for over a decade, and Akash could completely trust him. 'Judge Shilpa Singh … I want you to find out which car she had travelled in and then put it out of commission.'

'*Jee?*'

'Find her car without anyone realizing that you are looking for it. I don't care if you have to take the car's engine and drop it in the Yamuna River … her car shouldn't start when she leaves the party. Even a flat tyre would do. Okay?'

'Okay, sir.'

It was a childish plan, but Akash, being conscientious, hadn't given the instructions on the phone. The lawyer in him was acutely aware that Mandeep would be mixing with other drivers in the club's car park. Someone with sensitive ears could listen in to their conversation. But here, out in the garden, with his arm around his driver's shoulder, ensured a tête-à-tête no one else was privy to.

Vansh knew how Akash's brain was wired. They had known each other for over two decades now. He warned Akash again, and then left. Priti was waiting at home, he had said.

Thirty minutes later, Akash saw the judge say bye to everyone and leave.

He waited twenty seconds to make his exit. Shilpa was standing in the porch, talking to someone on the phone. She didn't sound impressed.

'Hello again, Judge,' he said as she finished her call. Then, as she turned towards him, he asked, 'Is everything alright?'

'My car, it's got two flat tyres.'

Two? Mandeep had certainly overdone it. One tyre would have done the job!

'That's odd – to have not one, but two flat tyres,' Akash recovered quickly. 'I mean what are the odds? Too many stray nails on the road, eh?'

'I know.'

'We can drop you,' he said, pointing to the gleaming black Jaguar Mandeep had brought around to pick him up.

'Thank you for the offer, but don't bother. I'm sure my

driver will fix the car somehow, or I will take a cab.'

'It's not a bother at all, and I'm not driving anyway; we'll drop you on the way. Where do you live?' he asked. *Saket*, he almost blurted out.

'Saket.'

'It's not too far. Come on, we'll drive you home.'

To his surprise, she accepted his offer. She called her driver to get the car fixed and bring it home later. Or leave it, go home, and get it up and running the next day, whichever worked.

'It's really nice of you to drop me home.'

'Your Honour, it's the least I could do.'

'Stop it. I'm not a judge here; this is not a courtroom,' she smiled.

'Okay, Judge.'

'Shilpa.'

'Okay, Shilpa.'

Bullseye!

3

FOR THEIR NEXT MEETING, Akash did not wait for a coincidence.

He called Shilpa on a Saturday morning, told her he was in the area and asked if she felt like a coffee. He mentioned he wanted to discuss a legal technicality, which didn't pertain to any case she was involved in. He had expected an excuse of some sort on legal grounds or an apology for being busy at the time, but he was delighted when she said that she was free to catch up.

They met at Select Citywalk in Saket.

The coffee was good. She liked it black, as did he. Making up a question on a moronic legal technicality was hardly a problem for Akash. She had come in jeans and a fitted shirt. Her three-inch heels gave her the same height as Akash, who considered himself tall. Five-nine. Which meant she was five-six. The bindi was conspicuously missing. Perhaps she only wore it when she met with people from the legal profession? Perhaps only when she wore Indian outfits?

However Akash looked, he found Shilpa Singh to be a remarkably beautiful woman, with her slender figure, high cheekbones, heart-shaped face and well-outlined lips. She had dimples when she smiled, which made her look like Simi Garewal from some twenty–thirty years ago. She had certainly got a haircut since Akash had seen her in court for the first time.

She was genial, not flirtatious at all. She gave him her opinion on the legal problem Akash had cooked up. If she understood that the point of this meeting was coffee and not the moot question he had posed, she did not show it. At least, she didn't show displeasure at his schoolboy tactic. All good. Somehow they began talking about how to discover good restaurants in Delhi.

'Have you been to the Dhaba?' asked Akash.

'Which *dhaba*?' Dhaba being a generic name for roadside eateries around the country, it was an obvious question.

'Okay, I won't ruin the suspense. Why don't I take you out for dinner at the Dhaba?'

She responded with a smile and a nod.

4

HE DROVE TO PICK her up – no Mandeep this time – for dinner at the Dhaba at Claridges on Aurangzeb Road. She wore a knee-length black dress, which hiked up to her mid-thigh when she got in the car, and he was left with his mouth agape. The moon shone through threadbare clouds, but enough light cascaded through the windshield for him to be mesmerized. Her skin shone like porcelain. She was a keeper, he instinctively knew. A Shangri-La moment. As he navigated the car through the roads choked by Delhi traffic, chicken drumsticks at the Dhaba were the last thing on his distracted mind.

She was wowed by the decor. Who wouldn't be? It was made to appear like a roadside – premium roadside, if there was anything like it – but the food and service were, of course, five-star.

'Are we on a date?' Shilpa suddenly asked, looking over the second glass of gin and tonic she was sipping from.

'What makes you say that?' Akash was taken aback. He wanted to say *yes*, he would have said yes if it were someone else, but he didn't know if he should. How would she react, and how would it impact their professional relationship?

'That's not the answer to my question, is it?'

'Isn't the food great?'

'Nope – that's not the answer to my question either.'

'Oh, you are a judge, aren't you?'

'Still not the answer to my question. Let me ask you again: Are we on a date Akash?'

'What does it look like?'

'Besides being bad manners to respond to a question with another question, it still doesn't answer my question, Mr Hingorani.'

'I'd like to think that we are,' he said softly.

'But?'

The waiter arrived with the hors d'oeuvres. Prawns for her, chicken wings for him.

And Akash was spared from responding.

5

THEY MET A FEW more times. Acutely aware of the fact that their relationship was akin to one of matches and gunpowder, that the consequences of the two of them dating was just the kind of fodder the media loved to scavenge on, that the conflict of interest could complicate things for them, they still decided to cross the line.

They were careful enough to meet at places where no one important could recognize them. At Pandara Road, for example, where the food was delicious without any hoo-ha. No one made them out, which made the evenings even more sublime. To Akash, it felt like the fulfilment of a sweet promise they had never made. It was pure bliss!

Had he found love? Finally?

THREE

1

THE STEWARDESS WAS BACK with Akash's dinner after a while: lamb chops with sweet potato mash, a side salad of beetroot and some other mix of indistinguishable veggies shredded thinner than rice noodles. But the best part was the bottle of Pinot noir that accompanied the food. Four shots of whisky and then a bottle of wine was the perfect recipe to induce sleep. He no longer had an appetite – what with all the liquid he'd swallowed and the news of Shilpa having been arrested and then no word from Vansh regarding her release. Nevertheless, he consumed the food. Once his stomach was full, he reclined his seat, got under the blanket and tried to sleep. He needed to be sharp when he got off the flight in the morning. But sleep was a long time coming. Memories flooded back yet again.

2

'I LIKE THE SECRECY of the whole thing, the shiftiness, the stealth, if you know what I mean. It makes me feel younger.

Like I'm in school, having a clandestine affair with my teacher, and no one should know about it. The cliché, stolen kisses are the sweetest, comes to mind. The whole thing has an air of mystery, don't you think?' Akash confided about his affair to Priti and Vansh.

'Oh, you are falling for the teacher. Mark my words,' Vansh highlighted, 'and which by the way cannot be a good thing.'

'Remind me how old you are again?' Priti asked. The three of them had been batchmates and were the same age. However, the two men looked considerably older than her. Her career as a corporate legal advisor was less stressful than her two friends' who would have to sometimes represent the scum of the earth in the courtroom. She was petite, five-four, and had the tanned skin tone of a Mediterranean woman. Her dark auburn hair – obviously coloured – was stylishly cut in steps for more volume. She was a demure, pretty woman in her forties, who exuded girl-next-door vibes.

'Only a year younger than you, gorgeous,' Akash retorted.

They were at Akash's residence in Vasant Vihar. The house was a strange juxtaposition of old and new. The building was an old one but the carpets were the only things from the bygone days. The rest of the items in the house were contemporary: paintings, decor and technology that would dazzle a geek. Akash Hingorani was one of the most sought-after bachelors in town. At forty-two, he was greying at the sideburns, but the rest of his head was more pepper than salt: long, straight hair worn back from his forehead. He was sinewy, but that was due to the time he spent at his home gym in the basement. The cleft chin on his perfectly symmetrical face, his charming smile and gentle eyes did the rest. Flamboyant, sharp-witted, theatrical, he was in the right profession. It was no surprise that he was the most expensive and celebrated defence lawyer in Delhi, maybe even in the country. But, despite the looks, image and wherewithal, he wasn't rutting around. He didn't have a playboy or a Lothario image in the press. He was, in his own words, *happy being single*.

'You're nuts,' Priti rolled her eyes in jest.

'You bet! He's got two, and they are going blue at the moment,' Vansh jibed. 'There's no future in what you're thinking, my friend,' he added. 'How do you see any of this working out for both of you? How would you represent anyone in her court? Forget that – with your spouse or partner being part of the judicial community, you'd be plagued with accusations of manipulation in the courtroom, day in, day out–'

'I'll quit.' Akash raised his glass to take a sip of the cognac the three had poured a while back.

'You'll quit what?' asked Priti.

'Quit practising law.'

'And do what?'

'I think I'll write a book.'

'You think? So, should I call up Pan Macmillan and tell them to start saving for an advance? The great Akash Hingorani is about to write the bestseller of the twenty-first century, the much-awaited sequel *To Kill All the Birds* maybe, or *A Mockingbird in Love*?' Vansh sounded part flippant, part flabbergasted at his friend's revelation. He shook his head in disbelief.

'I'm serious.'

'Why don't you write a graphic novel instead? Maybe some love scenes with—'

'Shilpa is a beautiful woman, not just on the surface but on the inside too. Real love comes along only once in a lifetime, don't you think so?'

'Do you know how crazy you sound?' Priti asked.

'Crazy in love.'

'How do you even know it *is* love?'

'You can't define love, but you know when it happens.'

'*Jai gurudev* …' Vansh folded his hands and let it go.

Several such interactions later, Akash introduced Shilpa to his friends.

3

'I HAVE A MAN in my life,' Shilpa told Akash when they woke up together one morning. She occasionally stayed back at his house after long evenings. 'Someone I've never told you about.'

Surprised as he was, he also found her admission intriguing. 'Do tell.'

'I'm surprised you didn't bother to dig into this. I've been married previously.'

Akash didn't say a word. He raised his eyebrows questioningly. He hadn't; he didn't think her past mattered to him at all.

'I married young. My husband was in the army, like my father. So, sometimes he would have to move to locations where he could not take his family. I stayed in Delhi for a while. That's when I enrolled in college and completed my law degree. Unfortunately …' Akash could see her eyes moisten, her voice was cracking. '… Major Rajendra Singh was posted in Jammu when he and three other members of his battalion were ambushed by an insurgent group late one night as they were driving back to their station. The four men succumbed to the crude bomb thrown at the jeep they were travelling in.'

'I'm sorry. I did not know about this ...'

'Technically, I'm a war widow.'

'So, who's the man in your life now?'

'I have a son.'

'Aha, so why haven't I met him yet?'

She pulled out a tissue from the box at the bedside and dabbed her face. 'Let me get us some coffee ...' Akash pecked her on the cheek, which tasted of the salty residue of her tears, and got out of bed.

Over coffee Shilpa told him about her son, Raghuveer Singh, who studied at Woodstock in Mussoorie. Since she had a demanding job, and there was no one else to look after Raghuveer, she had thought it best to put him in a boarding school, away from Delhi. It was also for security reasons, since what she did sometimes antagonized people who weren't exactly long-listed for awards for exemplary morals. It made sense.

Raghuveer was fourteen, and it was imperative that he and Akash got along for any kind of relationship between Shilpa and him to move forward, she explained. They came as a package, Shilpa was clear about that. She was a mother first, a judge second and a woman third, if she were ever forced to prioritize. It was not unusual for a single parent to put their child above all else, Akash could appreciate that; he had been a single parent's child.

'We should plan a trip to Mussoorie together,' Akash said after a brief pause.

'We should, but I think I should speak to him first before introducing you in person as his mother's … friend … or boyfriend, don't you think?'

Wasn't there a Yiddish saying: *If you want to make God laugh, tell him your plans*?

They worked rather well together on a personal and physical level. The lovemaking was intense; in the little time they had been together, they had come to memorize each other's curves and learn about the right switches to touch and hit. But Akash couldn't help but notice that the goodness of Shilpa's inner being was in stark contrast with his professional life.

Quitting the life of a defence advocate and writing a book were great romantic fantasies and good party lines, but the reality was different. Truth be told, being a defence lawyer didn't bother his conscience too much. There had been times Akash had defended serial criminals, people he knew were definitely in the wrong, but he had still gone ahead and done his job. Even the worst people on the planet have the right to a defence advocate. Shilpa's attempt at awakening his inner voice might have been good for him personally, but it was certainly bad for his career. This conflict of interest between a defence advocate and a judge were bound to surface at some point. And it reared its ugly head soon enough.

Did she think he represented vampires? Their conversations had started to head in the inevitable direction.

'But … you defend those who are guilty,' she said.

'We're all guilty … of something.'

'What do you mean?'

'If you saw someone pocketing a stack of stapler pins from your office, would you report it to the authorities?'

'No.'

'And if you saw someone stealing five lakh rupees from your office, would you?'

'Of course.'

'But they are both thieves since they stole something, so they are both guilty, aren't they?'

'Oh … puh-leeeese, don't go all philosophical on me. We both know what I mean.'

The strain eventually began weighing heavily on the relationship. Both had demanding jobs, and the added pressure of leading a cautious life to keep their affair hidden from the public became taxing. The brain, which is the most powerful part of the human body, was overcome by the stress. With their minds so out of sync, the physical relationship started to decline too. Lovemaking became mere sex – a mechanical activity.

Besides, tongues had started wagging in and around courtrooms. A judge and advocate romancing was certainly non-conservative, to say the least. And if rumours had started doing the rounds of the courtroom, the media couldn't be far behind.

The two were mature enough to comprehend which way the relationship was headed. They decided to part ways amicably six months after their first real date. A short-lived romance …

After they parted ways, two of Akash's cases were assigned to Shilpa's court, but he never made an appearance. He had decided to have no dealings with Judge Shilpa Singh in a professional capacity. He didn't want his client to win or lose because of his past with her. The first one, he let his junior take lead in the courtroom trial, and the other case he passed on to Vansh.

4

AKASH WAS UP BEFORE the flight was due to land at Indira Gandhi International Airport. He declined the breakfast that was offered. He had gone to sleep for a while after 11:00 p.m. UK time, so he'd had four hours of sleep, possibly less. He was also exhausted from the seventeen-plus hours of flying in the past twenty-four hours.

The moment they announced that the passengers could switch on their mobile phones, Akash called Vansh, who informed him that Shilpa's bail had been posted, and that he was waiting to take her to his residence in Defence Colony.

So, she had spent the night in a police station?

In light of what had happened, Shilpa had no doubt made it to the front page of most newspapers. It was a wise decision to take her to Vansh's house. The media circus would have indeed gathered outside her apartment. Vansh had sounded like he was with other people at the time, so he couldn't elaborate on the why or the what or the how. 'We should be home before you,' Vansh added before disconnecting.

Ordinarily, a defendant charged with a capital offence couldn't be released on bail if the proof of their guilt was evident or the presumption of guilt was overbearing. With the little information Akash had at the moment, he was certain there had to be an industrial-scale goof-up for the police to have arrested a judge on homicide charges. But these were anything but ordinary circumstances. One didn't come across esteemed members of the judiciary accused of murdering people on the street every day.

Once out of the aircraft, he rushed to the immigration desk only to encounter one of the few jovial officers there, just when he wasn't in the mood. The officer looked up at Akash as he glanced at his passport. 'Did you only go to England to deliver a parcel?'

'Yes, sir,' Akash responded, 'and you know what? I forgot to take it with me. I'm only back to pick it up and leave by the next flight.'

The officer smiled, stamped the passport and handed it over to Akash.

After collecting his bag from the luggage carousel, he walked through the green channel to find Mandeep waiting for him. But before the two walked out of the airport, Akash saw a couple of newspapers at a shop on the way. *The Times* and *The Express*. The headlines stopped him in his tracks:

JUDGE OR EXECUTIONER? DELHI DISTRICT JUDGE ARRESTED FOR MURDER.

But that wasn't all. The picture on the front page of the newspapers was one of Shilpa walking out of a restaurant on Pandara Road. It was obvious someone had cropped out her companion. Akash knew who had been cut off from the frame. The image was about a year old. Someone had photographed him and Shilpa together on one of their secret dates and and kept the photo all this while, waiting for the right opportunity. And this was as good an occasion to publish it as it could ever get.

Akash was outraged. Having been a lawyer for so long and being exposed to all sorts of evil and deception had invariably made him sceptical of coincidences. Coincidences were a myth. The man in him could let it slip as one, but the lawyer in him didn't permit it. Whoever it was, they knew Akash Hingorani would come to defend the judge, and they were rattling his chain, or was it a warning of some sort? Someone had leaked this particular image to the media; this wasn't happenstance at all, no, sir. It's funny when you think about it, that a picture is indeed worth a thousand words. But whoever it was who did this should have known that pushing Akash Hingorani would only make him come after them, not scare him.

'Mandeep, we need to go to Def Col.' Mandeep didn't need telling where in Def Col. He had driven Akash to and from the Diwans more times than he could count. *Had he heard the news?* Akash wondered. After all, Mandeep had known about Akash's short-lived love affair with the judge, but he knew better than to ask or mention anything. If he was surprised that his boss was back in the country in less than twenty-four hours, he didn't make it obvious.

'*Jee*, sir.'

The Delhi rush hour had begun. They weren't getting to Defence Colony anytime soon, Akash knew. He had bought four newspapers at the airport before exiting. At first glance, the reaction to Judge Shilpa Singh's arrest seemed mixed.

Some of the publications were unequivocal about their faith in the judge, some were slightly insulting, some abstained from commenting until they had completely gauged the direction of the wind, while others, having already picked a side, blathered nonsense. Akash settled down with *The Times* to read the details.

5

FOR THE VAST MAJORITY of the 1.3 billion people in India, crime means crime, and consequently, a criminal is a criminal. They were naive because they didn't deal with criminals day after day. The world of crime existed on the periphery for them. It didn't even occur to most of these people that when they paid an unauthorized broker to procure a driving licence for their children, it was bribery, which is a crime. The same principle applied when they greased someone's palms to move their loan application up the pile. When they availed out-of-turn favours …

Everyone's guilty of something.

However, for most people the biggest window into crime and the criminal world was the news they read or watched on TV. But there are different kinds of criminals, of course. Accidental criminals are the ones who end up doing something on the spur of the moment and repent it their entire lives. Someone passes a lewd comment at the lady you are with and you, in a fit of rage, attack and hurt him. Or when someone occasionally drinks and drives … these are all accidental crimes. Then there are opportunistic criminals like chain-snatchers, pickpockets – who strike whenever they get a chance. Then come the detestable offenders: burglars, rapists, child molesters, murderers, drug peddlers and the like.

There is yet another despicable variety – pimps of power, politicians, white-collar financial fraudsters. The psychopathology of this breed of criminals is starkly different from others; they are *mis-wired* to believe they aren't doing anything wrong. However, they are the most widespread, and the most overlooked. They are the ones who often manage to escape the law, since most often their crimes aren't against people. Well, at least not physically.

Kailash Prasad belonged to the last class of criminals. He was an MLA – Member of Legislative Assembly – from East Delhi, who had never lived in the ward he represented. He lived in a three-story palatial house in New Friends Colony. He had retained his constituency for three consecutive terms, and in the most recent election, he had won his seat yet again. But there were allegations and accusations of election fraud. His opponent, one Mr Deshmukh Das, had filed a petition in the district court in Saket. Serious charges of election malpractice, booth capturing, bribing and scaring the voters were brought up.

Over the last month, the case had been heard in the court of Judge Shilpa Singh. Kailash Prasad had also been cross-examined in the court, which was something he had abhorred. If the rumours were to be believed, he had sent *feelers* and then *threats* to the judge to avoid landing up in the witness box, since that would tarnish his image. Like many other politicians of his ilk, he held the highly aggrandized misconception of his own self-worth. He believed he was far too important and above the courts and judiciary of the country, but Judge Shilpa Singh wouldn't have any of it.

Akash figured, from the papers, that last Friday was the last day of the hearing before the court announced its verdict. But, with the judge presiding over the hearing now behind bars, that wasn't going to happen anytime soon. Mistrial. Apparently, Judge Singh, the newspaper highlighted, had been arrested for the murder of a material witness who had evidence that Kailash Prasad was innocent. If the media was to be believed – and Akash had no reasons not to since all the four newspapers encored each other – the police had practically caught her red-handed, with the murder weapon. *In situ.* The authorities had not yet made any further details available to the press.

Why would Shilpa murder an ally of Kailash Prasad, however abominable the politician was? Even if she was about to give her verdict against Kailash Prasad, which might be reversed in some superior court on appeal if someone had tangible evidence, why would she stoop to murder? It didn't sound like her. Anyway, as a judge she was supposed to be dispassionate, wasn't she? He acknowledged he was getting ahead of himself – he hardly had any facts. There were so many questions. If someone really had evidence favourable to the defence, why hadn't they presented it in court already … and how would Shilpa Singh even come to know that someone was in possession of any such evidence … how would she find out where he was at that particular place? And what was the police doing at the location, at the precise moment, to have nabbed her at the scene? Oh, this had fuck-up written in blood all over it. And it clearly explained the seven missed calls.

'Sir,' whispered Mandeep, indicating they were at the Diwan residence. Immersed in the newspapers and his thoughts, and with so many start-stops along the way from the airport, Akash hadn't realized they had arrived at their destination. Showtime!

The clothes he'd been wearing for over twenty-four hours chafed and stung in the wrong places, and had now even begun to make his skin itch as he got out of the car and walked towards the door.

Priti Diwan was already there to greet him. 'Pardon the cliché but you actually look like something the cat dragged in.' Her face was seamed with concern, but she still made a feeble attempt at humour.

'A very good morning to you too, Priti.' Not that he wanted to be rude or impolite, but humour was the last thing he had on his mind. He was plain numb.

'I'm sorry. Good morning.'

'No, I'm sorry, sweetheart,' Akash said and pulled Priti into a bear hug.

She embraced him and rubbed his back like his mother. This was a kind of reassurance he needed.

Before he stepped in, there was only one thing Akash Hingorani wanted to do: call his trusted private investigator DK Pentium. But he knew he'd have to wait. He never called Pentium using his own phone. He needed to get home. He had several unlisted SIM cards for this purpose. But, in a way this was better – it would be good to listen to the judge's story before involving an investigator.

When Shilpa and Akash were dating, albeit for a short while, they had been invited to the Diwan residence more than a few times. Not for intimate assignations, but for social interactions and dinners – there were only so many times one could eat at restaurants. Clubs were a strict no-no, although at times Akash pondered why they had to hide if it was love. They weren't outlaws or miscreants. However, the judge wasn't keen. Priti and Vansh were the only friends who knew about the affair, and the only ones Shilpa and Akash trusted enough.

Priti led the way into the living room. Walking behind her, Akash noticed that she had recently got her hair cut in a pageboy style, which gave her a chic look. 'You got a new haircut?'

'You noticed?'

'Yeah.'

'How does it look?'

'Pretty Priti.' Finding the right words proved that Akash still had a reserve of presence of mind somewhere. Some sanity had prevailed.

'You made my day, thank you.'

'How is she?' Akash asked, but it was a rhetorical question.

The Diwan residence was well-appointed. One step into the living room and it was clear that the opulence was all old money. The antique filigree furniture – not bought from antique shops, but passed down through generations. Heavy wood sofas with new upholstery, the twin-layered curtains, the taxidermy on the walls, the Afghan carpets – everything spelled class. The connoisseurs called it *fin-de-siècle* – like describing it in plain English would bring down the demand and crash their price. All this was quite a contrast to Akash's house. If the Diwan residence was a Jaguar with plush expensive leather, Akash's was *vorsprung durch technik* like an Audi. Albeit equally classy, Akash's place was a goldmine of the latest tech with its remote-controlled doors, voice-activated gadgets and music channelling through the rooms. But then, Akash's inheritance had been zilch.

FOUR

1

JUDGE SHILPA SINGH, EVEN after being in the lock-up overnight, looked like she was ready for a television appearance. No make-up required. Akash felt a slight welling of desire, a pang, an odd sensation that made him uncomfortable. His feelings for her were certainly present, but it wasn't what it used to be when they had dated. Instead, there was a wall of vacuum, invisible yet palpable. He wondered if she felt the same way.

'Hi Judge,' he said and walked up to her.

In her courtroom, Shilpa Singh was lethal like a tigress; today she looked a domestic cat under duress. She upheld her regal demeanour, but Akash could sense her fear. He had never seen her frightened before. Runnels ran down both cheeks when she saw him. Like she had been waiting for him to let them flow. As if she supposed he'd press a reset button and everything would go back to normal like before. Like he was the intrepid knight in armour devoid of any clinks. Without a word she ran into his embrace. Her anxiety was understandable: her life as she knew it was unravelling, leaving her with doubting associates, faltering relationships and a tattered reputation.

'I've aged ten years since yesterday,' she finally uttered after leaving Akash's embrace.

'I'd have to say you've aged well. It doesn't show at all.' Akash wanted to keep a calm front.

Priti asked them whether they would like coffee and left the two lawyers with the judge. If they needed to have a conversation in their professional capacities, it was only right that she wasn't privy to any information. And if Shilpa and Akash required personal space, she knew Vansh would follow her soon.

Vamini – Priti and Vansh's elder daughter – came down the stairs and into the living room. She was a facsimile of her mother, only slightly taller. She was all ready to step out of the house to go to college, and her demeanour revealed that she hadn't expected a sombre atmosphere downstairs. But Akash could sense her mind doing a quick recap. He was sure she'd picked up the news on social media by now, and done the math as to why the judge and Akash Uncle were whispering with her dad.

She wished the judge good morning and gave a quick hug to Akash, before turning and going into the kitchen to join Priti. Their other daughter – they had legally adopted Baby from their household help after a terrible calamity had destroyed their home – had already left for school.

'Smart girl, very pretty,' Shilpa commented, evidently attempting to take her focus away. 'Which college does she go to?'

'Lady Shri Ram,' Akash answered before Vansh. 'Now, does anyone mind telling me what's been going on, please?' He wasn't happy that the elephant in the room was being ignored. 'I leave the country for twenty-four hours and the sky starts to fall.'

After the coffee had been served, Shilpa narrated the incident of the previous evening. The police had taken her to the police station for formalities. They were supposed to put those arrested in the holding cell, but they had offered the judge better arrangements for the night. Obviously, they, too, sat on the fence. She had spent the night sitting in the station house officer's little office. They couldn't let her walk outside; it was too public a case to make that error. If she was inside the police station, no one would know, but if she was permitted to leave the premises without proper documentation, it would raise alarms. The media would get more fodder and ask questions. But she had hardly slept a wink, which was expected. She was only released after Vansh posted bail in the morning.

Akash smiled.

'You find it amusing?' asked Shilpa.

'No, and yes. I don't find this incident amusing, but what tickles me is you have only narrated the events since the arrest, and nothing prior to that or about why or what?'

'What do you mean?'

'What in the name of the dear Almighty were you doing at Lodhi Gardens yesterday afternoon?' Akash had picked up from the newspapers that the crime scene was the public park. 'I don't suppose you went there for a late afternoon stroll.'

Shilpa's eyes had started brimming. Shame? Regret?

But Akash had to do what he had to do. He carried on with his questions. 'The media says the victim had evidence that would have forced you to give a "not guilty" verdict for the high-profile case you were presiding, and that you had received an anonymous tip warning you of such evidence—'

'Is that what they are saying?'

Akash pointed towards some newspapers kept on the table. It wasn't surprising she hadn't read them yet. She bent down, picked up one of the papers and glanced through it. It took her a minute to read and compose herself. 'In my statement to the police I had told them the exact opposite – this is crap. Someone's done a complete one-eighty to malign me, Akash. And the media hasn't even bothered to check. I bet it is all quoted as "from anonymous sources", isn't it?'

'So … you're saying you didn't get a call?'

'How do you know about the call?' She appeared taken aback.

'The whole world knows about it.' Akash pointed towards the newspapers once again. 'Obviously, someone from the police leaked the info about the call you received …'

'I received a call, yes.' Shilpa admitted, then went quiet like she was thinking of something but couldn't compute what.

'You received a call from …?'

'Wait a minute. Are you signing up to take the case to represent me … as my advocate on record?'

What the flipping hell do you think I flew back for, he wanted to ask, but chose to nod instead. 'Vansh Diwan and I, Akash Hingorani, will be your defence advocates,' he said and looked at Vansh. He didn't need to ask Vansh. If the roles were reversed, he wouldn't have blinked if Vansh had signed him up for defending someone close without explicitly asking his friend. They were friends first; professional rivalry wasn't even a distant second.

Shilpa looked at Vansh. She had only known Vansh as a friend for the brief period she had dated Akash; she didn't know how strong their professional association was. 'I don't think I can afford two of the most expensive lawyers in the city—'

'It's a limited time buy-one-get-one-free offer,' Akash joked and realized Shilpa was too deep in her thoughts to take any humour.

'I don't think Akash is offering either one of us a choice here, Judge,' Vansh smiled.

'A Hobson's choice then?'

'Yes,' Akash responded and gently segued into, 'So you were saying you received a call from ...?'

'Should we move to my study?' Vansh asked. If they were about to get into the case particulars, it made more sense to do so in the study. 'We can take down notes.'

'Sure.'

'And you can take us through the whole thing from the beginning.'

2

VANSH DIWAN'S STUDY WAS as big as his living room. He was a pedigreed lawyer. His father and his grandfather had been lawyers. All lawyers invariably turned into bibliophiles – it came with the territory – and Vansh's legal library had three generations' worth of books. Dark mahogany floor-to-ceiling shelves covered three walls of the room, and there was a window overlooking the garden on the fourth. His writing table was large enough to play pool on. It had a Mac, two phones and a few box files on it. There were two chairs across the table, and a blue suede medium-sized chaise longue on the side opposite the window. Shilpa decided to sit on the chaise longue. She was still a sitting judge – there had been no notice of suspension yet – and she, maybe, felt awkward sitting across an advocate like a client, like a criminal. Akash followed her and took the other end of the sofa. Vansh rolled his own chair forward from behind his desk and sat down with a pen and a yellow pad. He looked serious about taking notes, it appeared.

'Do you know I had been presiding on the case of "State of Delhi vs Kailash Prasad"?' she finally asked.

'Yes, I heard about it,' Vansh said and looked at Akash who nodded in agreement.

'The case had been in my court and was near its conclusion. In fact, the advocates had closed their arguments, and I was about to announce the court's verdict early next week ...'

Silence. The two advocates in the room didn't see the need to interrupt, to break her rhythm. Neither did they ask what her verdict would have been. *Would have been.* It would be difficult, if not impossible, to find a precedent in the country where a judge, presiding over a trial, was accused of the homicide of a witness for the defence. However, even if it didn't have precedence in law books, the not-so-popular common sense would dictate the judge be taken out of the equation first, which would mean that the case would now be a mistrial, and a new case would have to be mounted against Kailash Prasad. And considering the circumstances, *if* he was powerful enough to implicate the ruling judge in as heinous a crime as homicide once, what were the odds that the case would even be brought to court again? And what was the probability that there would be any witness who'd be willing to testify against the defendant? The next judge appointed to handle the case would think twice before deciding on it. Moreover, there were a million methods and means to legally cause delays. A crucial paper could go missing, an expert witness could be travelling, there could be an untimely death in one of the advocate's families. Unfortunately, there was no upper cap on the postponement of court hearings or a trial's resolution. It could drag on for years, maybe long enough for Kailash Prasad to contest in the next assembly elections. Or perhaps, some circumspect magistrate might not permit the case to be filed for lack of evidence. Kailash Prasad, it appeared, had pulled off a brilliant trick.

Shilpa continued, 'I received a call yesterday, late afternoon from this Ashok Kumar—'

'The victim?'

Mritak nash, naam pata namalum was the literal translation of a dead body with no name and address. Ashok Kumar was the name the police sometimes assigned to such corpses to humanize and dignify them until the time they were identified and the relatives or science confirmed the same. The practice is followed in other parts of the world too; in some countries they are referred to as Jane Doe or John Smith.

'Yes. And he told me he had tangible evidence to prove, beyond reasonable doubt, that the defendant was responsible for the election fraud—'

'Hold on a minute,' Vansh interrupted this time around, 'this Ashok Kumar told you that he had evidence *against* Kailash Prasad?'

'Yes.'

'But the reports say you ki—' Akash faltered; he couldn't bring himself to say *you killed*. 'So it's is the total opposite that the media has been propagating – that you eliminated the defendant's witness?'

'That's bullshit. He said he had evidence *against* Kailash Prasad. The media has been wrongly informed.' One could sense Shilpa was getting worked up, now that she was privy to the story that the media had been fanning. Her voice clearly, revealed her annoyance.

'The other way around wouldn't make a good enough story, would it? Why would a judge bump off a witness against the defendant when the evidence only buried Kailash Prasad and reinforced my decision?'

But what in the name of God Almighty were you flipping doing there, Judge?

This was the principal question Akash wanted to ask, but he knew the deprecating question wouldn't go down well with Shilpa at the moment. It might indeed sound rude, if not reprimanding. Calmness and compassion were imperative here, not derision and conceit. Aloud he said, 'Hold on,' raising his palms to pacify her, 'so, this Ashok Kumar said he had tangible evidence against the defendant …?'

Shilpa nodded.

'Did he say what was the evidence?'

'You have to understand that it was an invitation to meet him. He did not reveal any information on the call. He told me, "Meet me if you want the evidence" and not "This is the evidence I have."'

'Thank you for the confirmation, Judge.'

'He did mention it was a tape-recording of a conversation where Kailash Prasad had asked his cronies to terrorize the personnel at voting stations into accepting fake voters – voters who were paid to cast their votes in his favour. He said he had other evidence too.'

'Then why didn't he do the logical thing? Why didn't he go to the police or the prosecution to deliver the evidence – that would be the standard operating procedure, wouldn't it? To bring such evidence to the court?'

'Yes, but he said he didn't want anyone to know *he* was providing me with the evidence.'

'Oh I see ...'

'I got a call yesterday afternoon ...' Shilpa narrated the events of the previous day. Ashok Kumar had sounded frightened on the call. He claimed to have enough evidence to bury KP – Kailash Prasad – once and for all, but he was scared to be seen anywhere near the courthouse or the judge's residence. He feared that if KP came to know of his transgression – him jumping ship from KP's camp to the opposition – there would be severe consequences for him and his family. It was a risk he couldn't afford to take. Hence, he suggested handing over the tapes to the judge on neutral grounds, in a public park. Ashok Kumar had been insistent that she came alone, without any devices to record the meeting or the conversation. He had been cagey and adamant about giving the tapes only to her, and not to any representative of hers. She had to promise him that she wouldn't name the source, he would remain anonymous, and that this meeting in the park would be their first and final one. She could take it or leave it, and she had agreed to take it. 'Now in retrospect, I know it was a hasty decision,' she concluded her twenty-five-minute monologue.

I think the word you're looking for is stupid, but Akash didn't verbalize his thoughts.

'Why didn't you tell him to just post the tape containing the evidence to you? That way he'd have stayed completely anonymous, wouldn't he?'

'I told him that, but he argued there wasn't enough time left, and if the parcel got delayed or damaged in transit, or got into the wrong hands, it would be a real shame.'

So Shilpa was, in her way, crusading against corruption. The murder ensured that anyone who was willing to provide evidence for the same simply vanished. And the crusader was now left bearing the cross. Her only mistake was to get suckered into meeting the witness alone. And that momentary lapse of reason had put into motion a chain of events that had put the judge behind bars, at least for a night. And the repercussions weren't over yet. One wrong turn from here could change the course of her entire life. The scale of the impending catastrophe was yet to be established.

'Did the call come to your office landline or mobile?' Akash asked.

'On my personal mobile; it came from an unknown number.'

'Do you think we could trace the number, Akash?' Vansh asked.

'Yes, I know someone who can,' Akash answered, then turned to Shilpa. 'Where's your phone?'

'The police took it from me last night. I have it back now but the battery is dead.' She dug into her bag and held the iPhone in her hand. Vansh took it from her and walked around his desk to plug it into the charger.

'Okay. What did the caller say?'

'I've already told you that.'

'No, close your eyes and think. What were his exact words?'

'Close my eyes?'

'Judge, it's not fiction. People often recollect better with their eyes closed. Closing your eyes helps you immerse yourself into a past experience and relive it. Imagine yourself picking up your phone. What exactly did Ashok Kumar tell you?'

Shilpa rolled her eyes, and then looked at Vansh. He nodded in support of his friend. Her face suggested she still thought it was all hogwash, but she closed her eyes nevertheless and tried to recollect her exchange with the late Ashok Kumar:

'Judge madam, I'm a friend. I know you don't know me, but I know you're presiding over the case that decides the future of KP – you know him as Kailash Prasad – and I have evidence against him.'

'What evidence?'

'A tape.'

'What is it – a cassette tape?'

'Yes.'

'How did you get that?'

'I'll tell you when I meet you.'

Shilpa recited the entire conversation as it had occurred. One memory led to another, which directed her to a whole throng of them. Her words came out as a waterfall as she recalled everything. Or whatever she could remember at the moment, almost twenty-four hours post the call that got her into this mess.

'Was there anything else?' Akash asked.

'Like what?'

'What did he sound like?'

'Like a man.'

'Thank you for pointing that out. Yes, I know that and I also know you told us he sounded scared, but close your eyes and think again. Did he sound anxious? Was there anything that could have given you an idea about his emotional state?' Akash could feel his pulse rising; he was getting into the case. Being a streetwise lawyer meant that part of his success could be attributed to sharpness, and the rest because he could think on his feet. He thought like a computer played chess, considering all moves to outthink the opponent before making his own.

'Not that I know … I mean I don't know how to make that out on a phone, but he was whispering as if he was afraid of being overheard.'

'You mean like he might be calling from somewhere close to Kailash Prasad or one of his cronies?'

'I wouldn't know.'

'What else can you remember?'

'I can't think of anything else.'

'Any background noises? Were there people in the vicinity, was it a public place? Cars? Horns? Close your eyes again. Think. Don't summarize, don't interpret, and just describe what you remember as clearly as possible.'

Shilpa closed her eyes and tried to glean more details from the memory, but she had told them everything she could.

'Do you guys need anything to drink?' Priti knocked and said as she came into the study.

'Drink?' Akash glanced at his watch. It was past noon. 'I don't know about these two but I need something to eat, if that's okay?'

Shilpa, and Vansh, too, agreed that it was time for a bite.

3

'SO, WHAT WAS ASHOK Kumar like in person?' Akash resumed after a brunch of poached eggs, bread, butter and coffee.

'Tall. Lean. Muscled. Two-day-old stubble, all black. Wavy hair. I wouldn't say he was model material but he wasn't bad to look at either.'

It was a well-established fact that women made better eyewitnesses than men. That was just it. No one had ever been able to explain the reason. Men have stopped debating and women never challenged it in the first place. But even they made bad witnesses when they were the victims themselves. Shilpa Singh, despite being an officer of the law, wasn't defying the standards. Her description of Ashok Kumar could well mean over a million men in Delhi itself.

'How did you recognize him? I mean what did he tell you on the phone as to how you'd make him out in a crowd?'

'He said he'd come find me when I reached the location. Like I told you earlier, he was jittery. He mentioned that he'd see me enter the garden, and once he was convinced that I was alone, he'd come forward to speak to me … otherwise the deal was off.'

'Did he tell you which gate to come in from?'

'Gate number two.'

Shilpa explained that she had parked the car a street away, as Ashok Kumar had directed, and then walked into the garden like everyone else. Kumar looked like he was in his mid-thirties; he wore square-framed photochromatic glasses, a white cotton shirt, blue jeans and blue Nike sneakers. Shilpa didn't get the impression of affluence from the man; he could have been from the upper middle class.

'He was on the ground, the knife in his chest, blood staining his white shirt. There was no coagulation; it was fresh blood. I dropped my bag and immediately ran towards him to help him—'

'Hang on a minute,' Akash intervened, 'you just stated that he didn't tell you what he looked like on the phone, and *he* was supposed to find you when you got there, right? So how did you know the stabbed man was Kumar?'

'I didn't. I rushed to help him like any responsible member of the public would have done. I had no idea he was the guy I had come all the way to meet. As I was trying to pull the knife out of the body—'

'You took the knife in your hands?'

'Yes,' she responded. The expression on her face told him that she recognized it was a dumb thing to do.

'This just keeps getting better.' Akash's sarcastic rejoinder made her conscious of her own naivety. The gravity of her situation seemed to be dawning on her as she narrated the incident to them. Her own words had begun to worry her. She looked concerned, even slightly annoyed at herself. No wonder the evidence against her had seemed conclusive to the police.

'Please carry on,' Akash urged.

'I think he'd been knifed merely moments ago – suddenly

three, maybe four people started screaming, "Murder, murder!" Before I knew it, a crowd had gathered and then, out of nowhere, a policeman, followed by another who might have been in the vicinity, arrived at the scene.'

'What, they just appeared out of thin air, but weren't around when Ashok Kumar was being murdered in broad daylight in a public place?'

She nodded. *Yes*. 'That's what it seemed like. And when they arrived, I was kneeling next to the corpse with the knife I had pulled out of it in my hand. I asked the people gathered to help, but no one came forward. And a few seconds later I saw the police.'

'So let me understand this. No one called the police, but they just happened to be in the area, strolling, having a jolly and they heard some people scream murder?'

'It could well be a coincidence,' Vansh spoke after having listened to the story. 'Criminals tend to visit the area after dark—'

'But it was daylight then, wasn't it?' Akash asked Shilpa.

She nodded.

'I know that. All I'm saying is it *could* be a sheer coincidence; we mustn't rule it out. It's just Murphy's law. Policemen could be patrolling there for some other reason and, hearing cries of "murder", they ran in the direction the cries were coming from. It could be as simple an explanation as that.'

'If you say so,' Akash said, but his mien suggested he didn't believe it one bit. Police presence in the park could have been a sheer coincidence like Vansh had suggested, but to him it all sounded a bit bizarre. He parked the thought for the moment.

Shilpa detailed that the senior police inspector who arrived after being called by the two constables and took control of the scene, instantly recognized her, but considering the public spectacle, with more witnesses than they could count, it was impossible for him to take any other action but to arrest her. She was permitted to make some calls – they didn't take away her phone. 'And I kept calling you all the way while they drove me to the police station.'

'I'm sorry, I was travelling.'

'Which I now know, of course.'

'Did you call anyone else?'

'No. Yes, I called my driver and asked him to pick up my car from where I had parked it.'

Shilpa seemed a victim of circumstances that she had herself created, so to speak. She had ignored the warnings from Kailash Prasad, and would be paying the price in months to come, maybe years, maybe her entire lifetime. Even if she won the case in court, there was a high chance the blemish would linger forever.

'Did this guy, Ashok Kumar, tell you *why* he wanted the campaign against Kailash Prasad to succeed so much that he was prepared to risk his life?'

'He said he'd tell me everything when I met him.'

'And he obviously didn't manage to murmur anything before he died?'

'He was already dead by the time I got to him.'

'Just in time, by the sound of it.'

'Did you find any tape on him?' Vansh asked.

'I couldn't check. Before I could pat his body down the police were there already. In any case, my guess is that if he was murdered for the recordings, the killer would have taken them, don't you think?'

'If he had any tape in the first place.' Akash commented. He seemed unconvinced.

'What do you mean?'

'When the random is too desperate to pass off as a coincidence, it's usually a lie.'

Akash's observation was lost on Shilpa.

'The whole anecdote is full of seemingly coincidental events, isn't it? Ashok Kumar being murdered right before you arrived at the scene to be seen by multiple witnesses just as you start to help him, and the police happened to be in the vicinity too. This has set-up written all over it—'

'Wait a minute, you think someone is trying to frame me?'

'I think the poor guy didn't know he was going to be sacrificed to catch the bigger fish – you.'

'I still don't know what you mean.'

'I don't know what I'm talking about either, I'm only trying to guess, but it is probably worthless since we have so little facts at this point.' Akash looked at his watch, which said it was 4 p.m. now. More coffee had arrived for them, and they kept discussing the events of the previous day for another hour. Akash asked some more questions, but got no new information. He didn't think the judge was hiding anything, and he knew she had nothing more to offer.

'We should call it a day,' Vansh, who had been quiet for a while now, jotting down points every now and again, declared.

Akash was exhausted from the travel, Shilpa appeared disoriented from her ordeal, and it seemed logical to wind up.

'I'll drop you on my way,' Akash suggested.

'That's probably not a very good idea.'

The judge and Akash looked at Vansh. The penny took a second longer than required to drop. The accusation of murder was already a complete chapter of humiliation in itself. There wasn't any need to gift-wrap another story for the media. A love affair that Shilpa Singh and Akash Hingorani had buried nine months ago didn't need to be exhumed. Someone had already started digging and had got hold of one of their pictures together. Why give the cameras another shot?

'You're right, Vansh,' Shilpa was the first to concede. 'Could you call a taxi for me, please?'

'You're surely joking, Judge,' Vansh attempted to sound hurt. 'I will drop you home.'

'Thank you, both.'

FIVE

1

WAS THERE SOMETHING CALLED mental atrophy? After all, some say that the brain is a muscle too. The sky was a deep purple when Akash got home around 6:30 p.m. He was tired to the bone, but he knew from experience that going to sleep would be impossible. Whenever he was involved in a major high-profile case, his fatigued brain still managed to force his physical self to work, not giving him a moment of respite. This was as major and high-profile as they came. And this time it was personal. His growing anxiety would have a doctor prescribe him some beta-blockers to calm down, but that wasn't the kind of help he needed at this moment.

He wasn't a heavy drinker like his friend Vansh, but he enjoyed his tipple every now and again. Cognac was always his chosen relaxant. He filled his snifter and sat in his study-office, or legal studio as he liked to call it. Unlike Vansh's wood-panelled officious set-up, this was more of a sanctuary than an office for Akash. It housed his diecast cars collection – over five hundred of them – state-of-the-art music system and over a thousand vinyls. In addition to the legal library, it contained books on various sciences – including physics, biology, chemistry, mathematics, statistics – and a small bar. Nothing in this large room was just for display. He enjoyed his collection, he found solace in music, and he applied whatever science he could in the trials at the court. His arguments, besides the oratory skill he was known for, always leaned heavily on science, which made him a formidable opponent. In most cases, science was indisputable. One didn't need to persuade a judge in a court, if a century ago Albert Einstein had already convinced the world of some principle that Akash was using to labour a point. With nuggets of science, arguments turned into bullets.

He sat behind his large desk, reclining on the tan leather chair turned towards the window facing the front lawn. He rested his legs to rest on the desk, which had on it a MacBook, models of an Aston Martin DB5 and '66 Mustang, and a desk phone that seldom rang. He had put on *Carnival of the Animals* – the French comic classic by Saint-Saëns – on the turntable and closed his eyes to think. 'Royal March of the Lion' had started playing. The strings provided the melody, and the piano suggested the roar of a lion.

He was ready to focus, to deliberate.

Judge Shilpa Singh was about to rule against a crooked politician, but she got framed in a homicide case that debarred her from making the judgement. Consequently, Kailash Prasad had won the first round. What possible connection could there be between KP and the unidentified Ashok Kumar? He opened the first drawer of his desk, pulled out a post-it pad and a pencil and jotted down the questions that still remained unanswered.

How had Ashok Kumar arrived at Lodhi Gardens to meet the judge? From what Shilpa had narrated – she'd called him upper middle class, hadn't she? So, Ashok Kumar didn't seem like a guy who travelled in a chauffeur-driven limousine? If he had driven himself, there should be an unclaimed vehicle somewhere near the park location of the murder. Had the police found it? If yes, where, and if not, why not?

Or did someone drop him off? Ashok Kumar didn't have to tell the person dropping him at Lodhi Gardens *why* he was going there. Maybe he took public transport? Where did he live? What did he have against Kailash Prasad? Did he really have something against KP or was he just a worm to catch the fish named Shilpa Singh? Maybe Ashok Kumar was only told the first part of the plan: he was to call the judge, lure her into a secluded part of the garden? Maybe he was told that when she got there, he'd have to give her something, maybe an empty tape – who uses cassette tapes anymore? There was no way for her to check what was on the tape until she got back to the car, at the very least. Maybe Kumar was told this was a simple con job, and that someone would photograph her taking something from him, and then blackmail her for taking some kind of a kickback? Who knew? And the second part of the plan, kept from Kumar, was to kill him off and pin the murder on Shilpa? To Akash, this is what seemed to have happened. Finding out more about the dead man seemed a good place to start. Who was he? What did he do? How did he get involved with the dirty politician? And why did he break away from KP? Did he have a family? More importantly, it had been a full day since his murder made it to the front pages of every major daily circulated in the city; why hadn't someone come forward to claim him?

The carefully cropped photograph of Shilpa walking down Pandara Road bothered Akash. His affair with Shilpa could have been a mere happy coincidence for whoever was pulling the strings. The media would bite at the scandal and be distracted from going beyond the obvious, to dig deeper for the truth behind the murder. They were already getting two scoops for the price of one. Why look for anything in addition to an accused judge who'd had a clandestine affair with a defence advocate? They'd bury her, and they'd bury him too. He had just got pulled into the vortex. But she couldn't have anticipated this. She was indeed not responsible for it. He didn't begrudge her. It was what it was. One couldn't alter or recreate the past. However, he had more than a hunch that their affair would turn up in the media now. Something told him the episode wasn't over.

The parodic movement of 'Tortoises' was playing now. He realized that he was no faster than the damn animal. His thoughts were breaking up. His brain, tired and anxious, was circling the drain. He got up, stretched and poured himself another drink – his last, he promised himself. He knew he had to do something extremely important before he retired for the day.

2

AKASH'S IPHONE ON THE desk vibrated. 'Judge' was calling. He had not changed it to Shilpa Singh even when they were dating. In public, he always referred to her as Judge; in private he almost always called her Shilpa Singh, never just Shilpa.

'Hi, sorry to bother you so late, Akash—'

'It's not late, the day is still young.' He picked up the remote and put the music on mute. 'It's only nine. How can I help?'

'I don't want Raghuveer to know about this incident.'

The judge's idea of keeping a lid on the news sounded like a fantasy. She'd made headlines in major national publications. And in today's world, it took seconds for news to spread like wildfire. The internet had no geography, no boundaries. If her son was on any social media platform – which in today's day and age was akin to breathing – he'd have read all about it by now. Keeping the matter from Raghuveer wasn't a viable option.

'But there's no way to stop the news once it's in the media.'

'What about damage control?'

That was more like it.

'If it were me, I'd call him up and tell him first-hand and explain that everything is under control,' Akash suggested.

'Is it?'

'Is it what?'

'Is it under control?'

'It's a figure of speech, Shilpa Singh, you have to be careful so that he doesn't get too worried. He's a child after all.'

'I guess you have a point,' she sounded like she had been pushed into a corner. Which wasn't untrue in many ways.

'What if I go to Mussoorie?'

'You mean drive up there and talk to him?'

'Yes, face to face. It would make more sense, wouldn't it?'

'I am not aware of the restrictions on the bail granted, but I can check with Vansh whether you're permitted to leave town.'

Some bails were accompanied by stricter terms than others when it came to free movement on the part of the accused. With the hot water the judge was already in, no detail was too small to overlook. It was a long row to hoe. Missing some minor legality or making a rookie error at this juncture could burst the dam of distress. Most times, waiting for a courtroom trial could be a prison sentence in and of itself.

'If I can't go up there, would you go instead?'

And what would I say? Hey, buddy, I am your mum's ex?

'But I thought you didn't want him to know about me until you told him about us first.'

'I know, but we're no longer *us*, and the circumstances are different now.'

'How so?'

'You're my defence lawyer … and a friend,' she added as an afterthought.

'Hmm …'

'You don't sound convinced, Akash.'

'Oh no, I was only thinking, why are we jumping the gun here? Let me check with Vansh, and maybe both of us could go to Mussoorie together?'

'You'll do that for me?'

'We are a full-service firm, ma'am. Client satisfaction is our only goal.'

'It's so good to have you as a friend, Akash. I really appreciate you helping me in my hour of need—'

'Stop it, Shilpa Singh. That's what friends are for. We'll get through this. It will take time, but it's not the end of the world, trust me.'

She thanked him again and said goodnight before disconnecting the call. Akash sensed that the initial shock had begun to fade. Good!

Shilpa being a judge made matters tricky. Most advocates despised judges more than they abhorred other advocates. After all was said and done, other advocates were kin. They allowed another advocate's criticism and folly as part of their jobs: *my learned friend*, *my colleague*, that's how they referred to each other in the courtrooms. Canines stick to their packs. Judges were felines; not pack animals at all.

They were the referees, they decided who the winner was in a trial. They managed to upset almost every lawyer on one occasion or another with their verdicts. On the face of it, advocates respected judges, but that respect was generally sired by fear more than anything else.

But no advocate – even if he was Akash Hingorani – could change what was already done now. Judge Shilpa Singh had been accused of homicide, and he and Vansh had agreed to defend her. Whatever the world said or did, Akash could sense she had been framed. He just needed the evidence to prove it.

3

DESPITE THE ABUNDANCE OF sophistication Akash Hingorani exuded, he was also a shrewd advocate. A mean streetfighter variety, unlike his friend, Vansh. Digging into the third drawer of his desk, he pulled out a burner phone.

He looked for a number in his contacts that had been stored alphanumerically. For someone going through his address book it would look like a password for some online account. He dialled the number, let it ring twice and disconnected. Then took a sip of the cognac and re-dialled. It was their code. Two short rings, then the call.

'Pentium,' the voice at the other end said.

Akash didn't say who it was. Pentium would know. Instead, Akash asked for something he had never asked Pentium before: 'We need to meet.'

There was silence on the other side for a few seconds as Pentium considered the request. 'It could be risky for you, *Janaab*.'

'So be it; let's take the risk.'

'Where?'

'My place.'

'When?'

'Midnight, tomorrow.' Akash was too tired to be up for another two hours, and then for another two to talk to Pentium.

'Roger that.'

Click!

Akash disconnected the call, took apart the phone to extract the SIM inside. He pulled out a pair of scissors from one of the drawers and cut the tiny card into even tinier pieces and dumped them in various bins around the house. His association with Pentium had always been hush-hush, and it was meant to be that way. Under no circumstances could Akash reveal that his prime source of information was an ex-criminal.

4

FOR THE FIRST TIME in his life, Akash was scared. He might have been one of the brightest defence lawyers in the country but there was a limit to his capabilities. He was a *vakil*, not Mandrake the Magician. Shilpa had been arrested red-handed; her fingerprints were on the murder weapon. With no dearth of eyewitnesses, and the police at the scene within minutes, it had all the bearings of a lost case, but he didn't think it was wise to apprise the judge that her future, even in his hands, seemed bleak. It appeared like the proverbial cut-and-dried case if ever there was one. But if you had a fertile imagination the speculations could be infinite, and quite frankly, none of them, at this moment, struck as positive for Shilpa Singh.

He failed to see how it could benefit any judge by killing a witness that only strengthened her ruling. As a matter of fact, whichever side's favour Judge Shilpa Singh had ruled was irrelevant. Why would it push her to a murderous extent? What was she to gain or lose either way?

However, to clinch the deal, the prosecution had already been provided with the motive. With Ashok Kumar dead, it was Judge Shilpa Singh's word against the entire gamut of media that had proclaimed that Kumar had evidence in *favour* of Kailash Prasad and not *against* him, which put Shilpa in an extremely tricky situation. It could be argued that Shilpa had a reputation for being impartial, but the question that was being asked – and rightly so – was what she was doing at the scene of the murder. If only they could find the tape or tapes that verified her claims. But what were the odds of finding them? That is, if they existed in the first place.

By all accounts, including hers, Shilpa had already decided to rule against Kailash Prasad, which signified there was enough evidence to do so. Then what made her succumb to an offer that only added another piece of evidence to the decision? Why had she rushed to meet someone who had been so evasive about it all? Stupid, rash decision! How could she, an officer of the law, be so reckless?

Akash hadn't been able to catch up with Vansh after their afternoon session, but he knew if Vansh had discovered anything new or stumbled upon some crucial information, he'd have certainly called and updated Akash.

As he lay in bed looking at the fan and the ceiling in the dim light, another aspect of the case worried him: the media-cawing, he imagined, was about to commence, linking the judge to him. Try what you might, you couldn't keep the media away from a story like this.

He remembered an old recording of a one-day cricket match he had seen ages ago, in 1981. Australia vs New Zealand. NZ needed six runs from the final delivery of the match to tie the scores. What did Australia do? Greg Chappell, the then Australian captain, asked his bowler to deliver the last ball underarm along the ground, which couldn't be hit for a six. It might have been against the spirit of fair play, but it was perfectly legal then. Australia won. Wasn't Akash's single goal here to win? As long as it was all above board, or he stayed vigilant to not get caught with his paws in the cookie jar, shouldn't he ...? Kailash Prasad was as dirty as used underwear anyway, so why not turn the media's attention towards him?

The media needed a story. And they already had one, but it was not one that would be in the interests of the judge or

Akash. He decided to dictate another story. Since the beginning of time, the world is known to favour the underdog. People cheered for a David fighting valiantly against a Goliath to survive until he could turn the tables. Akash had just the right person in mind to direct the media circus to another target.

Underarm bowling is underhanded. Not exactly fair play, but not criminal either. Well, if the choices handed down to you were substandard, any alternative you picked would be poor in any event. Garbage in, garbage out. Akash felt a momentary surge of anxiety and adrenaline. After a while, calmness ensued. With a pursed smile on his lips and content with the offence strategy he had come up with, Akash finally drifted into a much-needed state of slumber.

So many wise women and men had said it over the years: *if you can't win, don't lose.*

SIX

1

AFTER HIS CALL WITH Akash, DK Pentium lit a cigarette and took a large swig of local hooch straight from the bottle. In all his years – sixteen, seventeen – of dealing with Akash Hingorani, not once had the man ever asked to see him in person. This had to be something serious. He didn't own a computer, but he went online on his mobile to scout for news.

2

DK WAS DINESH KUMAR but he called himself Pentium to highlight that he was superfast, like the eponymous computer chip. The sobriquet 'Pentium' was, in fact, bestowed on him by none other than Akash Hingorani when the investigator had helped him crack a case by worming himself into a dirty hole to bring Akash evidence crucial to the case – all within an hour of being tasked with it and when the other private eye had been struggling to find anything for weeks.

However, it was painfully hard to locate Pentium himself.

And if you found him, there was an incredibly high probability – nine times out of ten – he'd be tanked up. Pentium came from the other side of the tracks; he had been in and out of prison more times than he could count. And once, he was arrested for aggravated battery that had sent two men to the hospital. He wasn't a gentleman, to say the least; his language was laced with words most people would find offensive. In fact, some of the anatomical impossibilities he suggested not only sounded crude but were also incomprehensible to most.

Pentium was a man of sharp mind and strapping build. A giant. And as if his sheer size wasn't menacing enough, he looked every bit as creepy as he was. No eyebrows; after one of them was burnt in an arson attack, he had deliberately shaved the other. Ergo, his deep-set black eyes looked even menacing. He had also discarded his mane to accentuate his big head, which could damage someone's kidney with a head-butt. He single-handedly shattered all romantic illusions that people might have about dapper sleuths they watched on Netflix or read about in novels. But he had one quality that was vital to his excellence in his profession: he was a private eye with no personal life.

Besides being an alcoholic, he was also paranoid. Then again, that was understandable since he had enemies who had tried to burn him alive once. As such, he had become a recluse – not that women were queuing up to date him – but his paranoia prevented him from telling anyone where he lived. He moved residences frequently. He disappeared like a ghoul for months only to surface to buy alcohol, smokes and ration to get by. Pentium was available for your service only if you knew him already or if you came through a reference.

He was neither listed as a private investigator anywhere nor was he licensed, hence, he didn't advertise his trade. If you needed to contact him, you needed to already know his mobile number. And of course, lots of patience was a prerequisite to get through to him. He decided to take your call or decline it depending on the mood he is in. He owed Akash big time and never failed to answer a call from the lawyer.

One of the biggest hardships someone who looked like Pentium faced was that his face was one that was difficult to forget. Most people who saw him once were able to describe him to some extent. He could be anything but inconspicuous. But Pentium was smart enough to acknowledge the problem and quickly learned to overcome or conceal his infirmities as needed. He had mastered the art of invisibility. He walked as quietly as a mouse, and moved stealthily enough to ensure that people around him were none the wiser. He was like a grizzly bear. Despite his weight and size, you wouldn't know he was near. Then he would be upon you if he wanted and you would be dead meat.

However, there was one positive attribute that no one could ever deny about Dinesh Kumar Pentium: if someone closely examined his long rap sheet, they'd see he didn't have a criminal mindset. All his arrests were for fierce and fiercer fights, which on almost all occasions were started by someone else. Pentium, being the muscled monster that he was, always came out on top and consequently, everyone around assumed that he must be the aggressor. His foul temper, use of the choicest expletives, villainous demeanour and the cynicism he had developed towards authority made it game-set-match for anyone who filed a complaint against him. Not once was he arrested for theft or burglary, not even for possession of stolen property, never for drugs or misbehaving with the opposite sex.

But it wasn't all bad: with every arrest, he made contacts on both sides of the bars. He knew exactly whom to bribe and which strings to pull at every police station across Delhi to get the information he required. In return, several police officers didn't shy from using him as a snitch from time to time.

SEVEN

1

CHAVI NAIR, INVESTIGATIVE JOURNALIST at one of the leading local New Delhi news channels, *Dilli Daily*, had been a star in the news media in Mumbai until a few years ago when an unfortunate incident burned down her career. She had been in love with a fine gentleman who – obviously unknown to her – had turned out to be a serial killer. Although she had no part in his evil life, the channel decided that she had to go, or they'd become a laughing stock in media circles. Imagine the star journalist of a channel that prided itself on breaking news and busting criminal conspiracies in the city not being aware of what her own boyfriend was doing? *Chirag tale andhera?*

Chavi took a break from her career and moved to New Delhi for some peace and quiet. Since no one knew her history here, there was no baggage, and with a sterling recommendation from the Mumbai Police, she was immediately hired by *Dilli Daily*. In the course of her two-year career in the city, she had crossed paths with Akash Hingorani on more than a few occasions, when she approached him for his comments on various cases. Ever-flirtatious, Mr Hingorani had been more than happy to oblige. Why wouldn't he? Chavi was a dusky, long-legged, gorgeous, curly-haired single woman who was always attired in a short pencil skirt. Every bit about her was stylish and chic. In fact, they had gone out to dine together soon after Akash and Shilpa had ended their relationship. If Chavi knew about his affair with the judge, she chose to keep it to herself. The attraction was mutual and the two complemented each other; there wasn't a conflict of interest between them either. But Akash abhorred her smoking; she was a walking chimney. Chavi explained she had succumbed to it after years of abstaining, when an old boyfriend passed away tragically. On her part, she loved six-inch stilettos and, Akash knew, she found him short. Neither confided their reservations to the other, and in the end, never dated either. Which was good in a way, since they remained close friends and helped each other behind the scenes.

'To what do I owe this privilege, Akash?' Chavi Nair asked as she answered her phone. 'It's not even seven-thirty in the morning.'

'I wanted to catch you before you went to work.'

'Pray, tell why? What does the best defence advocate in town need from a lowly, poor journalist like me?'

'This lowly, poor advocate wants a favour. Big time.'

'Ask and you shall receive, my dear. What is it? You don't sound like your usual self.'

He didn't want to tell her that someone had declared war against him by jerking his chain. Not on the phone. These kinds of matters were best discussed face to face. 'When can I see you?'

'What's it about – tell me something.'

'It could be the biggest story of the year.'

'You've got me already. But if you want me to see you this morning before I go to work you've got to give me some clue—'

'It's about Judge Shilpa Singh.' The revelation was met with silence.

Akash waited for half a minute before asking, 'Are you there, Chavi?'

'I am, and I'm listening …'

'What do you know about what happened the day before yesterday?'

'Judge Shilpa Singh was arrested for the homicide of some witness for the defence in a case she was presiding on.'

'Quite the opposite.'

'What do you mean?'

Akash could visualize Chavi's pupils dilating in anticipation. Could he trust her? If yes, how much? Could he trust her enough to divulge things that he had heretofore not revealed to people in his own office? Or would it be like poking at a beehive?

'Is the subject important enough for you to meet me before you go into the office today?'

'You bet.'

'One request though—'

'Say it.'

'No one should know you're meeting me.'

'Why?' It was a logical question.

'Why don't I tell you when we meet?'

'So, whatever you tell me – would it be off the record then?'

'Like I said, let's meet and discuss this.'

'Okay, when and where?'

'How about breakfast with me, say in an hour, at my place? How does that sound?'

'Sounds like a meeting not worth missing. Would you be cooking?'

'If you want me to.'

'I love naked chefs.'

'You got it.'

'No … please, no. I was just kidding, but if you … anyway I've just got up, give me an hour and half. I'll be there at about nine. That okay for you?'

'Most certainly. I could send my car to pick you up if you would like that?'

'That won't be necessary, Mr Super Advocate. I'll see you in a while.' She had been to Akash's residence before; she knew where he lived.

Click.

2

AKASH DISCONNECTED THE CALL and rang Vansh to inquire about the bail conditions that had been set for Shilpa. There had been no stipulation on travel within the country.

'She's still not been suspended from her position, not yet. There is a meeting today, the panel will most probably suspend her until the trial is over,' Vansh explained.

'Hmm …'

'Why did you ask? Is she planning on going away for a short vacation?'

'No, she called me last night. She wants to visit her son.'

'In Mussoorie?'

'Yes, that's why I called to check if she was allowed to travel.'

'Despite there being no restrictions on the judge's travel, my advice would be to inform the senior inspector at the police station where she was held after the arrest. I'm sure he should have no objection, but it would be wise to inform him about her whereabouts.'

'Good point, I didn't think about it.'

'Akash, are you sure you want to take this case?'

'Why would you ask that?'

'You – *you,* of all people – missed this simple courtesy? Does it not tell you that you are too close to the person you've signed on to defend?' Vansh was correct in his assessment. Akash hadn't thought of calling the senior inspector, which should have occurred to him without a prompt from Vansh. But it hadn't. 'Even the best doctors refrain from carrying out a surgical procedure on someone very close to them …'

'Are you telling me to just walk away?'

'No, but be my second chair.'

'I can't do that, Vansh.'

'I know how you're feeling, but that's precisely the reason I thought, as a friend, I should suggest this. You are extremely high-strung at the moment, even emotional. Emotions have no place in a courtroom or even in the preparation for a trial. One wrong decision could make all the difference, and you know that.'

'Thanks for the offer, Vansh, and I truly appreciate it. Let me think it over. I think I'm good for now, but if I feel like I can't handle the stress anymore, I'll let you know. Likewise, if you sense I'm losing it at any point, please step in. It's really good to know you have my back.'

'No worries at all, my friend. What's the plan for today?'

'I'm home, trying to get in touch with a few people. When are they going to charge her?'

Shilpa Singh had been arrested, not charged with a crime. The police had taken her into custody, but the charges needed to be brought up in court. Vansh had got a judge to sign an anticipatory bail. Typically, anticipatory bail was granted to avoid arrest, but in this particular case Shilpa had already been arrested at the scene of the crime. However, she was a judge, and no judge would have declined to sign a document that saved someone of their own clan. It's the way the world worked: save your own.

'Day after tomorrow, 18 January, 10:30 a.m. at Saket.'

'Whose court?'

'Vikrant Mathur.'

'Fuck!' Akash screamed.

'Why? What's wrong?'

'I can't stand him. He's a perfect asshole. Doesn't even have piles.'

'Is the feeling mutual? Does he have such equal high regard for you too?' Vansh scoffed.

'I think so. I'm sure he thinks I don't have piles either.'

'No worries, neither of you need to go around sniffing each other's piles-less bottoms on the day. We don't even have to put you down as the advocate on record for now. Let him charge her – which we know he will; there's no way out of that since she was arrested at the scene of the crime. She will plead "not guilty", of course. Let's get to that, and then see how it plays out. This will certainly be a quick one. At best, Mathur would be a temporary irritant.'

'Thanks again, Vansh. You're a—'

'Let me repeat your words: What are friends for?'

'Touché.'

'Going back to what we were discussing, I'd advise you not to leave town until after she appears in court.'

'Of course.'

'On second thought, do not inform the police of your intentions of travelling out of town until after she has been to court. No point in getting the inspector's panties in a wad. The last thing you want is a bent inspector relaying the info to whoever this KP is, and KP calling the prosecution to revoke the bail or mess with the conditions.'

'Got it.'

'Good, anything else?'

'Nope.'

'Bye, then. If you're not doing anything important this evening, come over for dinner?'

'I'll call you later and let you know.'

'Okay.'

3

CHAVI GOT OUT OF bed. She was all charged up. If Akash Hingorani couldn't wait for the day to begin before he had called her, it had to mean he had something monumental to share with her. Big story breaks were what journalists like her yearned for. Their careers depended on them. She stretched and looked at the time on her iPhone: 7:41 a.m. If she were to be at Akash's place at Vasant Vihar at nine, she would have to be out of her apartment around 8:40. On a good day it was a seventeen-minute drive from her apartment to Akash's place. If there was any traffic, she could always call him and apologize for the delay, but she couldn't just go out there without doing any homework. That would be disrespectful to her professionalism.

Still in her night shirt and bare legs, she carried her MacBook into the kitchen, fired it up and switched on the kettle for a coffee. She searched for 'Judge Shilpa Singh'. The first few pages Google brought up were the latest news of her arrest. Chavi already knew what was out there in the media. Their channel, obviously, hadn't covered the news yet, except for a mention in the day's headlines. No analysis had been done because the story had broken only less than forty-eight hours ago. There had been no comments from anyone yet. She saw pictures of Shilpa Singh doing the rounds.

Chavi dived deeper into the search results: the fifth, sixth, seventh pages of Google's findings. Judge Shilpa Singh had been a long-standing, respected member of the law community. There were no blemishes on her record prior to this incident. Some personal details sprung up on the tenth page. Shilpa was a young widow, with a son who studied in a boarding school, but nothing more. Not the son's name, not his age, not where he studied. But she was a pretty woman, Chavi noted. She did some quick math: it was obvious the judge had hired Akash Hingorani as her advocate. That's why Akash had a story for Chavi.

As she was about to close the browser, she had one last look at the image results. Something stood out in particular. One of the dailies had published a picture of Shilpa Singh, which suggested she was walking out of some place. Chavi downloaded it, blew it up. It became slightly pixelated, but it was evident that the picture had been taken at nighttime, without her knowledge and, therefore, without Shilpa's consent. The background was lit up by signages which, although indistinct, would have been recognizable to anyone who'd been to Pandara Road. Chavi had been there with none other than Akash Hingorani. In fact, he had suggested the place to her. Hmm ... maybe she was reading what wasn't even there between the lines.

Another detail that intrigued Chavi was that it was just one half of a picture. Somebody had edited it, and had indeed done a brilliant Photoshop job of eliminating whoever was alongside the judge at the venue. Nevertheless, at this magnification, and despite the deteriorated resolution due to excessive enlargement, Chavi could see Shilpa's right hand fingers interlaced with another hand. The editor hadn't cared to crop it or maybe found it too difficult to erase. Most naked or unobservant eyes would have missed it. It was either that or perhaps the person who edited the photograph wanted someone to make this discovery. Chavi guessed that the other person in the picture was a man. Shilpa's companion was on her right, his left hand holding her right.

Who was it? Chavi was good but recognizing the man from a blurred image of his fingers needed more than sharp observation skills. She would need to get the picture enhanced by professionals in her team back at her office to see if she could find something that could identify the man. Wouldn't it be better if all men wore unique signet rings so that they could be recognized at such times? Ha, she smiled. Could it, after all, be Shilpa's husband? No, she decided. The picture looked like it wasn't very old when compared to other official pictures of Shilpa Singh on the net. Her husband had passed away years ago. This was someone else.

Time was up. She walked into the balcony of her two-bedroom apartment and lit a cigarette. She smoked a Classic Milds, then another. Mindful of Akash's averseness to the smell, she decided to take a shower.

Before leaving her apartment, she called her boss – the chief editor of *Dilli Daily* – and told him she would be late to the office because she was working on a scoop. He knew her well enough to not ask what it was about. Sources were everything in the trade. He knew she'd tell him when the time was right.

4

ALTHOUGH AKASH HAD A swanky office in Saket, near the district court, most days he worked from his legal studio. He only ventured out if he had an appearance in court or to play golf with some of his associates. As per his schedule, he was supposed to be travelling to Cambridge. But with the trip out of the picture, his diary was blank for the week, which turned out to be a blessing. He called up his second-in-command at his firm, Sonia Pahwa, a few minutes before 9 a.m. Sonia was a young defence advocate who'd joined Akash a few years ago. She was sharp. And slick. And quick. A Ferrari on two wheels, everyone in the office called her.

'Missing us already?' she asked when Akash called. Mobile phones these days didn't reveal to the recipient the location of the caller.

'Yes, I missed you all so much that I'm back in town.'

'Seriously? What happened?' Sonia probably already knew Judge Shilpa Singh had been arrested, but she didn't know about her boss's affair with the judge.

'I've been called back, you could say.'

'May I know who dared?'

'We've been …' he had to word it appropriately for it to sound kosher, 'retained to defend a sitting judge—'

'Judge Shilpa Singh?'

'You've heard the news then?'

'If you've heard about it in the UK, of course I would have heard it here in Delhi. But why did she decide to hire us? I mean, did she call you … personally?'

'No,' he said. If you had to lie, lie smoothly. The best lies were the ones, which were laced with some amount of truth. *Ardh-satya*: half-truths were always far more believable, weren't they. 'She had called my friend, Vansh Diwan, whom you've met—'

'Mr Diwan of Diwan-e-Khaas? Yes, of course I've met him,' Sonia acknowledged.

'Vansh thought it would be a good idea if his firm and ours got together and mounted a joint defence. He called me, and here I am.'

'Gotcha. So, we'll be working together?' Akash picked up a faint note of dejection in Sonia's voice.

'Yes. Anything wrong?'

'Nothing, I was just thinking …' She went quiet.

'Come on, out with it!'

'I mean, if you and Mr Diwan are jointly working on this, my services won't be required, right?'

An epic case like this, defending a judge, came once in a lifetime. To be able to see the pie and not be able to get a bite of it would be understandably frustrating.

'Says who? You're involved. Three brains are better than two.'

'Don't you need to check with Mr Diwan? After all, he's the one who asked you to join him, and now you're picking an assistant without even consulting him?'

However smart and slick the lie was, it nevertheless came back to bite you in the ass. Akash, now, couldn't weasel out of the story he had so smoothly crafted only minutes ago. Sonia's worry was logical. If it was Vansh's case, he got to decide who joined the defence team. Or at least, he had more say in it.

If you're being questioned about a yarn of your own fabrication, there are two ways out: either you accept you were double-dealing, apologize, tell the truth and bail yourself out, or if you are a slick defence advocate like Akash Hingorani, you embellish it further to put more meat on the bones and make the dish juicier.

'We already spoke about it last evening when we met with the judge. He agreed that you were the best fit for the job.'

'Thank you, Akash, I really appreciate that.'

'You deserve it, Sonia. Vansh has seen you present in the courtroom; he acknowledges your talent.'

'Thank you.'

'Okay, whatever you are presently working on, see how quickly you can hand it over to Ali.' Ali was another member of Akash's seven-lawyer firm. 'I'll see you around two at my studio.'

'I'll be there.'

'Welcome aboard, and check your email when you get to work; I'll be sending some stuff for you to look into.'

'Will do.'

'See you later then.'

The wheels of justice were in motion. The best defence team in New Delhi was now on board. It was time to slant the game. Akash looked at his watch. 9 a.m.

His doorbell rang.

5

'THIS CASE MUST BE really important to you,' Chavi said, once Akash had ushered her into his legal studio. She sat with one leg crossed over the other on the sofa, with no writing pad to scribble on. Akash deliberately sat on the sofa, not behind the desk. The desk worked as a barrier – me and you, us and them. Wasn't that what had prompted Shilpa to sit on the sofa the day before, and not at the desk? Sitting on the same sofa somehow reflected that they were on the same side, the same team. Plus sitting behind the desk restricted a clear view of Chavi's legs. Akash was a cheeky bastard!

'What makes you say that?' His words sounded hollow even to his own ears. After having called Chavi early in the morning, promising her a story, asking her to skip her office and come here, questioning her premise was a bit pointless.

Chavi, it appeared, had read his mind. She just passed a smile.

'Yes, it is, just like every single case I sign up to take to court is important to me.' If Akash thought he had warded off her question, he was in for a surprise. Chavi was indeed an extraordinarily smart person. And she wasn't giving up or buying his lies.

'This has to be different in some way for you to be losing sleep over it. You might want to use some other adjective to describe it – how about "critical"?' She gave him another smile, one that had "I am not an idiot" written all over it. 'So why don't you try again?'

'What are you insinuating, Chavi?'

'Akash, either you trust me or you don't. The fact that you woke me up at seven in the morning—'

'Seven-thirty.'

'Let me guess: you were up at the crack of dawn, but you waited some time – no, a lot of time – to make it look like it was just another call. However, that doesn't change the point that it is significant for you and not just any other case. There is something else ...' she raised both her palms up to stop him from talking, '... something far more imperative or personal than what meets the eye, isn't it?'

'How much can I trust you?'

'It's a question you should ask yourself. As for *how* much – I'd prefer you either trust me completely or not at all.' She smiled yet again. 'What is the point of trusting someone halfway – trust isn't a percentage game. You can't be half-pregnant ...'

There was a brief silence in the room. Akash was hesitant to reveal too many details. Chavi was a friend. Okay, she was closer than some of his golfing friends, but how much did he really know her? She was fundamentally an investigative journalist. He could be unwittingly offering his head to the gallows.

'This is personal,' she said. Her voice seemed to come from behind a fog. Or maybe the sound only echoed in his mind. The fog lifted when she called it out the second time. It sounded like she had walked closer to him; it brought him out of his trance. 'That's the adjective you've been looking for, right? This case is personal. Judge Shilpa Singh is a personal friend.'

'You could say that,' he admitted.

'Akash, the passion in your eyes when you mention her name, the zeal, the fervour – this isn't just another trial for you, is it?'

'I'm at a loss for words.'

'And this?' Chavi bent, picked up her bag, unzipped it and pulled out the daily with the picture of Shilpa walking out of a Pandara Road restaurant. She turned the paper towards him, put her finger on the part of the picture where someone held Shilpa's hand.

'What is this?'

'Why are you doing this?' Chavi asked, straight-faced.

'To win the case, isn't it obvious?'

'Not just to win the case—'

'What do you mean?'

'Whose hand is it?' Chavi pointed at the picture in the daily yet again.

'Whose hand is where? What are you talking about?' He felt petulance rise in his chest and subside. It wasn't Chavi's fault if she was smart enough to have worked it out. He had been foolish to have believed that he could keep his past with Shilpa a secret.

Ignoring his questions, Chavi carried on: 'Mind telling me who the other person is?'

'I have no idea.'

'Do you mind if I take a guess who the other person is?'

'Be my guest.'

'I recognize the restaurant. *You* took me there.' Chavi seemed to have read his expression. 'Isn't this you?'

'Why do you think it's me?'

'Wrong answer; my question was: is this you?'

'It was a long … long time ago,' he conceded.

'You can trust me one hundred percent on this. You had an affair with the judge, that's entirely between you and her. I don't write columns on celebrity romances. It should have no bearing on the case at hand.'

'But it would, and you should know that. How could you be naive enough to think otherwise? The very fact that some sleazeball journalist has pulled it out and published this picture on the front page means they know about it. They—'

'Who is "they"?'

'I don't know for certain, but it has to be someone in the same camp that worked to implicate Shilpa Singh … I mean the judge in the homicide.'

'Care to elaborate for me please?

Akash gave her a *Reader's Digest* version of everything he knew about the case so far. 'It's all off the record.'

'Do you see me taking any notes?'

'I mean, a lot of it is conjecture.'

'I get it. Just so that you are aware, if I walked back to my office and narrated this to my editor, he wouldn't let me go on air with this without a source. Our editorial team is quite strict about such matters.'

'Coffee?'

'I was wondering when you'd ask. Yes, please, thanks.'

'My apologies, I should have asked earlier, but better late than never. How about breakfast? Have you eaten something?'

'Yes, I have. Coffee would be fine, thanks.'

The coffee was brought in by Akash's domestic help who quietly walked in, placed the cups down and left the office.

'What exactly do you want from me?' Chavi asked once they had settled down again. She had kicked off her six-inch heels, folded her legs under her and made herself comfortable on the sofa. Just how did she manage to do that in the tightest pencil skirt in the world, Akash wondered.

'Bring whoever is responsible for this to justice.'

'That's what the courts are for. What can I do?'

'Shift the media focus.'

Akash explained that the media would talk about the murder non-stop. Once they started digging, it was only a matter of time before they'd come across the judge's affair – if Chavi could figure that out with one printed picture, others would too – and then the whole narrative would veer towards the unimportant affair. He argued that it would do no good for the case, but it would crucify the judge's reputation. It might have started as something mischievous, but it wouldn't take long before it turned malevolent. She had an affair with an advocate and hence she must be secretive, conniving …

'You know how it is. The media will pronounce her guilty even before the trial begins. An about-turn at that point would be impossible. She'd be labelled as some depraved woman, which she is not. You following me?'

'I do, but I can't understand my role in the script so far. How can I help?'

'Like I said, I'm quite certain who's behind this. I want you to help me change the media focus. Kailash Prasad is no saint,' he said. 'All I'm asking is to add cream to the bowl of already-whipped eggs. More froth, more spillage, more filth, more visibility. Only this time the spillage would be to our advantage. I want the media to make the readers think that this is a smear campaign against a respected judge by a crooked politician, nothing more.'

'What's my source?'

'Ramesh told Ganesh who told Rajesh who, in passing, told Mahesh—'

'In other words, pure bullshit without a single bull in sight?'

'Yes, and you can blame Ramesh for that – he ran away with the bull before you could see it,' Akash returned Chavi's smile.

'I already told you, my editor wouldn't allow me to run this without a proper source.'

'Really? News needs a source, op-eds and opinions don't. Asking questions doesn't require sources. You just need to raise reasonable doubt in the minds of the public. This would give other media houses a story, and prompt the police to look into the case deeper too. Currently, they are focused solely on the judge. They think they've already cracked the case, which is not true.'

'Hypothetically speaking, even if my editor were to allow me to do this, what's in it for me?' Chavi asked. It was a good sign. Even if she had cautioned him with a hypothesis, it signified that she wasn't rejecting his request entirely. She was warming up to the idea.

'Me.'

'Eh?'

'I would owe you one. Big time.'

'Oh, I thought the great Akash Hingorani would finally be mine.'

'I'm all yours anyway.'

'Let me think before I talk to my editor.'

EIGHT

1

ASHOK KUMAR WAS DECLARED DOA: dead on arrival. It would have been a lot easier if Pentium had started from the morgue where the corpse now cooled. However, the police had been evasive about the whole situation. Even the constables who were thick with Pentium refrained from passing on any information, which was strange. Was it because this was a high-profile case? Maybe someone was pulling the strings in the background, maybe police personnel at the lower rungs weren't privy to the info themselves. End result: Pentium had nothing.

Except Pentium was the king of Ws: Who? When? Where? What? Which? Why? In his vast experience, the truth always lay in the answer to one of the Ws. Unlike the police, he didn't even believe that identifying the victim could solve the mystery. Although the name of the victim wouldn't necessarily tell them the name of the killer, it would certainly help.

Who was Ashok Kumar? How had his corpse been found with no form of identification? No wallet, no debit or credit cards, no visiting cards – neither his own nor anyone else's? No driving licence? What kind of a person doesn't carry a wallet? Then again, Pentium didn't leave trails either. He owned no credit cards, no bank account, no property, nothing that could be traced back to him. He accepted cash from everyone and paid in cash for everything. It was almost like he didn't exist. No one – not even Shri Sherlock Holmes – could ever figure out where he'd been. And no one could dig info like him either.

However, it was entirely possible that the killer swept everything off the body in the milliseconds after the murder.

With just one string of information – Kailash Prasad was an MLA from East Delhi, and presumably the dead man had some kind of a connection with the MLA or his constituency – the search for Ashok Kumar took Pentium to Shahdara, one of the oldest localities in Delhi and integral to what is called Purani Dilli, or Old Delhi.

Unfortunately, the answer to his quest wasn't painted on some wall. Without the name of the victim or his photograph, the search pretty much hit a dead end. He had called up whoever he knew in the trade – other private instigators, small-time crooks, snitches, even a constable or two – to find out if anyone they knew had gone missing. The man's physical description was the only lead he had. All he knew was that he was looking for a man in his mid-thirties who was tall and well-built and had wavy hair: talk about finding a needle in a stack of needles.

Something wasn't right. Something wasn't adding up.

How could no one have reported him missing? It had been over forty-eight hours since the incident. Shouldn't there have been family or friends somewhere who'd be looking for this guy who had clearly not made it home?

Maybe he needed to find the *where* first.

His worry was that the police didn't know anything about Ashok Kumar either. It only implied the police had made desultory inquiries and left it at that. They had passed on the task of finding the next of kin to someone really low on the totem pole, and it looked like the person had done a cursory job. With no one to claim the corpse, there was no one to bother the police about the investigation. The intensity of the search would fade quickly, if it hadn't already. The victim was a nobody, so why burn hours of resources when there were other pressing cases to pursue? And if the police didn't declare the name of the victim, it could be a while before anyone came looking for him. Quite a catch-22.

If the police had discovered his connection with Kailash Prasad, it might have been different. But KP was smart enough not to draw any attention to himself. The murder hadn't happened in his constituency. If he probed into the inquiry, it would only lead to questions he didn't want anyone asking. Or maybe there was no connection to KP at all?

However, if Judge Shilpa Singh was about to pass a judgement against the corrupt politician and the murder could get the trial dismissed, it was simple geometry that led Pentium to think that KP might have been involved in some way. And if there was no connection to KP after all, it needed to be ruled out on the basis of proof. The mystery of it all excited Pentium. One thing he was sure of was that he would find some answers in Shahdara. And there was only one way to find out.

Pentium knew he needed to scour Shahdara, but he would handle it later. His next stop was New Friends Colony. He had to find someone close to Kailash Prasad who would cough up something for the love of cash.

2

THERE NEVER WAS ANY quantification of *enough*. But merely one was certainly not, Akash Hingorani reflected. He was convinced that Chavi Nair would be able to persuade her editor to help Akash's cause. Given the reputation of his subject, Kailash Prasad, it would be easy to question his recent electoral scandal without mentioning the judge. Especially when the prize would be a scoop later from Akash. However, one journalist campaigning against a politician wasn't enough, he reckoned. Once Chavi & Co. broke the story, there should be several smaller media publications that should pick up the story and flare it up. One candle couldn't light up Delhi. Akash knew someone who should be willing to run it with their own interpretations and twists.

The name on his mind was Debashish 'Dev' Roy. Young. Ambitious. Splendid. Sublime. Ridiculous. Prudish. Pretentious. He was a freelancer with lots of contacts. He, too, was a powerful journalist who could make or ruin careers with mere adjectives. He formed opinions, decimated them.

Dev Roy was a loudmouth. He'd done it before. He'd used the power of his pen, and his presence on television. It could be debated if all the words he spoke or wrote were his own. Everything was up for sale. If a politician could be bought, why couldn't a journalist? If a judge could be implicated in a crime, why couldn't a politician be asked awkward questions?

But Dev could just select Judge Shilpa Singh as his next target. What then? It would be impossible to control the ripples he could create in the media. He needed to be contained, if not halted altogether. Better still if he could be charmed or convinced to pick a side early on. It was always better to have the dogs barking from your pavilion, than at you. In PR speak, they called it damage control.

'Hi Dev,' Akash called him around lunch.

'Oh, I must have missed it. Did the sun rise in the west today? Krishna is calling Sudama?'

'Ha-ha, if only you had been attentive at school, Dev, you'd have known that in the real story, too, it was Lord Krishna who called on Sudama and washed his friend's feet, not the other way around.'

'True that, but that still makes you Krishna, doesn't it?'

'Hardly. You're the true lord – you make news, my friend. I'm just a lowly officer of the law.'

'Oh my, my – the ever-self-deprecating man, Akash Hingorani. How may I be of any help?'

'Dev, I need a favour …'

'You need a favour? From me? Oh, I already have a hard-on, Akash … go on.'

3

PENTIUM TOOK A DETOUR to visit the scene of the crime before heading to New Friends Colony. The police had officially lifted the restrictions off the area now. There was only so much time they could spend searching for clues in a public place. It was impossible to guard the place around the clock, and there'd be no sanctity of the chain of custody if anything was discovered after it was left unguarded. They had taken photographs, collected whatever evidence they could and cleaned up the place. Even the tape that had been put up to mark the murder site had been removed, but the faded chalk markings led Pentium to the exact spot.

Although you could say this for many places in the world, Lodhi Gardens in the day and Lodhi Gardens in the night were two separate continents: beauty by day, menacing at dark. One inhabited, the other deserted. In most corners of the garden the only light was what the sun brought in and took back when it left at nightfall. No one stayed back during the night, except maybe some animals.

Pentium's first thought wasn't different from Akash's: what was the judge thinking coming here alone? But there must be someone who would have seen something.

During the daytime, there were usually a lot of people around. Families. Children enjoying a round of hopscotch, skipping ropes, playing all sorts of games. Pentium knew asking anyone anything at this time would bring no results. These were transient visitors. He needed to speak to those who resided here illegally. Despite the closed gates, Pentium knew that a lot of homeless souls spent nights here under the blanket of the sky in summers, winters and in heavy monsoons. Not by choice but because of the lack of it. He would have to return after dark to speak to these illegal residents, who were always present in the garden.

NINE

1

TO BE OR NOT to be: one way or another you cannot help but marvel at Shakespeare's insight to have asked such a pertinent question four centuries ago, one that served as a template for many of life's simple problems. Fast-forward to the twenty-first century when Akash Hingorani, sitting in his legal studio, sought an answer to the bard's question, but found himself at a loss about the correct response. *To be or not to be* alone with Shilpa on a trip to Mussoorie to meet her son. He had promised he'd go with her; no issues there. But his dilemma was if he should take his driver, Mandeep, for the trip. If Shilpa and he were alone in the car for a long drive – Delhi to Mussoorie was almost 300 kilometres, a seven- or eight-hour journey including rest breaks – he wasn't sure whether he wanted Mandeep to accompany them. He didn't want him listening in on their conversations, some of which might not be pertaining to the case he was handling, the ones about rehashing the past. It wasn't like Mandeep hadn't known about the relationship. Or that he would talk to someone about it. But still, Akash recognized that the quandary he had wasn't about Mandeep, it was about him; he realized he didn't have an answer because he was asking the wrong question. He still harboured feelings for Shilpa and wondered if their relationship could be reignited. The possibility of Mandeep accompanying them on the journey limited that possibility. Once the awareness of his true problem emerged, the answer was staring him in the face. Even if they rekindled the old flame, what was there to stop it from burning out again? The issues – the differences between them, the disparate outlooks, the professional incompatibility – still remained. Was there any merit in starting yet another verbal duel elaborating that everyone made poor choices, that one way or another everyone was blemished by sins? And everyone had, at some point, succumbed to temptation, however small. All it might lead to was another heartache.

Moreover, an affair with the judge, at this juncture, would be fodder for the media; it would add unnecessary complications to the trial. It was better to let Mandeep drive. He was indeed a better driver than Akash. The guy somehow always knew all the routes, irrespective of where they were travelling to, he instinctively knew where to park and, God forbid, in case of a break down, he'd be more than handy.

2

FRIDAY MORNING, THE DAY Judge Shilpa Singh was called to court, had been an uneventful one. There wasn't any brouhaha. As per the diktat from Judge Mathur, the press wasn't welcome, although if the prosecution had been given a choice, they'd have personally sent invitations to every member of the media.

They'd have organized a circus, maybe an event, called in Britney Spears to pull in more crowds and hired Mercedes Benzes to cart them around.

Unlike other clients, Shilpa didn't require any preparation or advice on how to dress or what to say. She wore a stylishly tied cream silk saree and heels to make her look tall and regal. She made it a point not to look under the cloud. She carried herself with dignity, indicating with every move that she had been wrongly implicated in this matter. She wanted Judge Mathur to know that she recognized that justice would be served by the end of it all. She wasn't a criminal. If anything, she was part of the elegant tribe that Mathur himself belonged to.

The case was presented in court, and as expected and agreed, Shilpa pleaded not guilty. As decided, Akash did not appear at the hearing due to his botched relationship with Justice Vikrant Mathur. Vansh Diwan and Sonia Pahwa were running the show. It wasn't clear whether Mathur was aware that Sonia was from Hingorani's team. He extended all possible courtesy to his peer and didn't lend his ear to the prosecution's plea of revoking her bail. Shilpa Singh fleeing the country, to him, must have sounded like a hyperbole.

'I personally know that the defendant doesn't even have a passport; how do you plan to purport your theory that she's a flight risk?' were his words that sealed the fate of the prosecution's request. Prosecutor Harsh Mehta's half-hearted attempt at revoking Shilpa's bail was, hence, quashed.

Judge Mathur was known for his egalitarian beliefs; he had little tolerance for theatrics, exaggeration or stupidity. Rumours in the courthouse cast him as a man in a hurry to run back to the little whisky-filled hip flask he carried around with him, although no one ever saw him taking a sip or smelled alcohol on him. Maybe he savoured vodka. In the end, Shilpa was let go on her own recognizance. No deposit.

'I haven't seen a case like this in over three decades of my career. Both the parties will hear from my office very shortly. Are there any more motions or appeals?'

Neither the prosecution nor the defence moved.

Whoever had masterminded this entire game was quite confident that the noose they had devised for Shilpa Singh was tight enough. They had neither made their presence felt in or near the courtroom, nor made their existence apparent in any way. It was a good strategy. But they would surely be watching from close quarters, and take note of Akash Hingorani's conspicuous absence. They might interpret it wrongly, and that would not be so bad for Akash.

3

'HOW THE FUCK DID she get bail on a murder charge?' Kailash Prasad barked at his three henchmen. His words echoed in every corner if the room. He was a large man. Correction. Kailash Prasad or KP sahib or KP bhai, as his cronies referred to him, was a gigantic man, like a water buffalo on two legs. He must have had zits when he was younger because pockmarks covered his face. Bald, large-headed, pot-bellied and a square, unpleasant jaw gave him the appearance of a *rakshasa*. Well, at least his looks matched his temperament and character.

'The judge, Mr Mathur, wasn't convinced she was a flight

risk,' Narendra Chauhan, his chief associate, responded meekly, like it was his personal fault the court of law hadn't ruled as KP had anticipated. The others, Jagjit Kumar and Alok Pandey, were equally nervous about facing their boss, who was indeed in an unpleasant mood. KP was known for throwing objects at people when he was angry and drunk.

'You said that big shot-lawyer, whats-his-name, didn't even come to the court.'

'He didn't, bhai, which was a surprise.'

'So, she didn't go running to him then?'

'But Akash Hingorani's junior was present in the court, so was Vansh Diwan.'

'How confident are you that she will be convicted?'

'Bhai, she cannot escape. It's a cut-and-dried case. Moreover, the police has discovered that Ashok Kumar had called her the same afternoon and asked her to meet him at Lodhi Gardens—'

'He was an angel, that Ashok Kumar, godsend even – may his soul rest in peace. Otherwise that bitch had caught me by my short and curlies. We need to ensure she gets prosecuted, and the case against me is shut once and forever, okay?'

The underlings nodded their acquiescence in fear.

4

AKASH AND SHILPA STARTED for Mussoorie at the crack of dawn. The earlier you got out of the limits of the vast megalopolis that was Delhi NCR, the better. The mood in the car was sombre. The night before, Shilpa's suspension orders had arrived as expected. She was not to attend to office matters and was not even permitted to enter her office. She had only gone there to retrieve her personal stuff under security. Since she was one of theirs, they hadn't cut her loose yet. But they, too, would sit on the fence and wait for the final outcome. It would inevitably be a media trial. Keen eyes would be watching to see if any favours were granted because she was cut from the same silk.

As Akash had planned, and envisioned, the headlines in the news had changed: JUDGE CAUGHT IN POLITICAL WHIRLPOOL. The theme was covered by a few dailies.

That set the tone. His contact Dev Roy had delivered the first shot, a hard-hitting one at that. And Chavi Nair, once she had the ammunition, had started the questioning too. Akash hadn't spoken to her since, but as anticipated, she had been smart enough to pick it up and run with it. She investigated into what all had been achieved in Kailash Prasad's constituency since he had become an MLA. The job wasn't done; it had only begun. Diverse media groups attacking a single entity would surely raise eyebrows. It was only a matter of time before everyone who was anyone raised questions pertinent to KP: a snowballing effect. The judge's case, fingers crossed, would slip down in the priority list and be relegated to the second page. Not making the headlines didn't mean a victory but it meant something.

News like this was a birthday present for tabloid editors. Other reporters, bloggers, TV anchors, photographers, shit-stirrers would soon lap it up. You had to give it to them. True or false or somewhere in between, the media always had bigger stories than the police. They also came with more mouths and louder voices. All in all, Akash knew his call to Dev had been successful.

Two hours into their trip, they had crossed Meerut and stopped at a highway restaurant.

'Promise me,' Shilpa said once they were out of Mandeep's earshot, 'if something happens to me, you will take care of Raghuveer.'

'Nothing will happen to you,' Akash responded promptly, but somehow he had a niggling feeling that he was maybe promising something he wasn't sure about. It hardly mattered whether you were a saint if you were in the lion's lair. The lion wasn't born to reason or empathize. Hadn't Akash, through the decades of his career, seen innocent people lose trials and criminals escape justice? There were no guarantees, no promises on which side the court would rule.

'Akash, sometimes the future one makes for oneself – even inadvertently – doesn't allow for any turning back. It was rather careless of me to go to meet Ashok Kumar the other day, don't you think? I should have let the moment pass without intervention.'

'It was rather impetuous of you, I would say.' He had wanted to stay careless or reckless but he held it back. Despite how hard he tried, Akash struggled to find a line of thought to follow. What had she been thinking? Why couldn't Ashok Kumar have posted the evidence if he really had any? Who used audio cassettes these days to tape secret conversations? And if it were indeed taped on a cassette, Ashok Kumar could have converted the file for electronic transfer and sent it to Shilpa? That would have provided him complete anonymity like he needed. It smelled like a trap from the get go, but then again, everyone's an Einstein in retrospect. A million questions came to mind, but none that he could ask her.

'I know. They say it is all written in the stars.'

'You believe in that?' Akash looked at her. He hadn't ever thought she believed in such things.

'One cannot help but believe in such things when one is put in a situation like this.'

'Nothing will happen to you, Shilpa Singh. You've got Vansh and me; we will sort it out. I'm sure any judge they put on the case would be able to see through the entire charade here ...'

'You can mount the best defence, but we don't know which way the ruling will go. It might take months, years.'

'We'll see.'

'Yes, let's not be too optimistic and lose the plot. Let's prepare for the worst-case scenario. Whatever the future, it's got to be faced. I'm only asking you to be there for Raghuveer in case—'

'You have my word,' said Akash, not wishing to extend the ungainly dialogue any longer. Shilpa looked distressed, yet Akash couldn't help but marvel at her inner strength. Even at a time like this, her priority was her son. Maternal instincts had made her ignore the perilous situation she was in herself. She could lose everything – her name, her reputation, her freedom, her life.

'The stress is ageing me faster than cocaine ...'

'How do you know cocaine ages people? You ever tried it?' he responded jocularly only to lighten the mood.

She smiled.

The memories of their time together needed little but a hint to come rushing back, but neither wanted to entertain them at this time. The atmosphere in the car wasn't tuned for them. Shilpa, Akash knew, wasn't one to show emotional fragility. Whatever she felt, she could contain behind the tough exterior she thought she had. To Akash, it was apparent she was troubled. But he was careful not to display any pity; it could send a wrong signal, hurt her pride which was undoubtedly brittle at this minute.

'If only I knew who's turning the dials here …' he said, but then went quiet and let the sound of the tyres on the tarmac take over.

5

THE CASE VANSH DIWAN had been buried under was now over, and that allowed him all the time in the world to focus on Judge Shilpa Singh's case. He knew Akash was travelling with her, so he had called Sonia Pahwa to his office on Barakhamba Road.

'Any luck?' he asked as they sat in his office sipping hot coffees.

'The police officer I spoke to, Senior Inspector Ajay Yadav, seems to be Kailash Prasad's ass-licker,' Sonia said, running her fingers through her hair. Her smooth, straight hair had been chopped off in the shape of an inverted V at the rear, exposing her beautiful, swan-like neck. A small tattoo rested there: the peace symbol. She had bark-coloured eyes, which were currently behind stylish reading glasses.

'Of course he'd be. He's from the same clan.'

'What do you mean?'

'Kailash Prasad Yadav – isn't that the scoundrel's full name?'

'Oh, I didn't know that.'

'Now you do, so you can appreciate where the bloody inspector's loyalties lie. Not to forget, Kailash Prasad is a big shot. He has power and money – the two things required to make things happen, conceal unfavourable incidents, win friends in the right places ... No, we'll have to go to court to get the details out of him or maybe call in our chips with other police officers for the information to prepare a solid case for the defence. He won't budge from his stance, trust me.'

'Did someone communicate any dates yet?' Sonia asked.

'No, but I reckon we'll hear something soon. They wouldn't want to delay a case like this. They'd rather close this file one way or another so that the entire judiciary isn't laughed at. If Judge Shilpa Singh is found innocent, they'll shout themselves hoarse that they were being targeted. If she is found guilty, they'll wash their hands of her as quickly as possible. It's the way of the world.'

'Do you think they might convict her – one of their own?'

'Sure, it all depends on the arguments in the court, and you know that.'

'What, according to you, are the chances she'll be acquitted?'

'Grim, if you want me to be honest. The evidence against the judge is overwhelming. She was caught at the scene of crime with the murder weapon in her hand. Hopeless odds, I have to admit, but we've all been wrong in our assessments before.'

He let his spiel penetrate the silence in the room. It was an eerie thought, even if it were the truth.

'Surely, you and Akash have represented clients some of the other defence lawyers wouldn't touch with a pole.'

'None where the accused was caught with a weapon in her hand … But I've always believed a courtroom trial is akin to a cricket match. Sometimes the last ball can change the outcome. We have very scarce info at the moment. Maybe there's something we don't know yet, which could change everything.'

Sonia nodded. The gravity of the situation was not lost on her.

'I haven't been able to sit with Akash and discuss anything yet,' Vansh continued, 'but I'm sure he is feeling the heat too. Things aren't looking as good as I would like them to. If it hadn't been for Shilpa's brief relationship with Akash …' he paused mid-sentence upon gathering that he had blurted out about the surreptitious affair. Embarrassed, he put the cup of coffee down and looked at Sonia, wishing he could take the words back.

'Mr Diwan, you must give me some credit. I know my boss was once close to the judge. A lot of us at the office know that. Akash doesn't know that we know, so we've kept it that way. I promise you I won't utter a word regarding this slip-up. It's okay, let's get back to discussing the case.'

'I'm sorry if I sounded too pessimistic.'

'Realistic, if you ask my opinion. My feelings are similar. I wonder what rabbit Akash can pull out of his fedora this time around.'

'It's sad. I know the judge personally due to her close relationship with …'

'Akash.'

'Yes … she's a good person, only a bit obstinate. It's sad to see someone like her getting accused of a crime like this. Murder, no less. But it is what it is. Let me dig around and speak to some people higher up in the chain of command and get some information. We should keep a skeleton of the defence arguments ready before they come back from Mussoorie.'

'When will they be back?'

'Tuesday.'

'Okay.'

TEN

1

THE JUDICIARY, NEVER KNOWN for administrative alacrity, seemed to have eventually got its act together. A date was set in six weeks – enough time for both sides to gather evidence and prepare for the trial. The shadow looming over the suspended Judge Shilpa Singh could spread darkness over the entire bench. Letting her go on bail with no bond posted was the extent of their compassion. They couldn't afford meting out special treatment. Or at the very least could not be seen showing clemency.

Judge Mohan Tripathi was the first judge approached to preside over the case of 'State of Delhi vs Shilpa Singh', but he recused himself. He used to be Shilpa's unofficial mentor when she had just started her career in law. Truth be told, most judges would shy away from taking charge in a situation like this where they'd be deciding on the fate of another judge who was a peer until only a week ago. But someone had to do it, and Judge Anshuman Durve was that someone who had been picked in this instance. Tall, lean, clean-shaven, a full head of L'Oréal dark hair, in his late forties, he was referred to as

AD by all his underlings in the court circuits. While he had a stellar reputation as an objective and impartial judge – not a single blot on his resume – and his selection was welcomed, his overloaded docket made him a nightmare to deal with. Finding time in his diary on short notice was nearly impossible.

Judge Durve was of the opinion that no advocate who practised law in Delhi NCR should be permitted to lead the prosecution. And he had the best intentions in mind. Anyone representing the State against *Judge* Shilpa Singh would have a jaundiced opinion – she or he'd have either a positive or a negative bias since they might have already been in her court. And when, he highlighted further – *when*, not *if* – she got reinstated into the judiciary after the trial was over, it would be impossible for the person prosecuting her now to ever present a case in her court.

The next question was: who was to be appointed as the prosecutor?

Ravi Nanda was an obvious choice. One of the most fearsome, the most respected and the most sought-after prosecutors in Mumbai – he'd taken on errant politicians, even ministers, mafia dons, film stars, too. He was slick, his conviction rate was close to one hundred percent, and he used the least number of witnesses: only those who were essential to the case since he didn't believe in wasting the court's time. Money didn't matter to him since he was the only child of a millionaire industrialist, and he knew he'd one day inherit more wealth than most people could earn or save in their lifetimes. In a perfect world, he'd have refused to take on prosecuting a sitting judge in New Delhi, but he was clever enough to know judges had their own web of influence. Declining a request – it was only veiled as one – from a judge in the capital wouldn't sit well on his resume.

There was some justice in the world, he convinced himself. After all, this trial guaranteed screen presence on television sets across the country and more column space in the press than any other case.

2

MONDAY MORNING IN MUSSOORIE: The wind was strong. The sun was bright. There was just a small translucent white cloud, which didn't seem to have any intent of bursting. Or maybe it wasn't capable of doing so. The streets were full of people with cameras. Picture-postcard Mussoorie. Just like Akash had imagined. He had never been to this quaint hill station before, despite it being not too far from Delhi.

By the time Shilpa and Akash had arrived the night before, the school's hostel had been locked for the day and there was no way the principal was letting any parent in, however influential she might be.

Raghuveer Singh was sixteen, but he was already six-foot-two. A boy in a man's body. Being short, Akash found it surprising to see the boy towering over him – the only complex the powerful lawyer had in his life was concerning his height. But Raghuveer was a calm giant. The hair on this face had started sprouting, but unlike other boys who try shaving at this stage, he'd bleached his facial hairs and they shone in the sun. Perhaps, this was the latest trend of this generation. His mother looked puny in comparison.

But he surprised both Shilpa and Akash. He didn't mention the tricky situation her mother had landed herself in, but it was evident to Akash that the boy knew about it.

For the first time in days, Shilpa finally broke down. It came as a surprise to Akash who was used to seeing Shilpa hold it together when the going got tough. They were in a cafe at the time, so Akash went out for a stroll with Mandeep, leaving mother and son to relay their fears and anxieties to each other. Whatever fears they experienced together needed to be quelled. In Akash's experience, fear was like hunger – if not taken care of in time, it had a tendency to grow exponentially.

When he returned, he saw the two of them holding hands, trying to comfort each other. Their faces looked like they had had a fair share of the waterworks, but that was expected.

'Raghu, why don't you show Akash around while I talk to the school principal?' Shilpa said on Akash's return.

Akash, not anticipating this immediately upon his return, looked at Raghuveer like he sought the boy's approval.

'I told him all about us. He's mature enough to understand his mother was dating you, but we are through with that now. He knows that you are representing me as my defence lawyer on a spurious murder charge ...'

'Yes, uncle. I kn—'

'Akash ... call me Akash. That's the only way to build a one-to-one relationship with anyone.'

'Mum told me you play golf. She's booked a nine-hole round for us nearby; why not go there? We'll rent the clubs and play?'

'That's fine by me.'

'Okay, you boys go, and I'll go chat with the principal.'

'Why don't you come along?' asked Akash. 'What is this conversation with the principal that cannot wait?'

'Like we had discussed on the way up here, I'm designating you as Raghuveer's guardian, should anything happen to me ...'

Akash nodded and asked Raghuveer to lead the way.

3

THE GOLF COURSE WAS windy; the game was okay. Raghuveer was a quick learner. Somewhere at the fourth hole, Raghuveer stopped, looked at Akash and asked him point blank, 'Do you think you can get Mum out of this mess?'

'I'm fairly confident—'

'You know she's not guilty, right?'

'I know.'

The two continued with the game without any conversation until the seventh hole when Raghuveer stopped again and asked Akash: 'Could I ask you a question?'

'Of course you can.'

'You still love her, don't you?'

Kids these days!

'What makes you say that?'

'So you agree you love her; you're only asking me why I'm asking?'

'Maybe.' It was quite an ambiguous response, but Akash didn't know how else to respond to his question.

'What's maybe? It's either yes or no.' He was his mother's son.

'Yes, but not in the way—'

'There is no other way, Akash. I appreciate your being here with her, taking guardianship of her son – you still love her.'

'Thank you.' Akash didn't want to unsettle Raghuveer by elaborating that the abyss between the judge and him was unbridgeable. Raghuveer looked composed, but only on the surface. If given a nudge, he'd break down; the boy was trying to be a man and Akash thought he was doing a real good job.

'You're welcome!'

They returned after visiting the nine holes, agreeing to keep in touch.

4

SHILPA AND AKASH STARTED for Delhi on Tuesday morning.

With each passing moment and kilometre, the feeling of despair continued to grow. As much as they tried to, they couldn't be certain of an optimistic eventuality in this case. How could there be one?

Mussoorie was in the rear-view mirror: the clouds hung low and appeared undecided about whether they wanted to rain or not.

'What did you tell Raghuveer?'

'That I've been charged with homicide, and you'll be representing me—'

'Not that, Shilpa, I wanted to know what you told him was the reason behind making me his guardian.'

'He knows the charges against me are bogus; he is confident they will all go away. He is convinced you're the best lawyer to handle the case, so I told him it was a precaution just in case I become unavailable due to legal reasons …'

Akash didn't know what to say next.

'You know, Akash, whether it's right or wrong or justified, you know, some mud always sticks. The doubt will remain forever.' She was talking about the repercussions even if she won the case. That kept the mood sombre throughout the journey. There was some truth to what she was saying. Even if she won the case, it was impossible to say that she would emerge unscathed and untarnished after the trial.

5

RAVI NANDA HAD BOOKED two executive suites at the Svelte in Saket for himself and his second chair, Diya Albuquerque. Rumours were aplenty that Ravi and Diya only pretended to be merely business associates. They were rolling in the sheets, but to keep up pretences, he'd booked separate suites. He was a state guest after all. And if anyone questioned his expenses, his pockets were deep enough anyway. Diya was wrapping up a trial in Mumbai and was yet to arrive in Delhi, but Nanda was already on the ground within twenty-four hours of the first call from the capital.

Harsh Mehta, the lawyer who had led the prosecution at the initial hearing, was told to provide all necessary assistance to Nanda as he was working in a new territory. Mehta had been the one who'd arranged for a taxi for Nanda to take him to meet Judge Durve.

Nanda thanked the judge for the opportunity and for his faith in Nanda's capabilities to ensure a fair trial. He hadn't heard of Shilpa Singh before he had been called and thus, there was no bias. He would fly back to Mumbai after the case, so Shilpa Singh – if and when she was reinstated – would not be presiding over a case where he was the trial lawyer.

Mehta took Nanda to the Lodhi Colony Police Station where they had taken Shilpa Singh after the arrest. With a judge from Saket District Court calling the shots, Nanda was accorded every courtesy and given access to all the evidence in police custody. SP Ajay Yadav almost genuflected to appease the prosecutor. He couldn't wait for Nanda to leave so he could make a call to relay to Kailash Prasad that they'd found the right match for Hingorani.

Mehta apprised Nanda about Hingorani. 'And he isn't alone either – he's teamed up with his old friend Vansh Diwan, who is an equally brilliant criminal defence advocate. The two of them can be quite intimidating. Vansh is good, but he's quite tame; it's Akash Hingorani you need to be wary of.'

'What do you mean?'

'Hingorani will rip open the carcass of the case. He'll crucify the police for poor crime scene procedures and call out their tunnel vision. He'll bring in premier experts. We need to get him out of the game,' he said effusively.

'Hmm ...'

'I know it might sound like an exaggeration, but without Hingorani, Shilpa Singh's toast, trust me.'

Nanda preferred to do his own research, instead of simply taking Mehta's word for it. After Mehta left for the day – he'd called his Mumbai office to get all the information they had on Akash emailed to himself. After perusing all the material, he was ready to accept that Akash Hingorani was a real threat in the courtroom.

And with Vansh next to him – however docile – they would be overwhelming, like Mehta had warned. But intimidating Nanda was no easy job either. He had to find a way to outsmart them – to show his mettle early on and get them on the backfoot, so to speak. From all that he had learned about Hingorani, the man was dangerous in every conceivable way. And he was playing on his own turf.

Ravi Nanda was as sharp as they came, but he wore a worried expression on his face all the time. Long frown lines had found permanent residence on his forehead like wickets on a cricket pitch. Since he had a large forehead, his eyes seemed to be set low on his face. He didn't have an ominous aura, but he didn't look like a friendly used-car salesman either. Even if he were the last man on earth, he wouldn't get the role of a romantic hero in any film, but he wasn't looking to act in one either. He was a bright lawyer. And, at this minute, sitting in his suite with his feet up on the table and a half-chewed pencil in his mouth – he acknowledged the fact that he was taking a knife to a gunfight. Even with his sharp wits, he recognized he was no match for Akash and Vansh put together; no way he was going to take the two of them head on. It was an uneven contest with the odds in his opponents' favour. He knew he had to eliminate one, if not both, from this trial, if he wanted to emerge victorious. He had nothing against Judge Shilpa Singh per se, but winning a case of this magnitude would put him in the national limelight like never before, causing his career to skyrocket even further. He had a long way to go, and he was still young. Thirty-eight was young, right? He was younger than both his opponents. Together, Akash and Vansh would put him at the bottom of a septic tank, no doubt about that. His law career could be over even in Mumbai. That bothered him to no end, but only until he received an anonymous phone call from a saviour, his guardian angel in this alien town.

The caller was a man, spoke in Hindi, refused to identify himself and was adamant that no one should know about this call ever. He provided a crucial nugget of information that could be confirmed elsewhere, but Nanda would need to act upon it without divulging the source.

After the short call was over, Nanda's face lit up. He called room service and ordered champagne. Then he called Diya and gave her the news.

'You're kidding me,' she said.

'Nope. I guess we need to confirm the same before I approach Judge Durve. But I honestly don't think it's a bluff.'

'But how did the caller find you?'

'I don't know. He just did. News travels fast here, I guess.'

'Hmm … I'll ask the team to dig into it. When do you want me to be in Delhi?'

'Tonight itself would be lovely.'

'I can be there by tomorrow night. I'll book an evening flight and be with you tomorrow.'

'Good – get confirmation about what I've told you, and let me know. ASAP, please. I'll ask the judge to make time in his diary next week. Let's present this petition together. See you tomorrow.'

'Love you.'

6

'*KAAM HO GAYA, BHAI*' – mission accomplished – said one of the many testicles Kailash Prasad carried with him, after he had called and delivered the tip to Nanda as he had been asked to do. KP wanted to bury Shilpa Singh. Now that his distant relative had supplied the nails to Nanda, they knew the prosecutor was more than capable of driving them into her coffin.

ELEVEN

1

RAVI NANDA HAD ASKED for an appointment with Judge Durve a week ago, and it took a good ten days before the judge's diary allowed a hearing for the petition the prosecution wanted to present. It wasn't something Durve would have considered ordinarily, but Nanda had highlighted it as *extraordinary circumstances* in the plea.

Diya Albuquerque, Ravi Nanda and Harsh Mehta were already chatting in Durve's chambers, when Sonia, Vansh and Akash were ushered in.

'Good morning,' said Judge Durve. Introductions followed, coffee was served, and for a while it seemed like they had gathered for a tea party of like-minded individuals. Which it both was and wasn't. Despite the courtesies, formalities and smiles on the surface, everyone in the room knew the hostile undercurrents could drown them all. The smiles faded the instant the court clerk moved in and Judge Durve announced that the meeting would go on record since the prosecution team had asked him to address a petition before the trial – a special case. Anshuman Durve was quite aware that he'd be under the media spotlight and was cautious to not be seen as being remotely partial to the defence.

'You can start, Mr Nanda … we are recording now,' Judge Durve smiled and looked at the court clerk – a mousy gentleman in his fifties who sat with a laptop to type every word he heard from this point onwards.

'Thank you, Your Honour,' Nanda's voice and articulation were pure honey. 'We've been put in a quandary …'

Something in Nanda's demeanour, not his words, was foreboding. Akash nudged Sonia, who in turn elbowed Vansh. They were all ears, ready for … what? They didn't know.

'I'm sure if we changed positions, my esteemed colleagues in the defence team would equally be at a loss for words like I am here, but I guess there's no way to circumvent the truth.'

'Mr Nanda,' Judge Durve, thankfully, called out, 'then, let's hear what your conundrum is.'

'It has been brought to our notice that Mr Akash Hingorani, the lead in the defence team, had a love affair with the defendant, Ms Shilpa Singh, a few months ago …'

Akash stood up. 'So, what has that got to do with the trial?' He found it hard to contain himself.

'Mr Hingorani, I request you to sit down and listen to what Mr Nanda has to say, please. Mr Nanda, even if what you say is true, and we'll come to that in a moment, may I ask why that should be a problem?'

'As I said when I began, it's a tricky situation we've been put in. I don't have to labour the point, Your Honour, that the prosecution will need to ask Mr Hingorani to be present as a material witness at the trial, which would most certainly be embarrassing for him, the defendant and the court …'

In India, if an advocate was called as a witness by the other side, it could safely be left to the good sense of the advocate to determine whether he should continue to appear as an advocate, or if by so doing he would embarrass the court or the client.

There was no *explicit* rule that gave the court the right to remove an advocate from a case, but in the case of 'Emperor vs Dadu Rama Surde' in 1938, Chief Justice Beaumont, speaking for the Division Bench of Bombay High Court, consisting of CJ Beaumont and CJ Wassoodew, observed:

> The question whether the Court has jurisdiction to forbid an advocate to appear in a particular case involves the consideration of conflicting principles. On the one hand, an accused person is entitled to select the advocate whom he desires to appear for him and certainly the prosecution cannot fetter that choice merely by serving a subpoena on the advocate to appear as a witness. On the other hand, the Court is bound to see that the due administration of justice is not in any way embarrassed … If a Court comes to the conclusion that a trial will be embarrassed by the appearance of an advocate who has been called as a witness by the other side, and if, notwithstanding the Court's expression of its opinion, the advocate refuses to withdraw, in my opinion, in such a case the Court has inherent jurisdiction to require the advocate to withdraw …

Ravi Nanda had chosen the words aptly. Adding embarrassment in the mix was enough for Judge Durve's eyebrows to go up.

In the case of 'Emperor vs Dadu Rama Surde', Chief Justice Beaumont had clarified that 'the prosecution in such a case must establish to the satisfaction of the Court that the trial will be materially embarrassed, if the advocate continues to appear for the defence …'

'Am I on the witness list?' Akash sprang up again.

'Yes, you are.' Nanda smiled at Akash and looked back at Judge Durve.

Nanda had hit where it hurt. 'Your Honour, as you can well imagine our dilemma – we had no intentions of casting aspersions on a fellow learned colleague by bringing him in as a witness, but I'm sure you will appreciate that we're obliged to follow all possible lines of questioning to come to the truth. There can be no compromise.'

'Your Honour, this is bull—'

'This might not be the courtroom; Mr Hingorani, but do I have to remind you that you are talking in the presence of a judge? I request you to control your emotions and mind your language. I will not caution you again, but hold you in contempt should I hear one such word from you again. Do we understand each other?' Anshuman Durve warned sternly. 'I want you to remain quiet until we have heard Mr Nanda's entire petition. Understood?'

'Yes, Your Honour.'

'Good, then please be seated.'

The earth slipped below Akash's feet. This couldn't be happening. He might have been a master of three-dimensional chess, but Ravi Nanda had worked out the ninth permutation. He had brilliantly checkmated Akash.

'I can't believe this, Your Honour, this is foul play.'

'Mr Hingorani, I don't speak to hear my voice. When I tell you to remain quiet, I mean it. Now, do I make myself clear? Another word from you and I will have to ask you to leave the chambers.'

> '... an advocate cannot cross-examine himself, nor can he usefully address the Court as to the credibility of his own testimony, and a Court may well feel that justice will not be done if the advocate continues to appear.'

It was a cunning ploy to eliminate Akash from the defence team. And for that, Nanda only had to prove to the judge, at this moment, why Akash could be a material witness in the trial.

'Mr Nanda, continue, and please enlighten us why Mr Hingorani's alleged affair that you've just quoted makes him a material witness in the "State of Delhi vs Shilpa Singh", bearing in mind you have just admitted that the *so-called* affair was a while ago,' Judge Durve asked Nanda to explicate.

'Your Honour, murder isn't a trivial crime as we all are well aware. It might be a crime of passion, but in the case of "State of Delhi vs Shilpa Singh", this isn't likely since we have no evidence of any past relationship between the victim and the defendant. They had met – and I quote the media and the police here – 'for the victim to pass on evidence in favour of the defendant, one Mr Kailash Prasad Yadav'. This is in relation to a case that was being tried in the court of the then Judge Shilpa Singh. So, the team feels, that for anyone to commit such a heinous act, it is possible that there were certain traits in the defendant's personality that should have been latently present, and that may or may not have been evident to a past lover.' Nanda paused.

Bastard! Akash wanted to flip a bird at Nanda but better sense prevailed. His Honour would surely have him struck off the register for that. Or impose some other severe penalty.

'And you think by questioning Mr Hingorani, those personality traits of the defendant – that he might or might not have noticed – would come to light?' Judge Durve asked.

'Your Honour, I wouldn't like to speculate on that aspect at this moment, but we can only be certain about that after we get to question Mr Hingorani as a witness.'

'Mr Hingorani, you are not under any oath, but we need an honest answer on the record here. Were you ever romantically involved with Judge Shilpa Singh as the prosecution claims?' Durve asked after a few seconds of contemplation. This was unprecedented for him, too. He had never sat on the trial of a fellow judge. He hadn't been asked to take a stance on the subject of excluding the defence advocate of the accused either.

'Your Honour, it's immaterial …'

'The answer I need, Mr Hingorani, is either a *yes* or a *no*. Essentially, any other response you come up with would be immaterial.'

'Yes, Your Honour.'

'Mr Hingorani, I cannot take away the constitutional right of your client to choose her advocate and hence, I will not forbid you to represent her, but I would strongly recommend that you step down …' Judge Durve raised his hand to stop Akash from interrupting him, '… rethink, re-evaluate, speak to your client – I'm sure your client wouldn't want to embarrass the court any more than I do.'

'But, Your Honour …'

Akash felt Vansh's hand on his shoulder. Vansh didn't utter a word but the shoulder press was good enough to let Akash know that he needed to shut up. No amount of pleading would change Judge Durve's decision.

Vansh wasn't surprised at Akash's reaction, but it was nevertheless embarrassing to witness his friend being emotional and irrational. He was moments away from crossing the line that could destroy his years of labour, his reputation and his relationship with the judge.

'Mr Diwan, we leave it to you to make the defendant aware of our discussion and let her decide who she wants to lead her defence. Is that clear?' Durve had turned away from Akash. The finality in the judge's voice made it clear that he had already decided that Akash had conceded.

'Yes, Your Honour.'

'Alright then, the prosecution's petition has been heard. Is there anything else either of the parties wishes to discuss at this point?'

'Yes, Your Honour,' Vansh said, and carried on without pausing for the judge to respond, 'we're having a hard time getting information to mount a defence in this particular case …'

'Mr Mehta,' Judge Durve scowled, lowered his voice and pointed at the lawyer, like he was chastising him, 'this is unacceptable.'

'But sir, we are only being told about this now—'

'And let this be the last time, too. I order you to carry out your duties responsibly by making sure the relevant evidence, autopsy reports, information about the police investigation are handed over to the defence team before the end of the week. Do not withhold any information, for your own sake – I hope I'm clear. Whatever you currently have on file, ask someone to send it to them, and whatever you receive should be sent to them without any delay. Is that clear to you and everyone in the prosecution team?'

'Yes, Your Honour,' the three prosecution advocates said in unison, like echoes of 'Thank you, ma'am' in a classroom.

'Also, I do not want anyone from the prosecution team speaking to the media about this meeting. The reason for Mr Hingorani's generous offer to step down should remain behind these walls. I will personally come after you if I come across any gossip in the tabloids. During the trial, of course, the relationship between the defendant and Mr Hingorani cannot be concealed but I don't want the media to start speculating for now. Am I understood by all parties?' If Judge Durve was attempting to assuage Akash's bruised ego in any way, he was missing it by miles. 'And now, if there is nothing else, let me remind you that we are going to trial next month. Mid-March. The exact dates should already be in your diaries. Have a good day.'

Nanda and team had won the first round hands down.

Akash Hingorani, apparently the best criminal defence lawyer in Delhi, had finally met his match. If he could, he'd have walked up and punched Nanda in his face, but thankfully, he restrained himself. His appearances at court were media events; his departure from the case would be a media story too.

3

'I CAN'T BELIEVE THIS shit,' Akash said as Sonia and Vansh walked him out of Anshuman Durve's chambers.

'I agree, but what's done is done now. We have to speak to Shilpa and get things moving.'

'I need to be part of the defence team,' Akash insisted.

'But you know you shouldn't be. Or rather cannot be. Although Durve *strongly recommended* you to step down, I don't think he gave you a choice,' Vansh said as they approached his car.

Akash looked crestfallen. He felt like he was being torn apart, like he was being forced out. He wouldn't be privy to information, to the files the police and the prosecution sent, he wouldn't be able to mount a defence. He wouldn't be authorized to, since it could lead to the weakening of Shilpa's case. A lawyer representing a client had the legal right to not reveal anything against the client and that was a privilege allowed by law. The entire communication between a client and their advocate was confidential and no court could force the lawyer to divulge anything. Unless, of course, the client confessed to the said crime or confided in the representing advocate about something that could potentially lead to a crime: it was then the responsibility of the advocate to inform the law. That was the primary reason why defence lawyers seldom asked their clients if they were guilty. Ignorance worked at all levels. What one didn't know, didn't matter.

However, this was an exclusive right and it wasn't extended to any other person.

Anyone put on the witness stand under oath was legally

obliged to reveal all information they knew about the defendant. This was not a choice, it was the law. A lie spoken or a truth held back, under oath, was perjury, which was a criminal offence.

If called to the witness stand, Akash would have to answer all of Ravi Nanda's questions. He couldn't hide behind the veil of advocate-client privilege. If he dared to lie under oath, Durve would be within his rights to hold him in contempt of court and send him to prison, issue a fine or worse still, debar him from practising law in the country.

'I understand that I can't be part of the team in the courtroom, but I still need to be able to discuss strategy with both of you.'

'We'll discuss that later, my friend,' Vansh deflected Akash's request as the three of them got into the car and left the district court.

4

'WHAT DO YOU MEAN you still want to be part of the team?' Priti asked in the evening when Akash insisted again. They had dropped Sonia off and were having a drink at the Diwans' house late in the evening. Priti, being a qualified lawyer, understood how Nanda had successfully got Akash removed from the race. She could empathize with her friend, but that was it.

'Why not? It's not that the case has been transferred to someone else. It's Vansh and Sonia representing Shilpa, isn't it?'

'Sonia is your employee, Akash,' Vansh pointed out.

'A loyal one at that.'

'Yes, I appreciate that, but loyalties can change. She might get a better offer one day and move on, or set up her own practice—'

'What are you trying to say, Vansh?' Akash, not usually a big drinker, picked up the glass of Macallan poured for him and drowned its contents. The frustration and the ensuing anxiety were jangling his nerves.

'Here today, gone tomorrow. She is ambitious; she isn't going to work for you forever. Employees are loyal only until they work for you. If, for the sake of argument, she is working for someone else tomorrow and gets an opportunity to represent a client as your opponent, she will use every trick in the book – all taught by you – to work against you. And then, it will be too late to go back on what you do today. She'll be the first in the queue to crucify you then. If you lie under oath and no one ever comes to know – that's one thing. Although I wouldn't say you should do that, but it's different when someone knows about it – do you get me?'

'No.'

'I am your friend – we've never been adversaries in a courtroom and shall never be; we made a pact two decades ago, and we have honoured it, right? So, we should speak to Judge Shilpa Singh and you can work on the strategy behind the scenes, but it will only be me who will talk to you, not Sonia. Do you get me now?'

'But even if I know the details, you know very well that Ravi Nanda will not dare to call me to the stand.'

'We don't know what we don't know. He's a rent-an-advocate for this case. He isn't here to make friends. We don't know how he operates; we cannot say for sure how suicidal he could get as things progress. What if he called you to the stand and asked you what we've discussed? How would it go then?'

'Akash, for you own sake, and for Shilpa's, please don't cross the line … Vansh is right. We are your friends. If anything goes wrong, we can take care of it.'

They were right. And they were putting their own necks on the block for Akash.

'I see your point. Could I have another drink, please?'

'Yes, but you'll eat dinner here and then sleep over. You're not going home.' Vansh got up to get the drinks. 'Also, we'll call the judge tomorrow morning to check with her if that's okay. No point in speaking to her right now.'

5

JUDGE SHILPA SINGH WAS shocked when Vansh and Akash called to fill her in about the events of the previous day, but she seemed to take the news calmly.

'If you're okay, Judge,' Vansh explained, 'I am happy to continue as your defence advocate with Sonia, who works in Akash's firm, as my second chair.'

'How's Akash taking the news?' she asked.

'Not very sportingly, I have to admit.'

'That bloody Nanda will never put me on the witness stand; it's just a ploy —'

'I know, Akash, but you have to give it to him for digging up our past and using it against us.'

'I know, but don't you worry – I'll always be working behind the scenes.'

'I am not worried about me, Akash. I'm worried about you jeopardizing your career for the sake of my trial. Vansh, do you think we could trust Sonia on this?'

A legal mind, after all.

'I explained the same to Akash last night, Judge. I'll make sure he only talks to me, if required. And I promise I won't let anyone know about that, not even Sonia.'

'Thank you.'

Shilpa was happy with Vansh taking charge. She said she'd sign the papers as soon as they were sent across to her.

6

'SEE, EVEN SHILPA THINKS the same way about it.'

'Thanks, Vansh, but between us friends, we are a team.'

'Of course. In a way it's not bad—'

'You wanted me out too, didn't you, Vansh?'

'To be honest, yes. And it was evident in Durve's chambers when you got emotional. Emotions need to be parked aside, my friend. We need to focus on the case. Just help me out – we will win this together.'

'But why keep me away?'

'If you look deep enough inside you, you will find the answer to that question, Akash. I'm not pleased about the way it happened, but I'm quite convinced of what happened, and let's be a team between us. Do you get me?'

Akash nodded, accepting that it wasn't his finest hour; it was best to trust Vansh and take a back seat this time.

'Being emotional is a luxury you cannot afford at this

moment, Akash; it will only come back to hurt you – and your client,' Vansh carried on. There was no asperity in his voice for Akash to react to; just pure friendship and concern.

'Maybe you're right.'

'Not maybe—'

'Beware, my lovely, *beware of running on adrenaline alone.*' Priti Diwan joined the conversation, and her little quip issued a round of laughter because the expression she had just uttered – 'beware of running on adrenaline alone' – was an expression used by one of their law school professors to warn his students and would-be lawyers about being mindful of their actions. Adrenaline was good, it was required, but it needed to be backed by a strategy. Priti walked up to Akash and he stood up for a much-needed hug. Priti and Vansh were the closest to a family he had ever had. They stood in a quiet embrace for a few minutes to let the longing to return to a simpler time pass. Does it ever truly go away?

'It's just that I feel I like I'm having a nightmare, and I don't think I'm waking from it anytime soon.' Akash finally broke away from Priti.

'This isn't something you should consider you're losing, Akash – you're merely passing on the baton to me, your friend who promises to win this fight for you.'

'Thank you, Vansh.'

'Dinner is ready whenever you two are.'

TWELVE

1

PENTIUM WASN'T HAPPY. SOMETHING was amiss. For one, the mystery of not being able to, so much as find out the name of the victim from any source was troubling him. Ashok Kumar had now been dead for over two weeks, and no one, not a single person, had come forward to claim his body. Was it possible for someone to be so unwanted that he had no family or friends? Secondly, after hanging around in New Friends Colony for over a week, he had not been able to locate anyone from Kailash Prasad's clan who was willing to talk to him; the man's clout was daunting. Moreover, his contacts in the constabulary remained tight-lipped too. His usual tactics failing, he realized he needed to work on the case from another angle.

The only other way to approach the challenge was to start with the corpse. He could pay the mortuary a visit; maybe speak to someone in the morbid pathology department who could help him somehow. He didn't know *how*, but there was no harm in reaching out for any kind of lead.

2

THE PROSECUTION MUST HAND over all evidence collected that could help the defendant. It was their duty. It was the law. There should no ambiguity in anyone's mind anywhere in the world that everyone was innocent until found guilty. And hence, concealing any evidence was an offence in and by itself. Advocate Mehta had no choice but to send across everything he had on the case to Vansh Diwan and his team.

As such, three large cartons of paperwork – witness statements, forensic evidence, expert opinions, police reports and what not – arrived at Vansh's office, which made him chuckle. Typical prosecution tactics. Bury the defence in so much paperwork that they couldn't distinguish wheat from chaff, forget about separating it. Somewhere in these stacks of documents lay a little gold needle that could prove Shilpa's innocence. The prosecution's task was to make it as challenging as possible for the defence to find the evidence that favoured their client without being obvious about it. Send more, not less. Sending less than the discovered material would be called duplicity and Nanda and Mehta understood that if Vansh went to Judge Durve again, it wouldn't be a pleasant experience in his chambers next time around. Neither could they manipulate any of the documents, legally speaking. However, sending an overabundance of material couldn't be argued against. *We didn't know if the defence would need this or not, Your Honour.*

However, that kind of chicanery only worked when the defence advocate was working with time and resource constraints. Vansh lost but one day. A team of two junior advocates sifted through the stack of documents and separated the essentials from the padding. Another team of two went through the inessentials to see if the first team had missed anything. Two small files were put together. Sonia Pahwa had temporarily moved into Vansh's office. Since Akash was out, it made sense for both the advocates to work together. Each one of them had a copy of the files to themselves. There was an ulterior motive, too. After work, Vansh would carry his copy to Akash and Sonia would be none the wiser.

3

'THE ANSWER IS BURIED in these files,' Vansh told Akash.

'I'm convinced she's innocent; are you?'

'Of course I am, but she did not do herself any favours by pulling out the knife from the victim in a public place and leaving her prints on the murder weapon—'

'She's a judge; she wouldn't have done something like that if she didn't think she was saving someone's life. Her conscience interfered at the wrong time, it seems. Had she left Ashok Kumar bleeding, she'd be home safe, don't you think?'

'True. That's a good argument to put forward.'

'Argue with me.'

'What?'

'Like a mock trial of sorts – we are both struggling here, we haven't been in a trial like this before, so why not? Treat me like a mock adversary, treat me like I'm the prosecutor here.'

'Really?'

'Why not? I'd do that if I were you.'

'Look at it from the prosecutor's perspective, now that you're playing that part, Akash. He's got a case that can kill his career, if not him. He doesn't have a clue about the truth; he's presently constructing a case based on the info provided to him by the police that are in turn acting on directions from Kailash Prasad. To take it a step further, the police have no real eyewitness – yes, they have eyewitnesses to establish Shilpa was there at the scene, with the knife in her hand but that's post the crime. That provides us with a crucial gap in the narrative. The only real eyewitness here is the accused so it's her word against the people who got to the scene immediately afterwards—'

'However,' Akash interrupted his friend, 'if Durve has to decide whom to side with, wouldn't he believe the witnesses instead of the accused – who has every reason to misstate the details. She's the only one who wins or loses and ergo, she has every reason to lie to keep herself out of jail. All the others are unrelated parties there. A she-said-he-said isn't something that would go in her favour here.'

'Hmm. We need more than her word against the other witnesses.' Vansh made a note. 'What would the prosecution have to say about the motive?'

'The victim had evidence that would have absolved Kailash Prasad, and Judge Shilpa Singh was about to give a ruling against him.'

'But, according to the defendant, the victim had evidence favourable to her ruling,' argued Akash.

'That's another she-said-he-said dead-end, isn't it? In any event, motive isn't a component of crime, it is something that might be obvious in linking the accused to the victim. But it's not obligatory for the prosecution to highlight if all other evidence is present. Even the best of motives is of little value without evidence and conversely, absence of motive won't fly in the face of overwhelming evidence.'

Although it was often said that the best green room rehearsal, more often than not, flew out of the window when the spotlights were turned on, the two friends knew one couldn't just get on stage without one either – not in this case, not when it was personal. They carried on for the better part of two hours like two good lawyers. All good trial lawyers closed all the possible lines of attack first. If you could see your enemy, your enemy could see you as well. Likewise, if you could already picture a fissure in your argument, be aware that the adversary has already seen it, and planned for it. And Nanda had already demonstrated that he had a sharp brain.

'I can only think of five justifiable defences in a murder case,' Akash got up to pour a drink for them both. 'Self-defence is always at the top, but we can rule that out since the victim in this case wasn't carrying any weapon. Two – if the accused could be medically classified as having lost their mind. A defence based on insanity, which won't work in Shilpa's case since she has no medical history. Three – establish that it was an accident; again, it wouldn't cut the proverbial mustard here. Why was Shilpa carrying a large butcher's knife in Lodhi Gardens? To prepare a tuna salad?'

'But maybe the victim had been carrying the knife, some kind of a scuffle ensued, the knife slipped out of the victim's hand and Shilpa used it against him?'

'Sounds like a film script, doesn't it?'

'Yes, it does.' Vansh knew it even before he had come up with the scenario.

'Fourth, that there was no murder at all; again, a futile

argument in this case because they have the corpse in the mortuary. The only thing is – and I'm quite surprised Pentium hasn't called me with a name yet – we don't know who died, but that isn't any defence. A dead body is enough for the prosecution. The *who* is irrelevant, and the absence of the name of the victim would hardly get her a "not guilty" verdict.'

'What's the last one then?'

'That someone else did it, which in my mind is the only way to move forward in this case.'

'But who?'

'Kailash Prasad – he's the only one to gain by taking Shilpa out of the equation.'

'But there's no evidence.' Vansh took a generous sip from his tumbler, before upending the glass. 'Wow, what whisky is this?'

'Macallan, fifteen years old.'

'Amazing. Could I have another glass, please?'

'Yes, of course.'

'And please put on some music. We always think better with music playing in the background.'

'Fair point.'

'As it stands, the prosecution's case is tight.'

'Come on, Vansh. We're both criminal defence lawyers. Nothing is ever as obvious as it seems. Just one more thing I wanted to mention before we have another drink – we need our own experts to analyze the scene, the murder weapon and everything. Money—'

'Isn't an issue, I know. And please don't put on The Rolling Stones and *Stupid Girl*, please.'

'Would *Paint it Black* do?'

'Of course. Cheers.'

4

IT WAS MIDNIGHT. VANSH had left about an hour ago after a long discussion about the case, a few drinks – okay more than a few drinks – some great music and two twelve-inch pizzas. Akash couldn't sleep. Vansh was right: Akash had lost about four kilograms since he began working on the case. Frustration at a personal level, the uncertainty, his own involvement with the judge that had led to his removal from the case was killing his appetite. Copies of all the documents were still in his legal studio. Option one was to toss and turn in bed until sleep took over; option two was to get up, make another drink and go through the file again. Option two was tempting. Wrong, but tempting – the case wasn't his anymore. It was akin to a dog's desire to pick up a neighbour's chicken. There was the fear of being caught, but he was attached to this case more than he'd been attached to any in his career. So what if reading them was illegal? If need be, he'd play the dog who'd even pee on the neighbour's front door for this.

Vansh had delivered them to him like a true friend. Vansh knew if he had missed anything, there was only one individual in all of New Delhi who could find that gold-plated needle to win the case. But Kailash Prasad, simply by virtue of elapsed time, was getting further away from them. Most homicide detectives believed that the case broke in the first twenty-four to forty-eight hours; after that the trails dried up, evidence became contaminated, perpetrators got away. While the police focused on Shilpa Singh, they had inadvertently let any and all other clues die by now.

He put on a robe and walked barefoot into his legal studio and heard one of the phones vibrating in the locked drawer. He unlocked the drawer to find the burner phone vibrating furiously like a neglected child. 12:30 a.m. Unknown caller. It could only be one person.

'Janaab?'

It was Pentium, no doubt.

'Hello,' answered Akash.

'Wrong, all wrong. Wrong colour of subject totally.'

'What is it, Pentium?'

'Red is not red, it is sharp-cut blue.'

'Really?'

'I've been to the workshop and checked it out. Wrong colour, wrong artist.'

'What are you saying?'

'Painter is concealing something here. Check documents.'

'Got it. Thank you.'

'Anything for you, Janaab.'

Click.

Conversations with Pentium were always cloak and dagger. Although they talked on mobile phones no one could trace, Akash always kept a distance. He didn't want anyone to know he used an ex-criminal for his investigations who procured information using ungodly means.

Akash had an inkling what Pentium's clandestine speak meant:

'*Wrong, all wrong. Wrong colour of subject totally.*' The corpse wasn't of the man they were saying it was.

'What is it, Pentium?'

'Red is not red, it is sharp-cut blue.'

Something was awry. Akash struggled to follow the sharp-cut-blue phrase but somewhere in the words there was one word that meant something, he knew.

'Really?'

'I've been to the workshop and checked it out. Wrong colour, wrong artist.'

Wrong colour usually referred to shade of skin, but wrong artist was baffling. Usually, Pentium was a bit more specific, but it wasn't the end of the world.

'What are you saying?'

'Painter is concealing something here. Check documents.'

Painter was obvious: the police. What were they concealing about Ashok Kumar? And then it struck him. The documents were stating something the prosecution's expert wanted them to know, but more importantly, they had camouflaged something there. Pentium had never let him down, and the key was there – he had to find the lock now. He spent the next hour reading and digesting the autopsy report included in the documents that Vansh had left for him.

5

AUTOPSY REPORT

- Name: Unidentified victim
- Gender: Male
- Age: under 30, possibly between 27–29
- Height: 185.4 cm
- Weight: 90 kilograms
- Body: muscled, lean and fit
- Skin colour: Fair, tanned; indicates the victim has spent a lot of time outdoors
- One approximately five-year-old scar (8 cm long) on right shin (possibly a knife wound)
- Several old lacerations (1–5 cm long); difficult to assess how old the wounds are, but they are irrelevant to his demise
- No tattoos
- No jewellery of any kind (chain, ring) found on the body
- Fingerprints match none on the criminal file sent over by the police
- DNA sent for further analysis to laboratory. Probability of finding a match: minimal (four weeks' wait)
- Teeth: None missing, no dentures, no filings, no crowns
- Medical history: No sign of surgical scars. Lungs and liver examination indicates the subject never smoked, never drank alcohol; no symptoms of substance abuse either. Heart seems to be commensurate with his age
- Others: Circumcised. Circumcision is practised in Judaism, Christianity (Old Testament) and Islam, so the subject could have been practising either of these faiths. Most

likely not a Hindu since the practice is not prevalent in Hinduism

- Cause of death: Heavy blood loss due to single stab wound in the chest – between the fourth and fifth ribs, approximately 5 mm left of the heart that severed the aorta and punctured the left lung
- Aorta being the main artery carrying oxygenated blood, death must have occurred within seconds. The victim's healthy heart would have accelerated the bleeding, thereby his death
- Absence of any defence wounds indicates it was possibly a spontaneous/surprise attack and carried out to deliver a single fatal blow, possibly with an extremely sharp knife
- The knife in evidence makes us lean towards the third aspect but it would be classified more as a speculation than an expert opinion.
- The weapon: A 20.3 cm long knife; in evidence, appeared to have been barely used
- Brand: Solimo Stainless Steel Chef's Knife
- Material: Sharp, high-carbon stainless-steel blade
- Handle: Black, triple-rivet and 12.7cm
- The weapon could have been bought at all retail stores selling kitchen items. Available online for approximately ₹399
- Wound: The knife's blade pierced the victim in an upward trajectory, the blade entered the victim's chest with the sharp edge on the bottom side and the blunt end on top. The wound measurement is 18 cm; the killer almost jabbed the entire length of the blade into the victim. Since the

knife wasn't inserted into the body of the victim to the hilt, no bruising caused by the handle

- Expert opinion at this stage: ????? (text missing)

The expert opinion had been classified as speculation and therefore, the prosecution team had struck it off. Which was stupid. If they had removed it entirely, it wouldn't have excited Akash as much as the missing text did. He looked at the clock. It was 3:21 a.m. He made a mental note to call Vansh and remind him to get access to the redacted expert opinion again. He sort of knew what Pentium had meant, but he needed confirmation.

The only link Akash gathered from Pentium's clandestine speak and the autopsy report was that Ashok Kumar could be anyone but Ashok Kumar; he could be Alex or Albert or Abdul, but not Ashok Kumar per se. What could that mean?

Nothing.

THIRTEEN

1

THE RINGING PHONE WOKE Akash up. He had dozed off on his chair while perusing case files the previous night. The screen announced: Chavi Nair.

'Hi Chavi.' Even to himself his voice sounded like it originated from the bottom of a dried-up well.

'Good morning to you too, Akash. Is everything alright with you?'

'Good morning. Yes ... yes, why do you ask?'

'Because your voice sounded like a sick toad's croak. The panache is totally missing, if I may say so, as a friend.'

'But you've already said it.' He let out a gruff scoff.

'That sounds more like the Akash I know. What's happening?'

'Nothing, I was up until late – you know the case is up for hearing next week.'

'Judge Shilpa Singh's case?'

'Yes.'

'How are you a successful lawyer when you're such a pathetic liar, Akash?'

'What do you mean?'

'Well, my sources tell me you are no longer the defence advocate—'

'Who told you that?'

Judge Durve had been clear about not informing the media until the last minute. Unfortunately, with the trial less than forty-eight hours away, the last minute had almost arrived.

'Is it true, Akash?' Chavi enquired.

'Yes, now tell me what, or rather, who's your source?'

'A good journalist never discloses their source. You know I can't do that. What I can offer instead is to take you out for dinner – my treat.'

'That sounds good, but—'

'No ifs, no buts – I'm not going to disclose my source to you or anyone, much like how you cannot reveal the intricacies of a criminal case you are trying in a court. So let's extend each other professional courtesies and have a meal together. So what case are you working on that's not Shilpa Singh's but is still keeping you awake?'

She knew he was off the case. She maybe also knew he was being called upon as a witness. He couldn't decide how much info to share, how much to hold back. He certainly couldn't share that he was working clandestinely alongside Vansh on the case. It would put Vansh's career in jeopardy along with his. He couldn't afford that.

Dinner? Did she say dinner? He was bored, sad, angry, frustrated and a million other things. Dinner sounded like a good outing.

'Will cognac be a part of the menu?' he heard himself asking.

'Yes, sir.'

'When?'

'Tonight?'

'I think I can do tonight, but let me check with Vansh. Vansh is the—'

'I know Vansh Diwan; he's the lead defence advocate in Judge Shilpa Singh's trial with Miss Sonia Pahwa – who works in your firm – as the second chair. But you can't be working on this case with them, can you?'

'Why not?'

'Because my source also told me you're on the witness list.'

'Wow. News does travel.' He was happy he hadn't opened his mouth earlier; his reading had been correct. She knew everything.

'Of course, why don't you call me back after you've spoken to Vansh?'

'That makes sense. I'll call you within an hour. Where are we going?'

'It's a surprise.'

2

CHAVI NAIR WAS DRESSED to the nines. In a polychromatic figure-hugging dress, which reached her mid-thighs and five-inch stilettos, she was a head taller than Akash.

Was she trying to intimidate him? He let the thought pass.

Mandeep drove them to Le Méridien at Windsor Place since there was no need to be surreptitious about this dinner. This wasn't Shilpa and Akash out on a date. Chavi chose the venue since she was picking up the tab. Le Belvedere at Le Méridien. Funny how some names stick. Le Méridien, before two American chains in succession acquired the brand and the properties, was an upscale, design-focused French hotel brand and hence the French names of the restaurants. No one ever thought – much less questioned – why an Oriental restaurant carried a French name.

Chavi and Akash got a corner table on the rooftop and ordered a bottle of wine. The waitress delivered the wine, took their orders for starters and retreated. There was a brief silence, the one that usually took over the conversation when two people struggled to proceed, not on account of lack of subjects to talk about but due to caution. How much should one open up with someone who was more than an acquaintance but less than a trusted friend? When silence has hung around for a while, someone always tried to fill the gap. If you kept your mouth shut long enough, you guaranteed the other person took the initiative. It could take minutes and those minutes might feel like hours, but patience wasn't dubbed a virtue for nothing.

'Tell me about you. Who are you?' Akash eventually asked.

'Chavi Nair.' She picked up her glass, clinked it with his and took a sip of the Rioja. 'Cheers!'

'Thanks, but you know what I mean. Who's Chavi Nair? And don't give me stock phrases like "I'm an investigative journalist", please. I'm trying to know you better.'

'You mean assess me …'

'You could say that.'

'To gauge whether you can truly trust me and my intentions?'

'Not my primary motive, but—'

'I was once one of the most sought-after investigative journalists in Mumbai, until I found out that the man I was in a relationship with was a criminal.'

'Criminal? You mean—'

'Not a criminal defence lawyer,' she joked. 'And not a financial scamster or something as bland as that. He was a psychopath, a serial killer.'

'What?' Akash was, for once, struggling to comprehend. 'How could you—'

'How could I not know? Well, in retrospect, it's easy to join the dots. We never slept together; he never stayed at my place or I at his. He avoided anything carnal because he was driven by different passions. But when I was dating him, it all made him seem like a gentleman.' Her eyes had welled up reminiscing about the ordeal she had been through. Akash could not even imagine what she must be feeling. 'So to answer your question – I never even doubted him, even when I was investigating the killer.'

'I'm sorry.'

'It's okay now … I've built a new life here …' She paused; her emotions were choking her.

'So, with that background, how did you manage a fresh start here in New Delhi?'

'The lead police officer on the case, DCP Rita Ferreira helped me move; she organized commendations from the Mumbai police commissioner. The rest is history.' She paused yet again, took a sip of her wine and said, 'Have I bared my soul enough?'

'I didn't mean to upset you, Chavi.' He placed his hands on hers to comfort her. 'What is it that you want from me?'

'I want you to talk to me about your affair with Judge Shilpa Singh.'

'You don't mince your words, do you? What about the affair?'

'Akash, I won't beat around the bush any more. Ths trial begins in less than thirty-six hours. In the first ten minutes or so, everyone will know that you – who was the lead advocate on the case – isn't representing her anymore. In the next ten minutes, everyone in the courtroom will know why. It doesn't matter whether you were asked to remove yourself by the Judge Durve or you recused yourself of your own accord. The media will have their story, everyone will. Anyone and everyone will talk about it in the way they see is legit. No one's going to bother about what's right or wrong, or consider your or Shilpa's perspective; they won't care as long as the story sells, which it would, trust me on that. But ...' Chavi stopped, brought her glass to her lips and let Akash process the facts she'd aptly stated.

Akash took a sip of the wine too. Seeing that their glasses were near empty, he picked up the bottle of Campo Rioja on the table, and poured some wine for both of them. 'Good wine,' he said like it was the most important thing at this point in the conversation.

'I'm proposing some damage control,' Chavi continued. 'I empathize with you and the judge. An affair, in the past, should not be anybody else's concern, but it makes a good story to write, read and gossip about, don't you think?'

'Thanks, Chavi, but I'm still not sure I understand what it is you're after really.'

The wine had started working. The starters had just arrived: sweet-and-sour prawns for the two of them.

'Let me break the story.'

'Say that again.' It wasn't that he hadn't heard her correctly; it was more of an exasperated comment. She had caught his tone.

'Hear me out, okay? All I'm saying is let me control the narrative rather than letting it spread across the media world like an epidemic. I want the story to break like it is: two consenting adults – both single – had an affair. How does it reflect on the moral character of either? Does it have any bearing at all? I'll handle the whole thing decorously – break the news like it was nothing out of the ordinary, nothing that the public should see as something that was morally wrong, nothing that should lead to one of them committing a murder, you know what I mean?'

'What if I say no?'

'I don't need your permission, Akash. I'm not here as a journalist, I'm here as a friend. I have your best interests at heart. I wouldn't be talking about this if I didn't believe in what I was asking for …'

'I don't know.' He took a bite of the prawn on his fork and savoured it. Chewing excused him from talking since he was at a loss for words. His thoughts were forming and disintegrating at great speed. 'And it's not just about me, is it? I need to speak to the judge about it.'

'This would benefit her cause more than yours.'

'May I ask you a straightforward question, Chavi?'

'Of course.'

'What's in it for you besides TRPs for your channel?'

Chavi forked a prawn, put it in her mouth and chewed it. 'You need to ask me that?'

'For the record, yes.'

'What if I said I love you?'

Akash was dumbstruck. Chavi's sudden outburst of her feelings had shocked him beyond comprehension. In any case, it was too soon; he wasn't really ready for another relationship, maybe because he was still licking his wounds.

She let out a laugh.

'Are you serious?' he asked.

'Akash, has it ever occurred to you that you might still be in love?'

'What do you mean?'

'It's evident. You can't love someone else until and unless you detach yourself totally. At this moment you are very much in love with her – Shilpa.'

'You are surely kidding.'

'It's written all over your face. You're still besotted by the judge – don't take this the wrong way. If you don't believe me, ask your close friends.'

Akash could feel his face redden.

'After this trial is over, if I were you, I'd go back and confess to her, see if things could work out between you two.'

'The presiding judge has categorically asked the prosecution and the defence to stay away from the media,' he finally uttered.

Chavi let out a smile. 'You aren't part of the defence team anymore. You're a witness, giving your side of the story. The rule does not apply to you, so it can't hurt.'

'What about our reputation? I can't risk putting her at the centre of a scandal at this time.'

'If you're in a firestorm, Akash, you are always at the risk of being singed. But trust me, I'll get both of you out without any major calamity.'

'What you're suggesting is akin to inviting a snake home for dinner.'

'Indeed. And the snake can bite, but at least we would have drawn out its venom by then. When it bites you in the courtroom, it will sting, but you will survive – trust me.'

3

IF YOU HAD POST-GRADUATED from Tihar like Mr Pentium, your brain would be wired to see the world in binaries. Something was either black or white. He didn't care for greys. He didn't like the greys. His mind was struggling to zero in on a possible suspect and motive. Besides the initial propaganda by the media that Judge Shilpa Singh had done this to silence a key witness in Kailash Prasad's trial, there seemed to be no motive for her. Quite frankly, Pentium was finding it hard to establish a motive for anyone in this case. How could anyone assign a reason to the murder when they didn't know who the victim was?

He instinctively knew that the first thing a criminal did after an offence was to clean the crime scene. Even as he was on his way to Lodhi Gardens, he believed there was little point in looking for clues at the crime scene. In any case, at Lodhi Gardens, the police would have searched every inch of the small piece of land and turned it upside down. It was unlikely that they would have found anything of consequence. Ashok Kumar's killer must have taken all precautions. Pentium was convinced that his assessment was correct because the murder weapon – the chef's knife recovered in the accused's hands – carried no fingerprints besides the judge's. There were no other prints on the weapon besides the main accused's. But an instrument of death wiped clean save for one clearly defined set of prints was telling Pentium a different story altogether. Someone had gone out of their way to frame the last person who held the weapon. Shilpa Singh had put her fingerprints on the handle of the knife by pulling it out of the victim's body. There should have been some prints from when the knife was handled before that.

However, for Pentium, being a criminal was an advantage. He could think like one. Even the coolest of cucumbers would melt under the heat of committing homicide. There was no way that the perpetrator had kept his senses after the murder and taken the time to wipe off his prints, whilst in a public place in broad daylight. The only theory that fitted was that the killer wore gloves.

Binary.

Black or white.

The killer had either run away with the gloves on or discarded them somewhere along the way. The murder weapon was the first thing any murderer tries to get rid of, and then anything directly associated with the murder. In this case, the weapon was left behind to frame someone else. But what about the gloves? It doesn't make sense for the murderer to hold on to them?

Pentium summarized that it was very unlikely that the murderer had kept the gloves on because there was a high probability that the gloves had blood on them, given the close encounter with the victim. They must have been discarded somewhere, at the first opportunity the killer got. But where would he look for them? If the gloves were thrown away in the vicinity or discarded in any of the bins in the park, the police should have surely found them. Nevertheless, it didn't hurt to search if he had the time. And Pentium was not short of time, was he? He decided that he'd spend a couple of hours looking around within a ten-metre radius of the scene of the murder.

Another thought crossed his mind – what if Judge Shilpa Singh had staged the whole thing to make it look suspicious? After all, she had ample knowledge of the law, investigations, murder weapons ... but the very idea of the judge going after a defence witness, like the media had stated, didn't have much merit. What could someone like Shilpa Singh have against Kailash Prasad? Could she have had an affair with the MLA in the past? Even the thought was ridiculous, repulsive. Forget about their backgrounds and the difference in status and polish, even a look at their respective photographs would tell anyone that the two couldn't have bonded over anything – physically, financially or socially. It was a virtual impossibility.

Clues very rarely popped up at the crime scenes. Whatever the police recovered from the scene of crime was generally used to nail the perpetrator only after he was apprehended – unless the perpetrator was already listed as a criminal in the police records. More often than not, the evidence from the scene helped establish him as the culprit but did not actually lead to him. Pentium himself always wore leather shoes with soles that carried no imprints; he even wore shoes a size bigger than his normal fit to avoid being identified by the police.

A lot of homicides are solved because the killer ends up boasting about his feat to someone. It only takes a snitch to pick it up and exchange the info to make some cash or curry favour with the police. In this case, no one Pentium had spoken to had heard anything directly or indirectly, which was another peculiarity.

The real clues are found when one traces the perpetrator's steps to the crime. Why did he kill? Where did he come from? Did he stop somewhere on the way to the crime scene, maybe for some *paan* or to light a cigarette nearby? Where did he go afterwards? Did someone send him? Ditto for the victim: why was he here in the first place? Unless the killer is reckless enough to leave his or her visiting card behind, these clues are the only way to nab him. In this particular case, Pentium was aware that the killer had planned ahead and called Shilpa Singh to the scene to implicate her for his work.

But the complete picture was still out of his reach. This was one mystery DK Pentium hadn't been able to unravel, and the more time he spent thinking about it the more frustrated he became. His pride wouldn't let him admit failure. He didn't want Akash Hingorani to contact someone else. Something had to give, he knew, he just knew it. He wandered around Lodhi Gardens after downing half a bottle of Indian-made foreign liquor. He was drifting into alcohol-induced sleep. He looked around. The sun had already set, there was a little light still, but he decided he wouldn't pack up for the day. But he was determined not to leave the scene. He walked out of

Lodhi Gardens to find the nearest shop selling cheap alcohol and picked up another bottle for the night.

Back at the scene of the crime, he tried to put his thoughts together. He was missing something, but what? Some of the hardest crimes in the world have been solved by luck – David Berkowitz aka Son of Sam, the dreaded American serial killer was caught not in the act, but because of a parking ticket. DK Pentium walked fifteen metres from where Shilpa found the dead body to find a place to sit and relax under a tree, possibly take a nap. As he sat down, his eyes fell on the piece of evidence he'd been looking for: a set of latex gloves, folded one into another with a small stone inside. What did this prove? Nothing? Everything?

Call it luck or call it Pentium's destiny. The two-by-two square foot place he had decided to sit on had revealed to him what could be the killer's gloves. He stared at them before examining them closely. He could feel a stone inside the yellowish ball of gloves and see more than a few specks of blood stains on them. The murderer was smart enough to flee with them on and had disposed them before making his escape. He must have thrown the gloves and run the other way. Smart man, this bastard!

It was time to call Akash Hingorani. A private lab could test the blood on the gloves before they were posted anonymously to the police, but that was up to Akash, not him.

4

CHAVI NAIR, WITHOUT REFERRING to the case on trial soon, or mentioning her sources, announced on air that Judge Shilpa

Singh – the accused in the homicide of an unidentified corpse – once *dated* the noted defence advocate Akash Hingorani. She had a diverse panel – celebrities, mainly – to argue that two consenting adults had every right to love each other and get involved if they wished too.

'It's a free country,' one of the loud ones proclaimed.

'It's their life.'

Others on the panel encored the sentiment.

The viewership of the hour-long telecast was one of the highest for any talk show in recent history.

Dev Roy, Akash's loudmouthed media contact had already been primed. He had a script to run in the press the following day. The rest followed.

If the prosecution was planning to score any points by damaging Shilpa Singh's character by highlighting her secret love affair with Akash Hingorani, the media had pulled the rug from under their feet.

The battleground had been evened out. Chavi had turned out to be right: sometimes the media fed on you, sometimes you fed the media.

PART 2

THE TRIAL

'There are so many things that life is, and no matter how many breakthroughs, trials will exist and we are going to get through it. Just be strong.'

– MARY J. BLIGE,
R&B and hip-hop singer

FOURTEEN

1

WITH THE PROSECUTION WITNESS list including both Judge Shilpa Singh and Akash Hingorani, the defence knew they could cross-question them to their advantage. If the prosecution wanted not one but two hostile witnesses, why not? The defence, on the other hand, had managed to come up with just two witnesses. The first was Mr Kailash Prasad Yadav, who wasn't at all happy to be called to the courtroom to testify in a trial that did not concern him whatsoever. *What would I have to say? Or do with the case?* He had asked. Some half-brained friend drilled sense into his thick head that it was better to show up at the court to avoid pointing fingers in absentia. It was important that he appear to be a model citizen. The other witness the defence wished to call was a premier expert, should the state's expert witness fail to ratify what the defence had in mind. A witness could be dropped from the list any time; there was no law against it. Adding a witness at the last minute was looked down upon by the presiding judge.

'Why not start with the expert, so we can establish Judge Shilpa Singh's innocence, and then build on from there?' Sonia asked. She and Vansh had been cooped up in his office since the afternoon, going over their theories, witnesses and strategy. They had stopped around seven and ordered pizzas. The remaining four slices in the opened box looked unappetizing – the cheese appeared rubbery, the meat and veggies looked uninviting when only a couple of hours ago they had tasted delicious. The leftover slices were probably as tired as the two advocates in the room. Vansh saw Sonia eyeing them with disgust and shut the box.

'I'd prefer the voice of science and reason at the very end, something the prosecution wouldn't be able to argue against,' Vansh explained. Akash and he had previously agreed the witnesses and the order in which they should be presented in the court, but he obviously couldn't tell Sonia that he was letting Akash consult on the case. 'An authoritative, logical deduction, which we'd like His Honour to carry the aftertaste of, when he returned to his chambers to think, to decide, before announcing his judgement.'

'So, like … save the best for last?'

'You got it. I think we should call it a day … or night rather.'

'I think so too, Mr Diwan.'

2

RAVI NANDA WAS A sharp man, no doubt. The fact that he had eliminated the biggest thorn in his path – Akash Hingorani – proved that he was indeed worth twenty-four carat. He was in the court flanked by Diya Albuquerque and Harsh Mehta, ready to take on his opponents. Sonia was already at the defence table when Vansh escorted Shilpa into the courtroom.

'All rise,' said the court clerk, Amitabh – 'no second name'. He was slim, tall, with a protruding paunch that would have appeared to be normal on a seven-month pregnant lady. He wore a standard white starched cotton shirt and black trousers that had been ironed more times than they should have been, leaving shiny marks on them. His black shoes were so well polished they could be used as a mirror to comb the scant hair on his head.

Judge Anshuman Durve arrived and took his throne.

The reason why a courtroom looks like it does is because that was how things were in a king or queen's court. The judges, just like the monarchs, sat on the throne; the ministers sat alongside as they determined people's fates. The peasants came in with their issues and problems. The arrangement in a courtroom is a replica of a royal court. The subjects came in to listen to their king or queen's declarations; fast forward a few centuries, the populace, along with the media, had replaced the audience of yesteryears.

'In the matter of "State of Delhi vs Shilpa Singh", what does the State have to say?' Judge Anshuman Durve said after he made himself comfortable in his big chair. His desk had a thick file in front of him, which he swiftly sifted through and closed after nodding to himself.

'Your Honour, we are ready to proceed,' Ravi Nanda stood up and said.

'And how about the defence?'

'We're ready too, Your Honour.'

'Let the proceedings commence then.'

'Your Honour, we are here to begin criminal proceedings against the accused, Shilpa Singh, for the murder of the unclaimed and unidentified Ashok Kumar—'

'Does this mean that the police machinery still hasn't identified the corpse?' asked Judge Durve. 'With such sketchy information, do you want to continue?'

'We are ready, Your Honour.'

'Okay. Please continue, Mr Nanda.'

'I'm Ravi Nanda, representing the State in "State of Delhi vs Shilpa Singh" in the homicide of one Mr Ashok Kumar – I know the corpse is still unidentified, but that does not change the fact that Shilpa Singh murdered Ashok Kumar in cold blood. The prosecution's second chair is Ms Diya Albuquerque, who has worked alongside me for about five years now ...'

Diya nodded. Vansh noted that the intensity in her eyes was no less than his own second chair Sonia Pahwa's. Both were young lawyers, trying to make their mark in the legal community and both would fight tooth and nail to win this battle. 'State of Delhi vs Shilpa Singh' wasn't making anyone money. Ravi Nanda and Diya Albuquerque were public prosecutors imported from Mumbai. They were working for their salaries, and if the rumours were to be believed, screwing each other's brains out every night in the plush hotel paid for by the Government of India. Vansh Diwan and Sonia Pahwa were doing this pro bono for Akash. Sonia was a salaried employee at Akash's firm and Vansh wouldn't take a paisa from Shilpa or Akash, irrespective of the outcome of the case. This was personal to his friend and thus, it was personal to him.

Nanda introduced and thanked Harsh Mehta for his contribution before continuing his pitch. 'It was a planned murder since Shilpa Singh knew the victim possessed evidence concerning the case she was presiding upon at the time: "State of Delhi vs Shilpa Singh". From the notes provided to us by this very court, it is quite apparent that the evidence that Mr Ashok Kumar was about to provide could put her ruling against Kailash Prasad in jeopardy, and show to the world that she had been reckless with her decision. To avoid the situation that could have harmed her career, she took the extreme step of eliminating the witness.

'The State and prosecution have no empathy for a judge like her. A person like her should be struck off the register. She could have acknowledged she was wrong, accepted the new evidence, but her ego was too big to admit her rash judgement about a respected politician. But her decision to take the extreme step of extinguishing the life of another human being perplexes the prosecution. There can be no room for mercy in such a case, Your Honour.' Nanda paused and looked at the defence table.

Shilpa Singh, dressed in a white cotton saree, sat calmly at the defence table, between Vansh and Sonia. She had been in such courtroom arguments for over a decade and nothing surprised her any more. She knew the opening statement from the prosecuting and defence advocates were mere spiels.

Opening statements were to lay the foundations of the case at hand. They may or may not be supported by evidence later on. All that mattered at this stage was to put forth a case that made the presiding judge think, to set a background. It wasn't so much about the content – she herself had, at times, discounted both sides of opening statements during her time as a judge – but she understood that some of these words stayed in the judge's subliminal memory and poked their consciousness when evidence was presented. But neither of the advocates typically objected to the opening statement of the adversary. It was more of a one-sided declamation and not an argument.

Nanda was still talking, 'Your Honour, we urge the court to take a decision that sets an example for everyone in the legal community, that deters anyone in power from taking the law into their own hands. The State fully appreciates that it will be a trying time for Your Honour since the accused,' Ravi Nanda paused, looked towards Shilpa to emphasize his point, 'is part of the same fraternity as Your Honour—'

Judge Durve raised his right hand. Not a good sign. He had heard enough and although Nanda had been on the mark, he had carried his discourse a bit further than he should have to make the last point. He had, in a mild manner, implied that Durve could be swayed by the fact that Shilpa was until recently a judge. Not good, not good at all. 'I get the drift, Mr Nanda. Anything else?'

'Your Honour, Shilpa Singh broke every rule in the book by taking the decision of going alone to meet up with a witness for the defence. Nothing else, Your Honour.'

'Mr Diwan, do you want to make your opening statements before the proceedings begin in earnest?'

3

VANSH DIWAN TOOK HIS time standing up, like he was in no rush. He walked out from behind the defence table to address the judge.

'Your Honour, I'm Vansh Diwan, and my second chair is advocate Sonia Pahwa …' he turned to look, and Sonia stood up for all present to see, then sat down. 'And we are here to defend the accused, Judge Shilpa Singh—'

'Objection, Your Honour.' Nanda stood up.

'Mr Nanda, could you save the rhetoric for later, please? This is just the opening statement of the defence counsel. He afforded you the courtesy of not interrupting your opening statement, so please extend him the same. And he's only started; I cannot even imagine what your objection could be at this stage.'

'I would if I could, Your Honour, but this is important.'

'Everything is important, Mr Nanda. That's precisely why we are here in this courtroom, and not in a movie theatre or in a park,' Judge Durve spread his arms to gesture around him. 'We'd be in a mock trial back in a classroom if this wasn't significant enough, don't you agree?'

'Yes, Your Honour … I completely agree with your assessment, but for this trial to progress, it is vital we agree upon some base rules before moving forward.'

'Base rules in my courtroom are decided and communicated by me, in case you have any misgivings about who's presiding here, Mr Nanda. And, more importantly, why now? You could have submitted a plea like you submitted another one, remember? The previous plea didn't stop you from asking for a unique, unprecedented meeting in my chambers, so you could have brought this issue along, too, back then.'

'Your Honour, at the time I didn't see this issue coming up at the trial,' Nanda doggedly soldiered on. He wasn't giving in, not even after he had heard Judge Durve's stringent words.

'Oh, I see. Please state your objection for the record, Mr Nanda.'

'Could we have a recess, Your Honour?'

'Why, if I may ask?' Judge Durve appeared intrigued. 'Never heard a prosecutor asking for recess before the defence has hardly uttered a word. Nevertheless, you've made me curious now.'

'I request you to indulge me for once, Your Honour. I wouldn't waste the court's time if I didn't think it was important. And it'll only take a few minutes, I promise.'

'Okay, both lead advocates, please approach the bench.'

Vansh looked back at Sonia. He knew what was bothering Ravi Nanda and the team. He had discussed it with Akash who had been adamant about it.

Akash felt that this would set the tone of the trial, it would underline if Judge Durve had any biases. Sonia, too, had independently come up with the same analysis.

Amitabh, the court clerk, approached the bench too. Nanda appeared uneasy to see him.

'Your objection, even if it is whispered to me, has to be on record, Mr Nanda, and you should know that.' Judge Durve smiled. 'Please state your objection.'

'Your Honour, the prosecution objects to the defence addressing the accused as a judge. She is currently suspended from her duties and hence, she's officially not a judge for the time being. The prosecution requests, that for the duration of this trial, this courtroom acknowledge just one judge, Your Honour, which is you. If anything, there'll be confusion as to who one is referring to every time anyone calls out, 'Judge.' That is all, Your Honour.'

Judge Durve was flummoxed. He looked at Vansh Diwan, then back at Ravi Nanda, but he didn't say anything or let his countenance betray his thoughts.

'We didn't want the media to pick up on our objection, and hence this request to speak to you in private, Your Honour,' Nanda continued, taking Durve's silence as a licence to carry on with this pitch.

'Have you noted this?' Judge Durve asked Amitabh.

'Yes, Your Honour.'

'Your Honour—' Vansh Diwan started, but Judge Durve cut him off.

'The advocates may recede to their respective desks and take their seats please.'

'The prosecution has made an objection concerning something this court does not deal with on an everyday basis. This is an extraordinary trial, and a very crucial one at that,' Judge Durve announced to the packed house, and pointed at the prosecution table, 'The State has raised an objection, and to be fair to both parties present here, I need to think regarding the validity of the objection made to this court. Maybe I'll consult a few senior officials as well. However, I forbid both the advocates and their teams from talking about this matter with any members of the media or the public other than those directly connected to this case until I take a decision. I am also warning the media to not pick this up before I share my decision. I shall come back with my thoughts on the objection made by tomorrow morning. Furthermore, I ask both counsel teams to meet me in my chambers tomorrow morning at eight-thirty before we recommence the trial in the court at nine. This court is now in recess.'

The sudden announcement from Anshuman Durve was startling enough to leave the audience in the courtroom open-mouthed in amazement. Loud discussions followed within seconds.

'Let's have some order please,' Judge Durve said before he left the courtroom.

'All rise …'

The rarefied atmosphere fizzled out instantly. It was quite disappointing for the media and the members of the public who were present in the courtroom to observe the day's proceedings. Upsetting, like they had come to watch a T-20 match and the umpire had lifted the bails and walked away without giving any reason. The needle hadn't moved a millimetre, and the judge had taken his foot off the pedal.

Why?

Speculations started as to what could be the objection: murmurs and whispers. The hush could be heard at the defence table. Vansh looked at Shilpa, then Sonia. Cautious not to utter a word that could be picked up by anyone in the crowd, they gathered their files and walked out to Vansh's car. Only once the car started moving did he provide details of what had occurred when Judge Durve had called Nanda and him to the bench to Shilpa Singh – she was after all directly connected to the case, wasn't she?

4

'JUST AS WE THOUGHT,' Vansh called Akash and conveyed the court's decision to break until the next morning, 'Ravi Nanda took the bait.'

'As expected, and I can understand why. I'd have done the same. Any lawyer worth his degree would fight hard to quash the defendant being addressed as a judge by the opposition. Let us wait and see what Durve has to say now.'

'How was your day?'

'Pentium called me, and I also met with the expert you sent over to my place.' Akash was cautious; he mentioned Pentium without a name. Always.

'And …?'

'How do you know there's more?'

'Your voice gave it away, Akash. The mirth in the tone suggests the goose has delivered a golden egg. You sound like the cat who got the proverbial canary, and a very large one at that.'

'Yes sir.'

'Go on then.'

'For now, let's just say we were right all along. The expert is of the opinion that he can prove that she didn't do it – that Judge Shilpa Singh couldn't have murdered the unidentified Mr Ashok Kumar. He still needs to confirm if he can take the stand confidently to prove her innocence beyond reasonable doubt. It's still iffy. And then there's some news from the private investigator we hired, but I won't say anymore on the phone.'

'Come over then.'

'See you for dinner at your place?'

'Can't wait … you know, I had no idea if I'd actually enjoy my secretive role in this case. Otherwise, every other case is unvarying in its rhythm – the trial, the strategy, the performance. Here, I feel like a co-director who doesn't get to see the performance, but it's only narrated to him after the act.'

'Yeah, like a non-playing captain.'

'Like a non-playing vice-captain. You're the captain, my friend.'

5

IF YOU WERE CALLED for a meeting to the chambers of a presiding judge at eight-thirty in the morning, you were required to be in attendance at eight-twenty. The last thing you wanted was to be late and be reprimanded for tardiness.

Diya, Nanda and Mehta were already there when Sonia and Vansh arrived. They exchanged smiles – Nanda wasn't a reprehensible guy; he had been put into the situation due to circumstances, an outcome of his own success in Mumbai. Diya and he walked up to their opponents and exchanged a polite hello before they were called into the judge's chambers.

Tea was served without asking for their choice of beverage. This wasn't the venue for a breakfast meeting; this was Judge Durve's private chambers at the Saket District Court.

Anshuman Durve walked in with a broad smile on his face and took the seat behind his desk. There were enough chairs in the room for everyone to sit and he gestured everyone to do so. The court clerk, the pregnant-looking Amitabh, tapped on the door and walked in without a response from Durve at precisely 8:29 a.m. and closed the door behind him. The meeting was in progress.

'I've been in a kind of whirlpool,' Judge Durve began, 'I spent the entire time thinking about your objection, Mr Nanda. And then I realized that I hadn't had the chance to listen to the defence team's argument on the subject, so Ms Pahwa or Mr Diwan, one of you should tell me why Mr Nanda's objection should be overruled, if at all?'

Judge Durve was stumped, Vansh thought. He didn't need this much time to end up asking for the other side's argument on the issue. Whether Shilpa Singh should be referred to as a judge or not in his courtroom was something he had already decided upon; this was a charade.

'Your Honour,' Vansh started assertively, 'this is a free country, and Judge Shilpa Singh should get to retain her title, irrespective of the fact that she has been temporarily suspended from her regular duties. That, in no way, takes away the rank and position she's earned in society. It's no different from the princesses and princes of India who lost their estates after Independence and the unification of the country. They are still referred to as Her or His Highness by the people in their local communities. And this isn't just about our country. Lord Jeffrey Archer – the famous English author – served time in jail for perjury; that didn't take away his Lordship. The crime Judge Shilpa Singh is accused of – a charge that will be proven false by the time we are done with the trial – does not take away her social status. Are we saying she dies a social death before His Honour even hears both sides of the argument, evaluates the evidence and takes a decision? The predicament she's unfortunately been put in is solely due to her involvement in a case—'

'Your Honour, this isn't the place to argue in defence of the accused.'

'I was wondering how long it would take you to object, Mr Nanda, and I totally agree with you on that. How the accused came into the position of being put on trial is what this trial is about, so it's best not to have those arguments in my chambers, but I've made my decision here—'

'Your Honour, we haven't been asked to present our side of the argument yet,' Diya Albuquerque stood up, her voice a few decibels higher than everyone else's.

Judge Durve looked at her, motioned her with a nod of his head to take her seat. 'Let's not go off the deep end, ladies and gentlemen. You can argue until the cows decide to come home but nothing you say now will change my decision, is that clear?'

Nods. No one spoke a word.

'It is this court's obligation to ensure that every defendant gets a fair trial. To that effect, robbing Judge Shilpa Singh of her title would be a kind of social opprobrium, which, unfortunately I cannot permit. I will allow the defendant to be referred to as a judge until the time the court decides that she's guilty. I will not ask the State to address her as a judge, and I will not stop the defence from addressing her as one. Motion denied.'

'But …' Ravi Nanda tried to reason.

'In any case, there will be no confusion in identities when you call someone 'Judge', since in my court you and the defence address me as Your Honour.' Judge Durve smiled. 'This meeting is over. See you in the courtroom in a few minutes, ladies and gentlemen.'

FIFTEEN

1

'YOUR HONOUR,' SONIA PAHWA rose up from the defence table. The court was jam-packed with more people than it could accommodate. There were people standing behind the last row like they were showing a new film starring Shah Rukh Khan for which they had paid a premium to stand and watch from the sidelines.

'Yesterday, my senior colleague Mr Diwan wanted to say that we don't want this to be a television-series kind of trial, full of histrionics and jumping on each other. Our esteemed colleagues in the prosecution have spared us by not providing us with an endless list of witnesses, and we sincerely thank them for that. We've done the same too. We want this trial to be over as quickly as possible, since there are lives and reputations at stake, which we need to be mindful of. We do not intend to engage in any unprofessional tactic of springing upon our opponents any last-minute witnesses or theories. This isn't about theatrics. This is about the life of Judge Shilpa Singh ...' she paused, looked at the defence table then turned to look at Diya Albuquerque and Ravi Nanda, daring them to object to her referring to Shilpa by her title, then carried on without any hesitation, 'we will prove beyond doubt that the defendant has been accused of a heinous crime she never committed, and for which she's been ostracized from her community, her social position, her job, her career.

'Your Honour, if nothing else, let's start from the presumption of innocence. Not in the least because the defendant is, or was a pillar of the legal community at the time of the said crime – to make it amply clear to my learned friends, I'm not asking for any allowances here. Presumption of innocence is the birthright of every citizen of India. It is our constitution that promises this.'

Nods all around the courtroom.

It was a good tactic, to appeal before going for the kill.

'Fact number one: the defendant has no history of crime. She's never been accused of any crime or even a misdemeanour of any kind whatsoever.

'Fact number two: the defendant has no history of violence, no history of mental instability and no record of any sort of mental or sociological disorders.

'Fact number three: the defendant is a respected member of the legal community that is sworn to defend the rights of those who have been victimized by others. She is known to dispense justice to parties who have been hurt, violated, mistreated or intentionally let down by others, among other things. She believes in the legal system and has never shown any inclination to take the law into her own hands.

'Fact number four: in all her years as a judge in this very district court, she has built a stellar reputation with no stains on any of her dealings whatsoever. She's always believed in justice over everything else.

'Fact number five: the defendant, Judge Shilpa Singh, received a call on her mobile – and the police has a record of the call – from an as yet unidentified man to say he had evidence in *favour* of the prosecution, that would have only strengthened her ruling against the then defendant Mr Kailash Prasad. I know that in the absence of the testimony of the deceased, it's a classic he-said-she-said situation, but we still need to keep in mind that someone has twisted the whole narrative. As per Judge Shilpa Singh's sworn statement submitted to the court documents, Mr Ashok Kumar had called to help her, not betray her, so the whole argument of the motive makes no sense at all. The prosecution here might have another version of the account, but we will hear that in due course.

'Fact number six: the police didn't consider the fact that Mr Kailash Prasad Yadav, the politician, had sent veiled threats – strike that – he had called and threatened Judge Shilpa Singh …'

'She's good,' Shilpa turned and whispered to Vansh who nodded in admiration of Sonia's opening statement.

Sonia had paused at the right juncture for Judge Durve to digest that the threat to Shilpa Singh hadn't been veiled: it had been blatant. All through her long monologue, Sonia had modulated her voice to emphasize points when required, clinically decimating the grounds on which the charges had been brought up against her client. She had learnt the craft of elocution from the master; her gift was that she drew in people and held their attention when she spoke. Each word measured and delivered well, exactly like Akash Hingorani himself. Brilliant!

'Akash wouldn't have had her in his team for so long if she wasn't this good,' Vansh acknowledged. He could see shades of Akash in her.

'As good-looking as him too,' Shilpa said with a smile.

'… Mr Kailash Prasad told Judge Shilpa Singh,' Sonia continued, 'in as many words that her verdict in the case upon which she was presiding needed a ruling in his favour or else … she'd pay for it,' Sonia carried on with suitable pauses to stress to Judge Durve that it could have been him in her stead – that it was simply a matter of Shilpa Singh being in the wrong place at the wrong time; nothing more, nothing less.

'All the defence would like to prove here in this courtroom is how a misdirected homicide investigation turned into an unfair murder trial, like a golf shot – a slightly wrong angle of the club when it hits the ball at the tee, Your Honour, multiplies manifold by the time the ball lands on the fairway. The investigation has been erroneous from the get go. A wrong start cannot lead one to the correct results, Your Honour. And that brings me to fact number seven: we shall bring to light what is not being said here in this court by the police and the prosecution. The police saw what they wanted to see or had been asked to see by someone influential. They decided that my client, Judge Shilpa Singh, was guilty and then looked for evidence to match their theory.' Sonia stopped talking. She stood silent in the midst of the courtroom for a full thirty seconds. And then added, 'That is all, Your Honour.'

'You were fantastic,' Shilpa murmured to Sonia as she took her seat next to her on the defence table.

'Thank you, Judge.'

2

'MR NANDA, PLEASE CALL your first witness to the stand,' Judge Durve said after a minute.

'Yes, Your Honour.'

The first witness in a homicide trial was more or less the same all over the world. It was either the police officer who made the arrest or the person who performed autopsy on the victim. The reason was simple: to invoke sympathy for the victim, and maybe elicit hostility for the perpetrator. Typically, the homicide victim's family or friends also attend trials and the judge, the media, and the members of the public tend to empathize with them. It isn't just the one life that is annihilated when someone is murdered, but many other lives are destroyed by the untimely loss of an individual. However, it was not the case this time: there was no one from the victim's family in the courtroom. They didn't even know who the victim was; he was still unidentified. It was a murder all right, but the focus of the media wasn't the victim in this particular instance; it was the defendant, Judge Shilpa Singh. Some wanted to crucify her, others wanted her to be exonerated. Some, as usual, were there merely for entertainment.

Kapil Kumar, an anorexic-looking man in his mid-thirties with long and shabby hair and thick, brown square plastic glasses took the oath and monotonously responded to Ravi Nanda's questions regarding himself and his commendable resume. He was an employee of the State and had carried out over one hundred autopsies, including the one on Ashok Kumar's body.

'So, in your expert opinion, Dr Kumar, how did the victim die?' Nanda pointed towards the pictures of the corpse at Lodhi Gardens, moments before it was bagged and carried away for the post-mortem, projected on the screen placed next to the prosecutor's desk. On the next slide, the corpse lay on a steel autopsy table. All to give a glimpse of the dead to the judge and the public, to bring death into the courtroom, to make it real for everyone how a life had been cut short. A flame extinguished before it was time.

Kapil Kumar rattled off what he had summarized in the autopsy report that had been shared with the defence. 'Death had occurred due to extensive blood loss … single stab wound … between the fourth and the fifth ribs … the trajectory of the wound, instantaneous death …' He wasn't one for creating a narrative; he was a man led by science and he delivered his findings in the most procedural and uninteresting way.

Nanda stopped him at different points to repeat certain things or explain them in layman terms. Dr Kumar gladly obliged. An hour after the tedious questioning had begun, there was little the lead prosecutor could ask or Dr Kumar could add. If they expected any objections from the defence table, they were off the mark. There was nothing to object to when someone stated bare facts supported by science. Truth be told, the testimony of Dr Kumar was so lacklustre that some people had lost interest in it within the first ten minutes or so. Maybe His Honour had too.

'We have no further questions for this witness, Your Honour,' announced Nanda.

If this had been any place other than a courtroom trying

a homicide case, the audience would have cheered about surviving the witness's testimony without dozing off.

'Mr Diwan?' asked Judge Durve.

'The defence has no questions for this witness at this time, Your Honour.'

'You may step down, Dr Kumar.'

Dr Kumar stepped down as insipidly as he had spoken.

'Let's take a break now and return to the courtroom after lunch. The court is now in recess until 2 p.m.' Judge Durve got up to leave.

SIXTEEN

1

THE PROSECUTION CALLED IN their next witness after lunch: Mohanlal Sharma, the policeman who had arrested Shilpa. Diya Albuquerque waited until Sharma took the oath before she walked up to him.

'Will you state your name and occupation for the record, please?' she requested. Her voice was as sharp as she looked. A budding yet confident prosecutor, well-groomed and well-prepared.

'I am Senior Constable Mohanlal Sharma assigned to Lodhi Colony Police Station. I arrested the accused, Judge Shilpa Singh …'

Vansh almost smiled at the mention of 'Judge' by the prosecution's witness.

He turned to look at Shilpa, who sat there mute. Angry. Resentful. Frightened. Ashamed of the reckless, knee-jerk reaction of driving out to see a man she had never met or heard of before. But she was composed on the surface if not completely relaxed: *sangfroid*.

'On the afternoon of the said murder, where were you?' Diya drew him into the case straightaway.

'I was on duty, taking a round of Lodhi Gardens—'

'Do you do this regularly, I mean take rounds of the park?'

'Yes, madam. There have been some complaints from people about illicit activities like use of drug and alcohol in the area, hence our supervisor has asked us to monitor the area. Two of us take daily rounds in the park during the day.'

'Okay, carry on.'

'I heard screams, "Murder, murder, police, police", and I ran in the direction of the shouts for help. At the time I thought it might have been another case of someone drinking or dealing or maybe a fight had broken out, but when I arrived at the spot I saw that there was someone lying on the ground bleeding and the defendant holding the knife she had killed him with—'

'Objection, Your Honour,' Sonia Pahwa stood up. 'Senior Constable Mohanlal Sharma may please keep his testimony to what he saw, not what he imagined had happened at the location prior to his arrival. He arrived at the scene after the murder, so he has no way of establishing who murdered Ashok Kumar.'

'Sustained. Strike off the witness's last statement from the record. And Senior Constable Sharma, please refrain from making assumptions of any kind.'

'So,' Diya took over almost instantly, 'you were saying that you arrived at the scene of crime and you saw what?'

'The scene suggested that the man on the ground had been stabbed in the chest. He had bled a lot. I pierced the crowd gathered around and checked his pulse; he was dead.'

Diya asked some other relevant routine questions: *What did you do next? What time did your supervisor arrive at the scene? When did the ambulance arrive?*

Sharma responded with facts – no chicanery there. He had actually been at the site; he had called his supervisor so there was no reason to doubt or object. He had pretty much done everything by the book.

'Did the police take statements from the eyewitnesses?'

'Yes, of course. There were four people who were there already and who had seen Judge Shilpa Singh next to the victim, and therefore they had *assumed*' – having had his wrist slapped by the judge once, he was careful in his articulation – 'that the person holding the knife *might have* stabbed the victim.'

'And what happened after that?'

'Once my supervisor arrived at the scene, he took charge, as you can imagine. He called for more people. The defendant was taken to the police station, and the investigation was assigned to a team of policemen.'

'Did you play any part in the ensuing investigation?'

'Yes, madam.'

'What was your role?'

'Since I was the first on the scene, I was an integral part of the search and inquiry. We had already recovered the murder weapon – I mean what we at the time believed was the murder weapon, which we were able to confirm later on – so we searched for other clues in the vicinity.'

'What kind of clues?'

'The usual clues that the police look for, like any signs of altercation that might have led to the murder. Any apparent motive, if there was someone else there who had run away before the accused and the eyewitnesses arrived at the scene.

Or if someone in the vicinity had seen any anomaly … things like this to help with the investigation.'

'And did you find anything?'

'No.'

'So, you concluded there was no possibility of someone else having committed the murder and got away before the accused arrived at the scene on the pretext of trying to save Mr Ashok Kumar by pulling the knife out of the corpse?'

'Objection, Your Honour,' Vansh interjected. 'The prosecution is leading the witness.'

'Sustained. Ms Albuquerque, please rephrase your question.'

'Of course, Your Honour. Senior Constable Sharma, do you think there was enough time for a murderer to escape before anyone – even the accused – arrived at the scene of the crime?'

'Objection,' Vansh was on a roll now. 'The witness just testified that he was among the third set of people to arrive at the crime scene. The first person to arrive at the scene was Judge Shilpa Singh, followed by the four people who called for the police before the senior constable got there. How would he know how much time had elapsed?'

'Sustained, Mr Diwan. Ms. Albuquerque please ask, the witness questions that he has direct answers for; do not direct him to make assumptions or hypothesize, please.'

'Apologies, Your Honour.'

Vansh looked at Ravi Nanda, who didn't look happy. Perhaps, he was wondering whether letting Diya take on the police witness had been a folly.

Diya was like a dog with a bone. She didn't give up. She was trying all possible angles to establish to the court that there wasn't enough time for anyone to get away from the murder scene, thereby ascertaining that the only possibility was that Shilpa Singh had committed the crime. If she could manage this feat, it would make a compelling argument in favour of the prosecution; the case would be as good as closed. However, each time she took a stab at that, either Sonia or Vansh screamed foul and objected to her line of questioning. There was no way the senior constable could have substantiated her argument, since he had already testified that he had arrived at the scene several minutes after the murder. No one could have determined the exact time of the murder. Even a morbid pathologist, after an autopsy, cannot pinpoint to the exact time of death. The post-mortem report always offers a timeframe. The defence was ready to go to war, if need be, to prove that the murder had happened around fifteen minutes before the arrival of the defendant at the scene. Shilpa Singh's initial statement to the police had clarified that the victim was dead before she was there. For how long? She didn't know then, and no one was any wiser now.

'No more questions for the witness, Your Honour.' After an hour of trying the unachievable, she threw in her hat. She looked at the defence table, her eyes piercing through Sonia, Shilpa and Vansh. Displeasure, discontentment and annoyance were written all over her face.

Judge Durve looked at his watch. It was coming up to 4 p.m.

'How long does the defence think they will take with this witness?'

'Not long, Your Honour.'

'Okay then, carry on without delay so we can all wrap up for the day by 5:30, please.'

2

SONIA STOOD UP, STRAIGHTENED her robe with a single stroke of her hands and walked closer to the witness stand.

'Senior Constable Mohanlal Sharma, are you familiar with the term "confabulation"?'

Sharma looked at the prosecution table, then shook his head. 'No.'

'Confabulation, in psychiatry, is defined as the replacement of a gap in people's memories by imaginary or false information that they might believe to be true. Does it make sense?'

'No, madam,' said Sharma.

By the looks on the faces of the majority of the people in the courtroom, it was evident that they were equally clueless.

'Let me explain in bite-sized parts to make it simple. Sometimes, with the passage of time, one's memory fades, do you agree?'

'Yes.'

'However, serious incidents, like homicide, for example, are recounted post-facto in newspapers, magazines, on television or, in your case, by colleagues and supervisors. They must have discussed it and thrashed it out during the investigation, am I right?'

'Yes, madam.'

'So, it is known to inadvertently happen in such cases – and there is sufficient science to back it up – that the gaps in a person's memory are filled up with the news or information she or he receives from various sources. Are you still with me?'

Sharma appeared distracted because he had realized that she had led him up the garden path into a well-laid trap. He didn't want to look like an idiot on the witness stand by admitting he hadn't understood her logic the third time around, but acknowledging the explanation and admitting he understood the same meant that he agreed to the holes in his testimony, and the eyewitnesses' statements.

'Do you understand me, Sharma-jee?'

'Y-ye-yes.'

'So, the eyewitnesses who called you and said they had seen the murder hadn't actually seen the murder occurring before their eyes or they would have certainly stopped it, is that not true?'

Vansh was exhilarated. Sonia's masterstroke was comparable to that of a seasoned advocate. Despite having the witness admit to the logic she had just presented, she didn't go as far as pointing the gun at him. She hadn't told him that he had made up the facts, possibly involuntarily. A lot of advocates made the rookie mistake of pushing witnesses so far into the corner that they ended up retaliating and fought back. In this case, all Sharma needed to do was agree that the four so-called eyewitnesses weren't, as a matter of fact, eyewitnesses at all, but they had come up with their story *after* the media exploded with intricate details of the murder, implicating Shilpa. Judge Durve had also grasped that Sharma had fallen into the same trap.

'You are correct. They hadn't witnessed the murder itself.'

So far so very good, Vansh told himself.

'So, you agree that the four apparent eyewitnesses had also arrived at the scene several minutes after the murder?'

'Yes, madam.'

'And what they saw was my client Judge Shilpa Singh holding the knife, correct?'

'Yes.'

'Which she has admitted to. She didn't drop the knife when she saw four people coming towards her. So …' Sonia paused to let the first part of her spiel sink in, 'the only two people who were present there at the time of arrival of the *supposed* eyewitnesses were the victim and Judge Shilpa Singh. Ashok Kumar, unfortunately, cannot tell us what happened, or we wouldn't be here, but we have Judge Shilpa Singh's sworn statement that she had pulled out the knife in an attempt to save Ashok Kumar's life—'

'Objection, Your Honour,' Nanda looked peeved. 'Is there a question there somewhere?'

'I was expecting you to object – I've been waiting for a question too, Ms Pahwa. Could you please move forward?' Judge Durve looked at his watch to highlight that the day was about to be over.

'Yes, Your Honour. Senior Constable Sharma, what tangible evidence do you or the investigating police officials have that establishes that what the eyewitnesses saw or told you was true, and what Judge Shilpa Singh said was untrue?'

Sharma looked at the defence table, then at Judge Durve, then at the prosecution table. But this wasn't theatre; no one was going to give him any kind of a prompt.

'The evidence is that we found a solitary set of fingerprints on the murder weapon—'

'But you weren't privy to that particular fact at the time, and the fingerprint expert will also testify at the trial, so we can leave that for later, shall we?' Sonia moved a step towards Sharma and stated politely but peremptorily. 'But for now, we're talking about witnesses and their statements here – what evidence do you have to prove that Judge Shilpa Singh didn't actually pull out the knife from the body of Ashok Kumar to save his life?'

'None.'

'Thank you. Moving on, I have just two more questions for you. When you arrived at the scene, what was the relative position of the defendant, Judge Shilpa Singh, vis-à-vis the victim, Ashok Kumar?'

'I'm sorry – I did not understand the question.' Sharma seemed to be in a daze.

Maybe he was still attempting to make sense of the logic Sonia had fed him minutes ago. Sometimes the brain froze after a long session like that.

'I'll repeat. When you saw the defendant with the knife in her hand next to the victim's body for the first time in Lodhi Gardens, what were their positions?'

'The victim was lying on his back and Judge Shilpa Singh was squatting beside him.'

'Was she near his legs or his chest or …'

'No, she sat near his head …' He closed his eyes to recollect: 'Yes, I remember she was on her knees, which were touching the victim's head. She was rubbing his forehead with her left hand … and held the knife in her right.'

'Rubbing his forehead? Hmm … do you think someone

who murders another person in cold blood would sit there rubbing their victim's forehead after such a heinous act?'

'Objection, Your Honour. This is totally unnecessary.'

'Sustained. Ms Pahwa ...' Although the Judge didn't complete his sentence, it was a kind of polite warning.

'My apologies, Your Honour. For my next question the court will have to humour me, since I will have to give you a background narrative to make matters clear, but it won't take more than five minutes ...'

'You may continue, Ms Pahwa.'

'Your Honour, the prosecution and the defence agree that Ashok Kumar had called Judge Shilpa Singh to Lodhi Gardens to hand over tangible evidence. Where we disagree is whether the evidence was in favour of or against Mr Kailash Prasad. If, for a second, we disregard the second point about which party benefited from that physical evidence, I'd like to ask Senior Constable Sharma,' she turned to Sharma, 'did the police recover any said evidence from the scene?'

'No.'

'Did you search the scene diligently, search the corpse, search Judge Shilpa Singh at the time of the arrest?'

'Not me personally, but yes, the team did all that.'

'And you recovered no audio cassette, video discs, papers or any such evidence that Ashok Kumar claimed to have brought to hand over to Judge Shilpa Singh?'

'No.'

'So, where did it go?'

'Objection.'

'Overruled. You can answer the last question, Sharma-jee.'

'I don't know.'

'Didn't you wonder if there was a third person at the scene—'

'Objection.'

'Overruled.'

'Senior Constable Sharma, didn't the police department, in the course of this homicide investigation, wonder if there might be a third person at the scene who took the evidence away after Ashok Kumar died and before Judge Shilpa Singh arrived at the scene? And that this third person could be the murderer?'

'Objection, Your Honour!' Nanda almost screamed this time around.

'No more questions for this witness, Your Honour.' Sonia stopped there. The message had been delivered to Durve. The evidence Kumar claimed to have couldn't have just disappeared. Someone must have taken it away. It was a simple yet powerful delivery by Sonia.

'You may step down, Senior Constable Sharma,' said Judge Durve glancing at his watch. It was 4:45 p.m. 'Who's the prosecution's next witness?'

'Mr Akash Hingorani.'

A soft murmur went around the courtroom. Ravi Nanda and team had put both Akash and Shilpa Singh on the witness list, but no one had really expected them to be called upon as witnesses. Who'd want hostile witnesses in a trial this important? It even surprised the three on the defence table.

'Let's have some order in the courtroom please,' said the Judge and then glanced at the prosecution table and said, 'there is little point in me asking how long that will take, is there?' He was smiling. 'Ladies and gentlemen, this hearing is deferred until tomorrow morning.'

'All rise ...'

3

'WELL DONE, SONIA. YOU were commendable today,' Shilpa broke the silence in the car.

'Yes, you were simply brilliant,' Vansh applauded her too.

'Thank you for the compliments, and thank you, Mr Diwan, for all the coaching.'

'I didn't imagine he'd call Akash as a witness. I thought it was a ploy to take him off the defence team,' Shilpa looked at Vansh and Sonia who looked equally baffled.

'Neither did I,' Sonia echoed.

'That makes three of us. And Akash didn't think Nanda was serious about putting you and him on the witness list. It's a very peculiar tactic, to invite hostile witnesses to the stand.'

'I still don't think he'll call you, Judge,' Sonia voiced.

'I think you're correct, but let's not take a chance here,' Vansh thought aloud. He wanted to agree with Sonia's logic but he didn't know if he could trust Nanda to follow any dictum.

'Is Akash prepared to be a witness?' Shilpa asked.

'We didn't work on it, but we have the entire night.'

'He's a quick learner,' Sonia jested, to lighten up the tense atmosphere in the car.

'That he is,' Vansh agreed.

'Should we all go to his place then?' the judge asked.

'I wouldn't suggest that you come along. We'll drop you and head off to see him.'

'I expected you to say that.'

'Sonia, do you mind messaging Akash to tell him we'll see him in forty minutes from now, please?'

'Not at all, Mr Diwan.'

'And tell him it's going to be a long night.'

4

'YOU'RE SHITTING ME,' WAS Akash's reaction to the news Sonia and Vansh relayed to him. 'That idiot actually, really, truly wants me on the stand?'

'Yes, so we're here to prepare you.'

'Oh, how sweet of you two. Should I open a bottle of champagne first?'

'Be serious, Akash.'

'What makes you think that I'm not? I'm serious, that's why I said champagne and not single malt – all of us need to be clear-headed tomorrow, right?

'We have time until midnight,' Sonia, once again, attempted at lightening the mood. 'So, we can have a drink. *A* drink, mind you.'

'That's my protégé.'

'Go on then, chill a pink one.'

'Nothing less would do, my friends.'

Akash and Vansh were conscious about Sonia being present. Lying, as always, was tricky business. The secret that Vansh had shared the intricate details of the defence's strategy with Akash could come back to bite them if a single word slipped out of either's mouth. Not that Sonia would run and make a complaint right this minute, but as Vansh had warned previously, it could become a contentious issue at some point in the future. But their two-decades-long experience as advocates had taught them how to expertly lie by omission.

SEVENTEEN

1

AKASH HINGORANI WAS DRESSED in an elegant pinstripe charcoal-grey suit and open-collared white shirt. As he walked to the witness box, he turned to Shilpa and gave her a reassuring a smile. Although under duress, to him she looked pristine in the silver-grey saree she was wearing, quietly seated between Sonia and Vansh. She was fighting her emotions and winning at it, at least for the time being.

Maybe Chavi was correct in her assessment, maybe he was still in love with the judge. Why had they moved away from one another? What if there were professional differences? Life was more than one's profession, wasn't it? He wanted to rush to her, take her in his arms and promise her that all this, these false accusations, this sham of a trial would soon be over and they could start all over again, now that their love needn't be burdened by secrecy. They'd make a beautiful couple; they'd make fantastic parents to Raghuveer. If professional differences still existed, one of them could give up the damn profession – it didn't matter to him which one of them quit. He made a lot more money than her, but she was in a significantly more prestigious position. Maybe it could work out in the end – it wasn't that if he gave up his practice, they'd have to put less butter on their toast or sacrifice the marmalade at breakfast. And it wasn't that he couldn't switch from being a criminal defence advocate into some other field of legal consulting that would certainly be less at odds with Shilpa's ethos.

'Are we ready?'

His reverie broke when he heard Judge Durve's voice. He took the oath.

'So how does it feel to take the oath in a courtroom?' asked Judge Durve with a broad smile. Laughter ensued in the packed courtroom at the judge's comment, which for once Durve didn't mind. After all, it was his joke that had invoked it. He let the laughter and murmur die down naturally. There were more people in and outside the courtroom today than there had been on the last two days of the trial. Everyone and their dog had read or heard about the romance between the accused and the witness on the stand today, and people had come in hordes like it was some film set where a Yash Chopra classic was being remade. Since the media wasn't permitted to bring cameras into the courtroom, Akash had been totally blinded by the camera flashes that lay in waiting at the room's entrance. Clichéd headlines – 'Witness for the Prosecution' and 'Hostile Witness' – would accompany his photographs with articles about the day's developments across media platforms.

'I've been waiting for this moment all my life, Your Honour,' Akash replied to the judge. Jest for jest.

'The prosecution may begin with the proceedings.'

Ravi Nanda got up. 'Will you state your name and occupation for the record, please?'

'I'm Akash Hingorani, I'm an advocate by profession, like you, although we usually represent different sides—'

'Mr Hingorani, may I request you to keep your answers short and concise?'

'My apologies, Mr Nanda.'

'How long have your practised law, Mr Hingorani?'

'Almost two decades. Do you need the exact date on which I started?'

'No, this much information is enough.'

Vansh and Sonia looked at each other and giggled like schoolgirls. As much as they had tried last night, they knew Akash wouldn't stick to the script. They couldn't imagine why Nanda would want him as a witness; a reputable, more-than-successful defence advocate. Professional suicide came to mind, and they had laughed it off over a glass of champagne.

'What exactly is your relationship with the accused Shilpa Singh?' Nanda turned and gestured towards the defence table in case Akash wasn't sure which Shilpa Singh he was talking about.

Nanda and his assistant Diya had not once referred to Shilpa Singh as judge. Harsh Mehta seemed to be under a self-imposed embargo; he sat at the prosecution table like a statue and didn't talk or blink or move or confer. He was there since the court had appointed him as the local advocate assisting the Mumbai-imported prosecution team. He was smart enough to keep his bridges from burning should Shilpa return to the courtroom as Judge Shilpa Singh.

'We work in the same district court, so that makes us colleagues,' Akash responded.

'Are you sure you were just colleagues and nothing more than colleagues?' Nanda asked.

'We also socialize in the same circles, so yes, you could even call us friends.'

'Friends?' Nanda nodded like he was on to something. 'Friendship between an advocate and a judge—'

'Objection, Your Honour. There is nothing in the Indian Constitution that prohibits a judge from being friends with an advocate.' Vansh stood up.

'Sustained.'

Nanda pretended like he was crestfallen. 'You're right, even Lord Krishna was friends with Sudama. I got carried away. My apologies.' He flashed a wicked grin. 'Mr Hingorani, can you highlight what exactly was the nature of your friendship with Ms Shilpa Singh for the benefit of the court?'

'I'm not sure I understand – the nature of our friendship?' Akash was a consummate actor too. Years of practising the same tactics in a courtroom accorded one with adequate training to manage such situations with élan. 'The nature of friendship is being friendly.'

'I mean was it just friendship or more than that?'

'A little more than friends.'

'Before we get sucked further into this needless debate, Mr Hingorani, let me ask you a direct question: are you having a clandestine affair with the accused, Shilpa Singh?'

'No.'

'Did you, at some point in time in the past have a clandestine love affair with the accused?' Nanda changed the tense.

'You could call it that, but—'

'I could call *it* that? What would you call *it*, Mr Hingorani?'

'We were romantically involved for a short duration.'

'Isn't that what they call a love affair?'

'Not really.'

'Oh, pray do tell us all and enlighten the court – what is the difference between the two terms?'

'Objection, Your Honour. The witness is a qualified defence advocate and not some linguistic expert who should explain synonyms and antonyms to my learned colleague and waste the court's precious time.'

'I agree, but I'll allow it, Mr Diwan, simply because my curiosity is getting the better of me. I'd very much like to know the difference too.'

'Thank you, Your Honour. So, Mr Hingorani you think having a "love affair" and "being romantically involved" with someone aren't synonymous?'

'To begin with there are no synonyms in any language. It's all about the nuances—'

'Please stop, Mr Hingorani.' Judge Durve raised a hand to stop Akash from talking. 'Mr Nanda, I advise you to buy yourself a copy of *Wren & Martin* and some dictionary and complete your language lessons in your own time. Maybe you could order copies for the court and for me too. Let this be on record that I sustain Mr Diwan's objection in retrospect. Mr Nanda, I urge you to put this little discussion on semantics to bed for now and move on, please.'

Durve had grasped that Akash would meander away from the prosecution's questions, lead them down some superfluous path and waste as much time as the prosecution provided him by engaging in a word duel. It was enough having two advocates argue in the court – having one on the witness stand, too, was turning out to be His Honour's nightmare.

'As you wish, Your Honour. So, Mr Hingorani, without engaging in an exchange of words – no pun intended – I am happy to use your terminology in the interest of time.'

'Which terminology are you referring to now, Mr Nanda?'

'The fact that you were *romantically* involved with the defendant.'

'Yes, thank you.'

'You're welcome. Now, when were you romantically involved with the accused?'

'Do you need me to provide you with the exact dates?'

Nanda didn't look too happy. He turned to the judge to intervene to bring Akash in line since he was evading the prosecutor's questions by countering them with his own needless queries. The judge simply shrugged in a you-should-have-known-that-before-calling-a-hostile-witness-on-the-stand way.

Truth be told, Akash hadn't dodged any of Nanda's questions so far.

Nanda had asked for a timeline and Akash had enquired how specific the prosecutor wanted the response to be. Nor had Akash been rude or non-deferential to the prosecution or the judge in any manner. There was little that Durve could do about it.

'No, just an approximate timeframe would do.'

'The romantic involvement concluded about ten to twelve months ago.'

'Ten or twelve?' Nanda almost bit his tongue but the words had left his mouth.

'You just said I need not be precise.'

'But surely remembering the number of months is generic, not precise.'

'Objection, Your Honour. The prosecution is harassing the witness,' Sonia Pahwa could hardly hide her smile when she raised the objection.

Laughter followed. By now everyone in the courtroom had started to enjoy the banter between Ravi Nanda and Akash Hingorani. The crowd had come to see this very repartee. The media found it juicy too. All in all, it was more entertaining than any legal drama on screen.

'Sustained,' Judge Durve said; he was part irritated, part amused.

'Mr Hingorani,' Ravi Nanda, the professional, continued without breaking his stride. 'How long did this so-called romantic involvement with the defendant continue?'

'Almost nine or ten months, I would say. I'll have to check my diary if you are particular about the start and end dates—'

'No need for that, this is enough,' Nanda responded, not intending to get into another verbal confrontation. 'In the nine or ten months that you were romantically involved with the accused, I assume you two shared some private moments?'

'I'm not sure I follow what you mean by private moments.' Akash wasn't giving in. He intended to make this session as difficult for Nanda as possible, and he was doing a great job at the moment.

Nanda looked at the judge pleadingly, but only for a second. Upon realizing he wouldn't get much assistance, he rephrased his question. 'Did you and the accused, Ms Shilpa Singh, spend time in the company of each other?'

'Yes, we did.'

'Mr Hingorani, how would you describe that time you spent alone with the accused?'

'Sublime comes to mind—'

'Mr Hingorani, did the defendant ever appear down or depressed to you?'

'No.'

'Never?'

'No.'

'Mr Hingorani, did you ever get this feeling that the defendant had any violent tendencies?'

'No.'

'Did it ever occur to you that the defendant was concealing something from you – like a violent part of her personality? Or something else? Anything?' This was a double-edged question slipped in by Nanda.

'No, there is not a single violent or mean streak in Judge Shilpa Singh.'

'You mean to say she never kept anything from you?'

'I don't believe she did, and in any case—'

'Mr Hingorani, please keep your responses short and to the point.' Nanda sounded annoyed now. Getting Akash on the stand was his first victory as it removed him from being Shilpa's advocate, but as a witness Akash wasn't letting Nanda accomplish the second and more crucial purpose. Since the police had not been able to identify the victim yet or establish a clear motive for Shilpa to murder Ashok Kumar, Nanda wanted to portray the defendant as someone who had a short fuse with a tendency towards reckless behaviour. He wanted to suggest that Shilpa Singh had lost control on the day of Kumar's murder.

'Mr Hingorani, did you know Ms Shilpa Singh is the widow of a war veteran?'

A wave of whisper went around the courtroom. This little piece of information hadn't been widely circulated in the media.

'Yes.'

'Did you know that before you were romantically involved with her?'

I have a man in my life. Shilpa's words echoed in Akash's mind. He remembered that he hadn't known about her marital status before they had started dating. Or about Raghuveer. He wasn't aware if this particular aspect had come up in court before this time; this was something Vansh and Sonia hadn't discussed with him. He looked at Shilpa. He thought about the implications of him lying on the stand under oath, the risk of perjury. Getting caught could do more harm to him and to Shilpa.

'Mr Hingorani ...' he heard Nanda call out to him. 'Did you know that Ms Shilpa Singh was a widow before you were romantically involved with her?'

'No.'

'Did you know she had a son before you were romantically involved with her?'

'Objection,' Vansh stood up. 'Your Honour, Judge Shilpa Singh's marital status or the fact that that she's a mother to a son is irrelevant to the case.'

Judge Durve nodded. 'Where is this headed, Mr Nanda?'

'Your Honour, please indulge me for a few more questions, and I'll prove their relevance.'

'Okay, you can answer that one, Mr Hingorani.'

'Mr Hingorani, did you know Ms Shilpa Singh was married

and had a son before you were romantically involved with her?' Nanda repeated the question.

'No, but—' Akash now understood what Nanda wanted but he couldn't evade the questions.

'Objection, Your Honour. At the time my client and the witness were romantically involved, they were both single. Their short-lived involvement was the same as of any other pair of consenting adults. There is no reason for the prosecution to bring their relationship into the courtroom to berate or judge my client. The fact that my client is a widow does not disqualify her from living a normal life and falling in love. My learned colleague is making it all sound like it was some adulterous relationship when it was anything but. We are living in the twenty-first century—'

Judge Durve raised his hand to stop Vansh from talking. 'Mr Nanda, how long before we see the relevance of your questions?'

'Your Honour, I agree with Mr Diwan – I wasn't trying to criticize or pass any judgement on the romantic involvement between the defendant and the witness here. My sole purpose of this line of questioning was to prove to the court that Ms Shilpa Singh did, in fact, conceal some parts of her life from Mr Hingorani—'

'Objection, Your Honour.'

'Overruled.'

'If she concealed her past from someone she was romantically involved with, what makes Mr Hingorani so confident that she didn't disguise her violent tendencies?' Ravi Nanda had trumped the defence team once again. 'No more questions for this witness, Your Honour.'

'Mr Diwan, do you have any questions for Mr Hingorani?'

'Yes, Your Honour,' Vansh said. He hadn't planned to question Akash and he wasn't prepared for it either. They hadn't expected Nanda to be so brutally brilliant. 'But may I request the court to take a small recess, please?'

'We'll meet after lunch then. This court will reconvene at 3 p.m.'

'Thank you, Your Honour.'

The crowd was reluctant to leave their pews despite the announcement of the recess. They didn't want to lose their seats when they returned to watch the second half of what had turned out to be the most entertaining part of the trial.

People around the world were obsessed with secret affairs, sex and morality. They would have loved this discussion to carry on for a few days, maybe forever. Who died, who was murdered and who was responsible for the cold-blooded homicide was secondary. Who cared? Especially when no one in a world of eight billion inhabitants had come forward to claim the orphan corpse …

2

THE PROSECUTION TRIO WERE positive they had damaged the defence case. In any case, after getting Akash Hingorani removed from the defence team, the prosecution had no option but to put him on the stand even if it had led them nowhere, or Judge Durve would have admonished them.

'You were fantastic, Ravi,' said Diya.

'What do you think the defence team wants Hingorani on the stand for?' asked the local prosecutor, Harsh Mehta.

'They aren't left with much choice after this session. I made sure I cornered the lover boy into accepting that he'd been lied to, even if by omission. My guess is that Sonia and Vansh will try to salvage whatever they can to reinstate some of Shilpa's credibility,' Nanda responded, 'because at the moment she looks like a crafty woman who lies and holds onto information when it suits her.'

'Well done, Mr Nanda,' Mehta conceded. He had never seen Akash bamboozled in a courtroom.

'Thank you.'

EIGHTEEN

1

'YOUR HONOUR,' VANSH STARTED after lunch. 'Forgive me for saying this, but in my opinion, what my learned colleague attempted before lunch was an extremely low-end tactic that doesn't befit this court: exploiting someone's personal life for—'

'Objection, Your Honour.' Nanda was standing at his table.

'State your objection.'

Nanda looked like he'd got punched. His mien reflected that he had half-expected the judge to uphold his objection, but instead it was he who was being questioned.

'Your Honour, does the defence advocate have a question here?'

Advocates – prosecution or defence – need to ask questions to the witnesses, and not preach or lead the witness and to that effect, Nanda had a valid point. However, Vansh, too, had been careful with his summary of the prosecution's tactics. Shilpa's defence team had taken two extraordinary sucker punches since the beginning of the trial – in fact, one of them was delivered even before the trial commenced, and Vansh wasn't going to let Nanda and team spoil their party anymore.

He had carefully directed his statement at the judge and not at Akash, the witness.

'Mr Nanda, I think the defence counsel here was talking to me. Do you want him to start asking *me* questions now?'

'Your Honour, I thought—'

'You may take your seat, Mr Nanda.'

'I apologize, Your Honour.'

'And … Mr Diwan, your opinion is duly noted. You may proceed with questioning the witness now, please.'

'Yes, Your Honour.' The point had been made. Vansh knew better than to labour the argument anymore.

He walked towards the witness box and addressed his friend. 'Mr Hingorani, before the lunch break my learned colleague asked you if you knew about Judge Shilpa Singh's past life – her being a widow with a grown-up son – before you got romantically involved with her, right?'

'Yes.'

'If it's not too intrusive, may I ask you which one of you made the first move to romance the other?'

'If you must know, it was I who made the first move, which she initially declined and later reluctantly accepted,' the verbose Akash responded without any fear of being interrupted by Vansh.

'And as per your own testimony, you weren't aware of Judge Shilpa Singh's marital status at the time, is that correct?'

'Yes, that is correct.'

'Tell me something – if you had known that she was a widow with a teenage son, would your decision to be romantically involved been any different?'

'No.'

'So, am I correct in understanding that there was little reason for Judge Shilpa Singh to intentionally conceal her past from you—'

'Objection, Your Honour. Shilpa Singh couldn't have read the witness's mind to know how he would have reacted if she had told him the truth at that specific point in time.'

'Sustained.'

Nanda conveyed the impression that he had no desire to let Vansh walk over the brilliant inference he had drawn from Akash's testimony before lunch.

'Mr Hingorani,' Vansh didn't let the objection derail him whatsoever, 'when was it that you came to know about Judge Shilpa Singh's past life?'

'It was in the early days, maybe when we were barely a month into the relationship.'

'Who told you about her past life?'

'Judge Shilpa Singh told me about it all.'

'She told you?' Vansh made it sound incredible. 'The defendant,' he turned and gestured at Shilpa, 'told you that she had been married earlier?'

'Yes.'

'What else did *she* tell you?'

'That she had a teenage son who was studying at a boarding school.'

'And how did *you* react?'

'Nothing changed. We were mature enough to not let this revelation affect our relationship—'

'Objection,' Nanda cried. 'Your Honour, the prosecution requests the court to strike the defence advocate's last question and the witness's response to it, please.'

'On what grounds, Mr Nanda?'

'Your Honour, discovering such fundamental details about someone a month into a relationship is an entirely different scenario than knowing them upfront. This line of questioning by the defence advocate is mocking the court by attempting to rationalize that lying by omission is acceptable, that it is a norm when it is not. The fact remains that the accused, Shilpa Singh, withheld this detail at the beginning of the relationship. It doesn't matter what she told the witness later once they were romantically involved, since she couldn't have concealed the truth forever once she was in the relationship.'

'And,' Judge Durve responded rather sternly, 'the fact also remains that the witness, Mr Hingorani, didn't throw a fit when he was made aware of it, and that he didn't walk away from the relationship after finding that out.'

'Thank you, Your Honour,' Vansh jumped in. 'You just summarized *my* argument, Your Honour.'

Nanda looked deflated. His entire premise, of proving Shilpa Singh to be a conniving woman who operated deviously, had been overturned. And that was the sole reason why Vansh had made Akash take the stand after lunch. There was nothing more satisfying than throwing a trump card on your opponent's ace.

'Your Honour,' Vansh continued. 'The prosecution seems to have taken a small part of Judge Shilpa Singh's life and blown it way out of proportion. The fact that she is a widow who was once romantically involved with the witness does not have any bearing on the case at hand whatsoever. The entire session was to fan unfounded allegations of a homicide merely because of her affair with the witness: how far could one go with this kind of flimflam? This trial is about the murder of Ashok Kumar. Nothing more, nothing less—'

'Objection. My learned colleague is sermonizing again, Your Honour.'

'Sustained.'

'That's all, Your Honour. I have no more questions for this witness.'

The buried love affair between Judge Shilpa Singh and defence advocate Akash Hingorani would now be the topic of conversation until the next juicy piece of news was delivered from some other quarter. The prosecuting team could well have asked for testimony from other experts than dragging this into the court, and the trial would have been a lot less muddy and concluded considerably sooner. But as it went, Nanda had wanted to sow the seeds that Shilpa Singh was capable of odd and abhorrent behaviour, and that she operated on the sly and he had been provided the opportunity. To be fair to him and the prosecution team, they had done their jobs brilliantly.

At the end of the day, the prosecution carried the burden of proof; they had to prove, beyond reasonable doubt, that the accused had committed the crime. As such, they always had the first go at any trial – irrespective of the crime, irrespective of the country – and that was the law. What Judge Durve thought of the day's session when he reflected on the testimonies and arguments later was anybody's guess.

'Mr Hingorani, you may step down,' Judge Durve said. 'I think we should close for today. I don't know about all of you, but my brain feels totally sapped. I'd like to see both the lead advocates in my chambers in five minutes. The court will take a recess until tomorrow morning.' Then he briskly walked out.

2

NO JUDGE EVER ASKED the advocates to see him in chambers after a day's trial to plan a weekend retreat. It indicated that he had something serious to discuss with them.

'How do you think the day went?' Judge Durve was seated behind his desk when Ravi Nanda and Vansh Diwan arrived. 'And before you ask me the same question, let me tell you how I feel: if at all it was permitted within these premises, I'd have ordered a double Patiala peg of the most potent whisky in the world and had it neat in one go. I trust that tells you my state of mind.'

Vansh glanced at Nanda who seemed equally baffled by the judge's disposition.

'I'm sorry if it was something I said, Your Honour,' Vansh started.

'So am I, but our intention had never been to make any trouble as such but, if in the course of—' Nanda joined in.

'Okay, I appreciate that neither of you went out of bounds as far as the proceedings were concerned, but a lot of it was uncalled for nevertheless, wouldn't you agree?'

'Your Honour—'

'I am still the judge, and I haven't finished yet so it would be good if both of you gentlemen listened to me first – is that too much to expect?'

Both glumly acquiesced with nods.

'Here's the thing. We knew Mr Hingorani would be a hostile witness and he turned out to be very much so, no surprises there. For the love of the law and the Lord, I cannot bear another day with another hostile witness on the stand.

'The curtain needs to come down on this spectacle soon. And although I cannot, by law, forbid you from calling the defendant to the witness stand, I strongly advise you against it. If tomorrow turns out to be a repetition of today, I will not be a happy man, I can tell you that.' Judge Durve stopped, picked up a glass of water from his desk and took a few sips. 'Without going into details, what does the prosecution expect from the testimony of Shilpa Singh?'

Vansh noted that Judge Durve had mentioned Shilpa Singh by just her name – no title whatsoever. But him being a peer, he had the right to do so.

'May I, Your Honour?' asked Nanda.

'Yes, you may speak now.'

'Your Honour, as for today, we had to establish that Shilpa Singh has a tendency to conceal—'

'Yes, that was today, Mr Nanda,' Judge Durve sounded insistent. 'You gave the media enough material to fill columns with lurid news, which was nothing less than defaming the defendant. Your argument is duly noted. Yes, she had a love affair and she didn't mention she was a widow in her first meeting to her beau. Too bad. However, if that is all you're going to furnish tomorrow, I expect the defence,' he looked at Vansh, 'to state continuing objection and I'll withhold all of them without letting you ask another question on the same topic or with the same impropriety. Could we put that affair to rest and focus on the case – it's a murder trial, for God's sake.'

He must really be livid to be cursing, Vansh thought. But one couldn't blame Nanda for what he'd attempted earlier. Every prosecutor worth his degree, however stealthily, always harboured a desire to try a historic case. A celebrity – and who could be more celebrated in a courtroom than a judge? – defendant in a murder trial, in a packed courtroom with a scandal thrown in: the media had unlimited ink for such cases. It had all the possible ingredients for Nanda's wet dream to come true. Would Vansh have done anything different if he was in Nanda's shoes? Of course not!

'Understood, Your Honour, but there is also the matter of the defendant breaking every rule in the book by going alone to meet the witness in a case she was presiding over—'

Durve raised both his hands to stop Nanda in his tracks.

'Mr Nanda, no one knows the truth – whether she went to Lodhi Gardens to meet the witness for the prosecution or the defendant – it's her word against media speculations and who do you think I, or any judge for that matter, would be inclined to believe? And how do you plan to establish to the court, beyond reasonable doubt, that the verdict that Shilpa Singh was about to give in the case of Mr Kailash Prasad mattered so much to her that she ended up stabbing the witness – a witness that to date the police force has been unable to identify?' Judge Durve picked up his glass and upended it. 'In any event, what possible motive could she have had in stabbing a witness whether he was with the defence or the prosecution?'

'Your Honour, it seems like the prosecution is on a fishing expedition in a lake with no water …'

'Mr Diwan, I shall ask you when I need your opinion.'

Slap! Vansh could feel his face reddening. Why did he have to be a wise-ass?

'Your Honour, I don't think that will be fair. For instance, we now have on record that Shilpa Singh had lied to Mr

Hingorani; maybe she's lied about something else, too. Maybe she has violent tendencies—'

'Too many *maybes*, don't you think, Mr Nanda? There isn't a motive. If you want to prove she suffers from episodic insanity, you'll only be helping the defence.'

The insanity plea, in murder cases, is usually filed by the defence, and backed by a psychiatrist to prove mental imbalance of the defendant. Once established, the defendant could be considered 'not guilty by reason of insanity' and it may result in the defendant being committed to a psychiatric facility instead of a prison.

'In any case,' Judge Durve continued his lecture, 'where is the psychiatric evaluation that she has any mental illness? Is there any past incident of insanity or violence or outburst or such untoward occurrences in the docket that you've filed in the court?'

'None, Your Honour.'

'I thought as much. And I'm sure you know the date to file for insanity has long passed now for both the prosecution and the defence, so I'm not sure what your game is here?'

Nanda took the dressing down quietly.

'Today's session with Mr Hingorani was nothing more than muckraking, and unfortunately, I will not be able to bear it again tomorrow. Mr Nanda, you have other witnesses. The experts. I will go out on a limb if I have to, and not let anyone or anything subvert or throttle the truth, but get the evidence to support your arguments and proceed with the case instead of smearing people. I cannot disallow you from doing it, but once again, I strongly advise you to refrain from calling the defendant to the witness stand as your second hostile witness and make a mockery of the system.'

Nanda looked furious but he bit his tongue.

'Mr Diwan – now, what is it you were saying?'

'Nothing, Your Honour, I apologize for interrupting earlier.'

'Thank you, gentlemen … and not a word of this conversation to anyone. Not even to your team members.'

'But your Honour, how will I explain this sudden change of tactic to my second chair?'

'Your problem, not mine. Have a good evening.'

With their tails between their legs, the two advocates retreated from the room.

3

'What did Anshu have to say?' Diya asked when Nanda reappeared after the meeting in the chambers.

'Anshu? Who's Anshu?' Mehta looked surprised.

'Anshuman Durve, the judge,' Diya said with a chuckle.

'Oh.'

'Nothing, he impressed upon both parties that he wanted the trial to conclude soon; doesn't want it to stretch too much since it is one of "theirs" on trial.'

'And how does he propose we do that? At the end of the day, it's a murder trial and not a case of a missing dog. These things take time.'

'I have an idea,' Nanda told them. 'Maybe we could drop Shilpa Singh from the witness list, now that we have already compromised her integrity in the court.'

'Why would you do that? It would only benefit our case if she lied on the stand or stumbled when you asked her direct questions,' Diya insisted.

'Okay, let's think about it later.' Nanda was conscious of Judge Durve's warning. There was no way he was revealing to Mehta why he planned to drop Shilpa Singh from the witness list. Diya, he knew, he could talk to later in the hotel room.

4

'How do you think it went?' Chavi asked in the evening. She had come over to Akash's house for dinner.

'I don't know. I wish you were there.'

'I was.'

'I didn't see you.'

'And I made sure of that.'

'Is this a journalist talking or a friend?'

'A friend.'

'But if you were present in the courtroom, why ask me? I should be asking you that?'

'I think it went fine. Ravi Nanda had cornered you in the first half, but Vansh got credibility back for the judge, methinks.'

'And ...?'

'So it was a zero-sum game to be honest. I don't think the defence scored any points as such, in my opinion. I sincerely hope Vansh Diwan and your pretty assistant—'

'Sonia Pahwa. Not a difficult name to remember unless you

have a grudge against pretty women. She's an ace of a defence lawyer.'

'As I was saying,' Chavi ignored his comment, 'unless the defence team has some real evidence besides reacting to Nanda's offensive tactics—'

'I am told they do,' Akash responded.

'Great.'

'Tell me something, are you in any way jealous of Sonia?'

'Why should I be?'

'The other day you told me you love me and then gave me a lecture on how I was still in love with the judge, so I thought maybe, you know …'

'I know, and I admit if we had met a few years back we would certainly be dating.'

'But?'

'Like I said, you're still in love with the judge and I still have emotional scars from my previous relationship. I love your company a lot; maybe we'll stay friends forever and never date, maybe one day we might. In any case you are allergic to my smoking.' She let out a chuckle to lighten the mood.

'That's true. Maybe one day you might give up smoking, who knows?'

NINETEEN

1

THE COURTROOM WAS IN order before Judge Anshuman Durve took his chair and asked for the proceedings to resume. Shilpa Singh had taken her seat between Sonia and Vansh. When the trial had just begun, only her eyes betrayed her, but now even her disposition seemed a bit shaky to say the least. Akash's testimony might have discredited her for no fault of hers or his, but because of the affair that the prosecution was determined to condemn. When did honest love become so vile?

'Dr Joshi,' Nanda started, 'tell us about yourself.'

Dr Vivek Joshi wasn't a doctor of medicine. He had a doctorate in forensic science and was an expert in fingerprints. He had been called to testify as an expert in more cases than anyone could remember. At fifty-eight, he stood ramrod straight, a full head of salt-and-pepper hair coiffed to invoke envy in any teenager. He wore stylish rimless glasses and was dressed in a charcoal-grey suit, a white shirt with a magenta tie. The only thing that dampened his style was the walrus moustache from the seventies, but he looked confident.

'I've been in the forensic sciences for almost four decades now,' he responded with aplomb and carried on summarizing his resume, which left no doubt in anyone's mind that the man knew what he was talking about. Try as hard as you could, there was no shitting him.

'Dr Joshi, did you lead the evidence team in the case of "State of Delhi vs Shilpa Singh"?'

'Yes, I did, and thank you for giving me the opportunity.'

'Do you recognize this knife?' Nanda pointed at the knife that had been brought in as an exhibit and displayed on the table in the middle of the courtroom. It was wrapped in clear plastic, preserved with stains, as it might still be carrying the fingerprints, which weren't visible to the naked eye.

Dr Joshi took a quick glance. 'It appears to be the same.'

'It is the same,' Nanda said, then turned to the Judge: 'May I, Your Honour?'

Judge Durve nodded.

Nanda held the exhibit at one corner of the plastic and carried it towards the witness stand for Dr Joshi to give it a closer inspection. 'What do you think now, Dr Joshi? Does it appear to be the same or *is* it the same?'

'I can confidently say that it is the same knife.'

'Just to be clear, this is the same knife that was procured by the police in the investigation from the scene of crime in which one Mr Ashok Kumar was murdered in Lodhi Gardens, the trial for which is in progress now – "State of Delhi vs Shilpa Singh?"'

'To the best of my knowledge, it is.'

'And what did you find on the knife?'

'We found blood, which matched the blood of the victim, Mr Ashok Kumar, like you mentioned, and just one set of fingerprints.'

'And do you know who that one person was whose fingerprints were found on the knife?'

'Yes, I do.'

'Is that person present in the courtroom today?'

'Yes, she is.'

'For the record, could you point at the person whose fingerprints you recovered from the murder weapon, please?'

Dr Joshi pointed at the defence table and said, 'Judge Shilpa Singh.'

'Thank you, Dr Joshi.'

'You're very welcome.'

'Dr Joshi, you mentioned you found just one set of fingerprints on the knife, am I right?'

'Yes.'

'Does that mean no one else had ever touched the knife handle before?'

Vansh squirmed. Nanda was stealing his thunder right under the defence's nose. Vansh and Sonia had decided to challenge Dr Joshi about the lack of any other prints, and hence establish that whoever had used the knife had deliberately eliminated the prints. But Nanda had the first shot and he'd turn the whole theory upside down, making it difficult for the defence to rebuild on it. Or twist it.

'I am not sure what the question is,' Dr Joshi said.

'Dr Joshi, it can be one of two scenarios here: one, that the knife was brand new, taken out of its wrapping by Shilpa Singh and used for stabbing Mr Ashok Kumar—'

'Objection, Your Honour.'

Mentioning Shilpa Singh here, at this point, was way out of order. 'Sustained. Mr Nanda, choose your words with caution.'

'I'll rephrase, Your Honour. Dr Joshi, as I mentioned, either a brand-new knife was taken out of its wrapping and used for the first time at the scene of the crime or the only alternative is that the miscreant who used the knife to stab Mr Ashok Kumar was diligent enough to wipe off all previous prints on the knife before the accused arrived at the scene. Do I sound correct in my assessment?'

'You seem to be.'

'Seem to be?' Nanda repeated. 'All previous fingerprints couldn't have vanished on their own, so what could be the third scenario?'

'I never said there was a third scenario.'

'But you didn't seem entirely convinced of my deduction either, did you?'

'Oh I am. I am sorry if I led you to somehow believe that I wasn't.'

'Dr Joshi, have you ever come across a situation like this before?'

'Objection, Your Honour. What has any previous situation got to do with this? Past statistics have no relevance in such matters,' Sonia got up to point out.

Durve looked nonchalant like he couldn't care less which direction the witness's response to this particular question went. He looked at Nanda. 'Where is this headed, Mr Nanda?'

'Your Honour, to put my learned friends in the defence team at ease, I am not establishing any pattern here by using statistics. I'm merely trying to understand if there has been a similar case in the past and what were the readings by Dr Joshi as an expert witness.'

'Overruled. I'll allow it. You may sit down, Ms Pahwa.'

'Dr Joshi,' Nanda resumed, 'have you ever come across a murder weapon that has simply one set of clear fingerprints, and nothing else?'

'Lots of times.'

'Really?'

'You see, most times the perpetrator – if they have a little time on their hands after the crime – attempt to wipe off their prints from the weapon. Sometimes they are successful, but most times they are not. In this case, what I gathered from the police was that the defendant did not have time since members of the public were quick to arrive at the scene—'

'Objection, Your Honour,' Sonia stood up again. 'The witness should stick to their area of expertise and not draw conclusions based on hearsay. Your Honour, the defence requests the court to strike that comment.'

'Sustained. Please strike off the last part of the witness's response. Dr Joshi, I request you to please keep your answers brief and to the point.'

'My apologies, Your Honour.'

'Dr Joshi, while you pointed out that most criminals attempt to wipe off their fingerprints after the event, certainly there could be some residual fingerprints on the knife from before the event?'

'There may or may not be.'

'Could you elaborate for us mortals, Dr Joshi?'

'It would be a lot easier for someone to clean the knife off any prints before the event. They would have all the time in the world and no pressure of being caught in the act.'

'So, let me rephrase it for my learned friends and the court: the accused Shilpa Singh carried a clean knife to the scene of crime, stabbed Mr Ashok Kumar—'

'Objection.'

'Overruled.'

'… Shilpa Singh carried a clean knife to the scene of crime, stabbed Mr Ashok Kumar, and before she could wipe off her prints she was caught by members of the public. Does my assessment sound correct to you?'

'That would be my summary too.'

Nanda dwelled on the topic for another twenty minutes. He asked similar questions from all possible angles to seal the deal. He was good. He wanted the court and His Honour to bear in mind that there just wasn't enough time for a third person at the scene to stab Ashok Kumar, to wipe off his prints – one needed time and presence of mind to ensure they wiped off all prints – and get away, leaving Shilpa Singh holding the knife like a saviour of a fellow citizen, as she wanted the world to believe. No one in the vicinity had seen anyone running away. Nanda desperately tried to prove that Shilpa Singh hadn't – like she said – pulled the knife out of Ashok Kumar but rather put it there in the first place, and then she had concocted a story when she had been caught red-handed. The State witness, Dr Joshi, had been primed for this. His carefully measured responses underlined every word Nanda spoke.

'No more questions for the witness.' Nanda finally sat down.

Judge Durve, in his typical manner, glanced at his watch. 'I can imagine that the defence has a lot of questions for Dr Joshi, but the court will take a short break. See you after lunch, at 2 p.m.'

2

'DR JOSHI,' SONIA STOOD up. They had agreed in advance that Sonia would take on the state expert. If she could break the case here, very good, and if not, Vansh would need to up the ante and their own expert would need to be called upon. It would be expensive, but that was hardly a concern; however, that could cause delays. 'Your record is impeccable, so looking for any inconsistencies in your outstanding resume would be futile.'

'Thank you.' Dr Joshi blushed.

'I wish someone said that about my credentials too.' She smiled, but continued without breaking stride, 'But moving on Dr Joshi, before we discuss the murder weapon,' Sonia glanced at the knife that had been brought into the court again after the recess, 'did it ever occur to you that the murderer might not have taken as long as you think to wipe off the fingerprints after the murder and before he got away from the scene?'

'I'm not sure I follow you, miss.'

'Dr Joshi, what if the murderer had cleaned the knife before the act, and worn gloves during the stabbing – in that case the person didn't need any time to wipe off the prints, am I correct?'

'That is a possibility, but the police found no gloves at the scene of crime.' Akash had mentioned the gloves, but only Vansh had known about Pentium's discovery. He hadn't revealed it to Sonia or Shilpa. That Akash was carrying on an investigation on the side wasn't something he could reveal without disclosing that he was also working alongside him on the trial.

'There could be a million reasons for that – maybe the perpetrator walked away with the gloves, maybe the police didn't look hard enough—'

'Objection,' Diya called out. 'My learned friend should tackle the case rather than finding faults with the police investigation.'

'Sustained. I agree. Ms Pahwa, please continue.'

'Dr Joshi, all I am saying is that it isn't beyond the realm of possibility for someone to be wearing gloves, stab Mr Ashok Kumar, and get away without leaving any prints on the murder weapon, am I correct?'

'It is possible, however—'

'It is certainly possible. Moving on, Dr Joshi.' Sonia didn't let Joshi introduce another *but*. 'The fingerprints on the knife … you said in your testimony for the State that you found the defendant's prints on the knife, correct?'

'Yes.'

'Right or left hand or both?'

'The right hand.'

'Hmm …' Sonia paused. 'Your Honour, I'd like the witness, Dr Joshi, to demonstrate how the defendant had gripped the knife.'

'Objection, Your Honour,' Nanda cried. 'How is the witness supposed to know that?'

It was an objection made for the sake of it, and Nanda knew that too. One could easily tell how a particular object had been held by examining the fingerprints.

'Overruled.'

'But Your Honour—'

'Considered and dismissed, Mr Nanda,' Judge Durve said

it a bit louder this time. Then turned to Dr Joshi, 'The witness may respond to the defence's question.'

'Your Honour, we need a dummy knife for the purpose, which we have arranged for. If the court permits, we would like to use it for a demonstration right away in order to save time. The defence isn't planning to establish the weapon per se in this demonstration, but we'd very much like to understand how the fingerprints of the defendant were recovered on the weapon.'

'Does the State have any objection?' Judge Durve asked.

'It is all a waste of time, Your Honour.'

'Noted, but that's not an objection. Anything besides that?'

'None, Your Honour.'

'In that case you may proceed, Ms Pahwa.'

'Thank you, Your Honour.' Sonia walked to the defence table where Vansh handed her the knife they had brought in – similar in length and breadth to the actual murder weapon, but entirely made of wood. She took it to Dr Joshi on the stand. 'Dr Joshi, based on the recovery of fingerprints on the knife's handle, how would you say the knife was held by Judge Shilpa Singh?'

Vansh turned and looked at Nanda's table, and it was quite apparent that the prosecution had known this and discussed this among them, but it couldn't be refuted.

The dummy knife was quite a good replica. The wooden blade had a sharp edge and a blunt edge just like it's real counterpart. The measurements were exact too. Dr Joshi took the knife from Sonia and looked at it by rotating it in his hands. Sonia let the expert play with the toy for a while before she repeated her question: 'Dr Joshi, the fingerprints on the murder weapon must tell you how the defendant had held the knife, correct?'

'Of course.'

'If you may please tell the court: how was it that Judge Shilpa Singh held the knife?'

Dr Joshi turned the knife in his hands several times yet again. 'This way.' He raised the dummy knife in his right hand for everyone in the court to see. The way he held the knife revealed that the sharp end of the knife was upwards and the blunt end downwards.

Sonia walked up to Dr Joshi, took the knife out of his hand and held it exactly like he had held it seconds before.

'Like this?' she asked again to reconfirm.

'Yes, miss.'

'Isn't that contrary to the trajectory of the murder wound, Dr Joshi? The knife that pierced the victim's body had the sharp edge at the bottom, and the blunt end on top.' Sonia had been amazing so far. 'If Judge Shilpa Singh held the knife with the sharp end facing upwards, it corresponds with her version of the truth that she held the knife when she pulled it out of the victim's body and not put it there, doesn't it?' Sonia held the knife in her hand, enacting a pull-out motion.

'Yes, but—'

'There's hardly a but here, Dr Joshi. We've already established that there wasn't enough time for someone to wipe off their prints from the knife, so there is little possibility for Judge Shilpa Singh to wipe off her prints one way, and then put them back again. Only this time the other way around. So how was it even possible for Judge Shilpa Singh to murder Mr Ashok Kumar?'

'I couldn't tell you that,' Dr Joshi was finally beginning to concede.

'Isn't it possible, Dr Joshi, that Judge Shilpa Singh has been telling the truth all along. That she arrived at the crime scene seconds or minutes after the real perpetrator had left and she actually – like a good and upright citizen of this country – bent down to pull out the knife from the victim's body?'

'Objection, Your Honour. How is the fingerprinting expert supposed to hypothesize what exactly happened at the crime scene?'

'And Judge Shilpa Singh's prints on the knife handle emphasize the fact that she had pulled the knife out of the body and not put it there,' Sonia continued since His Honour hadn't stopped her. 'She was seen bent at the side of the victim's head – as the police confirmed, which supports her claim that she pulled out the knife with the sharp edge upwards because it had been put in sharp edge downwards by whoever stabbed Ashok Kumar from the front – exactly in the reverse trajectory if someone was positioned on the side, where she was. Am I correct?' Sonia held the knife with the sharp edge downwards and stabbed the air in front to demonstrate.

Leave the presiding judge with the most damning thought. Deliver it powerfully so the image was etched indelibly. 'All I'm asking you is that she couldn't have stabbed the victim holding the knife with, sharp edge facing the sky since the wound pathology is exactly the opposite, isn't it?'

'Objection, Your Honour,' Ravi Nanda almost screamed.

'Overruled. You may answer that one, Dr Joshi.'

'You may be right,' Joshi muttered with reluctance.

'*Maybe? Really?* Please highlight what could be the other possibility then, Dr Joshi?'

Joshi looked at the prosecution table, but there was little that the three lawyers could offer.

'What do you mean?' Joshi sounded confused.

'You just said I *may be* right, which also means I may be wrong. If I'm wrong, then there must be some explanation as to why – is that not correct?'

'I wouldn't know,' he said.

'Maybe' was enough to raise a reasonable doubt. Sometimes one should know when to stop. 'I don't have any further questions for this witness,' Sonia said, looked at the prosecution team, and returned to the defence table. She had single-handedly destroyed the State's case. She had been better than good.

'You may step down, Dr Joshi. I think we have some time left. Who is your next witness, Mr Nanda?'

'The prosecution rests, Your Honour. I think we have provided enough evidence for the court to rule—'

'Mr Nanda, the prosecution may have rested, but the defence still has to bring in their witnesses, so please save your closing speech for later.'

'My sincere apologies, Your Honour.'

'Mr Diwan, who is your first witness?'

'Mr Kailash Prasad Yadav.'

'Hmm ...' Judge Durve deliberated. 'See you all in the courtroom at 9 a.m. tomorrow then.'

'All rise...'

3

ALTHOUGH SONIA HAD DONE a fantastic job of destroying the only credible evidence that the prosecution had, it still didn't mean that Durve wouldn't consider all the other evidence and testimonies. Proving Kailash Prasad Yadav had a motive to derail the case against him by framing Judge Shilpa Singh would go a long way in getting a 'not guilty' verdict.

'Do we need to call our expert witness to the stand after this?' Akash asked when Vansh briefed him later.

'I doubt it. It would simply be a repetitive exercise, I think. Totally unnecessary, I'd say. Our expert will not be able to add to what the State's expert has already accepted, and it's far better coming from the prosecution's expert, don't you think?'

'Thank you, Vansh.'

'Thank you for what?'

'For being such a good friend and a fantastic advocate.'

'Save your gratitude for Sonia; she's the real gem.'

4

TO SAY SHRI KAILASH Prasad Yadav, MLA, wasn't happy would be the understatement of the decade. He was outright livid. Try as much as he could, he couldn't understand why he had been called to the courtroom for a case that had nothing to do with him. He had been called as a witness in the previous case, which he was defending, and that was acceptable, but this … why?

'Why now?' he barked at his cronies like they were responsible.

'Because the court has issued an order for you to attend the trial as a witness, bhai.'

Kailash Prasad picked up an ashtray kept on the table beside him and flung it hard at the wall. 'And you are saying this fucking advocate has the balls to take me on in the courtroom? I'll fucking peel his eyes out ... *chutiya-nandan, sala.*'

'Bhai,' one of the cronies started reverentially, 'please be careful, bhai – Vansh Diwan is protected by Akash Hingorani, who is a dangerous guy to take on.'

'I don't give a flying fucking fuck – those bastard sons of bitches.'

TWENTY

1

THE CAMERA FLASHES BURNED as expected. Akash Hingorani was back in the courtroom. Not as an advocate, nor as a witness either. He had come as a spectator of the biggest drama in his own life – now that his part as a witness in the trial was over, he was free to attend the trial proceedings. Feelings for Judge Shilpa Singh, which had been abeyant for a while, had started smouldering after Chavi Nair had ignited them. She had accompanied him to the courtroom. Let the world make any conclusion, she didn't care; he didn't care. The two of them sat right behind Shilpa who was flanked by Vansh Diwan and Sonia Pahwa at the defence table. Shilpa was dressed in a steel-grey silk saree with paisley patterns. She looked as gorgeous as ever. She hadn't lost her demeanour with all that was happening around her. Tough girl. Akash was never attracted to weak women – he loved authoritative women who could stand up to powerful men like him. Chavi was right. He was still in love with Shilpa, that much was true. Maybe, after all this was over, he could convince her that they were meant to be together. Lost in his thoughts, he missed the part when Judge Durve walked in and took his seat.

'State your name for the record.' They had decided it was best to let Vansh handle Kailash Prasad since the misogynist politician might find it even harder to respond to Sonia. Big man, extra-fragile ego. In any event, Sonia had done her part astoundingly well.

'I am Kailash Prasad Yadav, MLA …'

'Is MLA part of your name, Mr Yadav?'

There was a faint murmur in the courtroom. A wave of suppressed laughter. Akash and Vansh had worked on the strategy until midnight and arrived at the conclusion that Vansh would poke this witness at every given opportunity, instigating him to explode. Once KP lost his temper, the rest would be easy.

'What do you mean?' KP asked.

'Never mind. For the record, state your profession, Mr Kailash Prasad Yadav, MLA—'

'Objection, Your Honour,' Nanda cried foul. 'The defence is ridiculing the witness.'

Tumhara naam kya hai, Basanti? What did Vansh expect, asking the witness's profession by referring to him as an MLA?

'Mr Diwan,' Judge Durve called Vansh out as a warning. 'Don't push it.'

'My sincere apologies, Your Honour.'

'Mr Yadav, you were recently elected as an MLA from East Delhi, is that correct?'

'Yes, four times in a row.'

'So, you must be reasonably proficient in manipulating the electorate by now—'

'Objection, Your Honour.'

'Sustained.'

'Mr Yadav, is it true that your opponent in the previous elections, Mr Deshmukh Das, filed a petition accusing you of charges of election malpractice, booth capturing and bribing and scaring the voters?'

'To be honest, Deshmukh Das is a nutcase—'

'Focus on the question here, Mr Yadav. We aren't gathered here to assess the mental faculties of Mr Das. Did Mr Das or did he not bring charges against you in the recently concluded elections?'

'Yes he did, but—'

'Mr Yadav, I humbly request you to keep your answer short and precise, and please do not attempt to embellish every response with an explanation. If the answer is a straight yes or no, please do not add your commentary, is that understood?'

Kailash Prasad's face had turned beetroot-red. His fragile ego had been crushed by a man half his size. Considering he was the size of a grizzly, he could have crushed Vansh with a simple bear hug, but he was bound by circumstances. He just nodded.

'Thank you,' Vansh said, 'so let me repeat the question. Did Mr Das raise a case of malpractice against you in the recently concluded assembly elections?'

'False case, totally fabricated.'

'Your Honour ...' Vansh pleaded.

'Mr Yadav, could you respond to the defence advocate's questions without any additional qualifiers, please?'

'But, Your Honour—'

'And please do not even attempt to argue with me.' Judge Durve was already enraged. If it hadn't been enough for the prosecution to have called in a hostile witness, the defence had gone ahead and repeated it, maybe upped the ante by calling upon a crooked politician to take the witness stand. The pissing contest was about to get a lot messier with Durve having to mediate in every damn question like a school teacher.

'But Judge Sahib—' Kailash Prasad wasn't accustomed to being interrupted.

'Another word and I'll hold you in contempt of court, Mr Kailash Prasad, so I warn you to be very careful here. I'm the judge here and my word is the law.' It seemed Judge Durve was losing it faster than Kailash Prasad.

'Mr Kailash Prasad, were you or were you not accused of malpractice in the recent elections?' Vansh lost no time in shooting his question yet again.

Kailash Prasad nodded.

'Mr Yadav, I need a verbal response for the record, please.'

'Yes, and I say it under protest.'

'What protest?' What Vansh indeed wanted to say was *what fucking protest*, but he refrained from doing so.

'It was that bloody Deshmukh Das's story.'

'Mr Kailash Prasad, is that a yes or a no?' Judge Durve intervened.

'Yes.'

'See, it wasn't that hard after all, was it?' Vansh called out.

'Mr Diwan, I suggest you proceed with the questioning,' Judge Durve slapped Vansh's wrist for his little wisecrack.

'Yes, Your Honour.' Vansh realized Judge Durve's words were indicative of his foul mood and that he wouldn't tolerate any deviation from the straight and narrow questions. No latitude for frivolities now. He turned to the witness. 'And the case was tried in the court of the defendant …' Vansh pointed towards the defence table where Shilpa sat alongside Sonia, 'Judge Shilpa Singh?'

'Yes.'

'And do you remember that you were asked to be a witness?'

'Yes,' Kailash Prasad barked. If Vansh were any closer, KP would have bitten too. Maybe Vansh's hand, maybe his head.

'Why do you think you were called by the prosecuting advocate into the witness box?'

'Objection, Your Honour. Speculative. How is the witness supposed to know why the prosecution invited Mr Yadav as a witness?'

'Sustained.'

'Let me refresh your memory, Mr Yadav. Isn't it because the prosecuting advocate told you that your absence would mean that you consider yourself above the law?'

'Objection, Your Honour. In the absence of any material evidence, my learned opponent is propagating wild theories. It doesn't matter if the prosecuting advocate called Mr Yadav as a witness in another case. How does it have any bearing on the material evidence for this trial? It seems the defence is trying to subdue a gentleman MLA for some vicarious pleasure.'

Kailash Prasad Yadav appreciated being called a gentleman. The State seemed to have scored a point with the witness, if not with the judge.

'Sustained. I am leaning towards the State's reading, Mr Diwan. Is this just a fishing expedition or do you have something tangible here?'

'Just indulge me for a few minutes, Your Honour.'

'Your Honour, the defence is merely wasting the court's time.'

'Do you need to be anywhere else, Mr Nanda?'

'No, Your Honour.'

'Then your time cannot be more important than mine, so please remain seated. Let's see if the defence can satisfy our curiosities. You may continue, Mr Diwan, but be aware that my patience is running thin. Is that understood?'

'Yes, Your Honour.'

'Mr Yadav, did you in any way threaten Judge Shilpa Singh to issue a favourable verdict in the case of "State of Delhi vs Kailash Prasad?"'

A loud babble erupted in the courtroom. Eyes raced from the witness box to the defence table where Shilpa Singh sat. Journalists scribbled furiously. Allegations which were doing the rounds in whispers and closed rooms, were being openly discussed in an open courtroom. This was real masala. *Garam masala!*

'Objection.' Nanda stood up. 'This is all irrelevant to the trial in progress.'

'They're linked, Your Honour. Like I just requested, humour me for a few more minutes, please,' Vansh pleaded.

'Overruled. Please answer the defence advocate's question, Mr Yadav.'

'What was the question?'

'Did you or did you not send threats to Judge Shilpa Singh to give you a favourable verdict in the case of "State of Delhi vs Kailash Prasad?"'

'No.'

'No?'

'I had sent a request that she be objective about the whole thing.'

'Oh I see,' Vansh articulated sarcastically. 'Wasn't your request phrased something along the lines of … "If you go against me, you will regret it" or "I know which school your son is studying in"?'

'She's a lying fucking bitch—'

'Order, order,' yelled Judge Durve. 'Mr Yadav, mind your words or I'll have you arrested for being in contempt of the court. Take this as my first and final warning. That kind of language is not acceptable in my courtroom.'

Vansh knew he had succeeded. He and Akash had wanted to establish that KP had a motive to remove Shilpa from the scene, and while a circular argument like that might not prove his direct involvement in the homicide, it surely cast a doubt in Judge Durve's mind about Shilpa's guilt: *Kailash Prasad may have had a motive*. Finally there was someone who had a clear motive, which until now had been totally absent from the trial. No one up until now appeared to have a clear motive for eliminating Ashok Kumar.

'You threatened Judge Shilpa Singh and when she – as an honest guardian of the law – refused to give in to your threats, you concocted a story, called her under the pretext of providing evidence and framed her for homicide—'

'Objection, Your Honour. This is preposterous. This sounds like an elaborate conspiracy theory – or fantasy rather – in the absence of any alternative that the defence can provide.'

'Is it?' Vansh soldiered on since Judge Durve hadn't intervened yet. 'Why would an upright member of the law community go to pick up evidence in a park and then murder the witness? She knew the law; she knew she'd look guilty.'

'Is my learned friend here trying to tell the court that she's not guilty merely because she looks guilty?' Nanda stood up again.

Judge Durve might have expected the arguments to die, but they didn't. 'Enough gentlemen, I've had enough. Mr Diwan, do you have any more questions for this witness?'

'No, Your Honour, the defence is done with this witness. We can only apologize for his misconduct—'

'Apology accepted,' Judge Durve interrupted satirically. He could appreciate that Vansh was attempting to malign Kailash Prasad further by apologizing on his behalf. 'Mr Nanda, do you have questions for this witness?'

'Yes, Your Honour.'

'You may proceed then.'

2

NANDA KNEW HE HAD to walk on eggshells. KP was already fuming. Nanda asked about his candidature, the good work he had done in his constituency, the reason his electorate loved him so much that they had voted him the fourth time around. In an hour of questioning – with no objections from the defence table – Nanda asked and established Kailash Prasad's whereabouts on the day and time of the murder in January. Pointless really – no one had even imagined, much less accused Kailash Prasad Yadav of having murdered Ashok Kumar first-hand. Anyone who had seen this King Kong once wouldn't have forgotten the sheer size of Kailash Prasad – someone would have seen him in Lodhi Gardens and remembered.

Moreover, for someone as bulky as him, it would have been impossible to get away in the short time the murderer had to escape before Shilpa had arrived at the scene.

Akash sat there wondering what the crux of the questioning by Nanda was, as it amounted to nothing. It was meant to whitewash KP's obnoxious behaviour in court. Maybe he wanted to show that KP wasn't a completely loathsome figure – that he was a normal, gentle individual who had, in a heated moment, lashed out at Shilpa for being drawn into a trial that had nothing to do with him. Did Nanda succeed in convincing Judge Durve? Akash had his doubts. Years of experience in the courtroom taught you to read the judge's mien and mind. And Akash could recognize that Judge Durve didn't see KP in the best light here. But who knew?

After an hour Nanda came to a halt, thanked Kailash Prasad Yadav for his testimony and sat down.

'Is that all?' asked Judge Durve. 'No more witnesses?'

'None for the defence, Your Honour. The defence rests.'

'This case might go down in history as a homicide trial with the least number of witnesses,' Judge Durve remarked to let some cheerfulness return to the courtroom, which had been tense since morning. 'Let's break for lunch. Since it's already late, the advocates can present their closing statements tomorrow at 3 p.m.'

'All rise …'

3

THE TRIAL WAS OVER, and the advocates had done as much as they could with their arguments. Closing arguments were more of a monologue, like the opening statements, by the advocates on both sides to merely summarize the case, their perspectives, and their opinions to – for the lack of a better word – *refresh* the presiding judge's memory of all that had been presented at a trial. No new evidence was presented at this stage. The judge – Durve in this case – was supposed to take into consideration all the facts and evidence and testimonies, decide and communicate his judgement. There was no more room for debate.

Sonia, Priti, Vansh, Shilpa and Akash gathered at the Diwan residence the evening before the verdict. It no longer mattered if those not directly related to the case were present now. The mood was tense since Judge Durve had been extremely cautious about betraying his thoughts. They discussed everything except the elephant in the room. It was at dinner that Vansh broached the subject.

'I think Sonia should deliver the closing argument.'

'Great idea,' Akash promptly replied. He was quite confident Sonia could deliver with élan. Shilpa, too, having seen Sonia's performance throughout the trial, was equally convinced it was a splendid idea.

'Go girl power,' Priti, who had been the only one present with little or no privy to the case, chimed in.

PART 3

THE VERDICT

'You aren't sure if you're making the right decision – about anything, ever.'

– JOAN DIDION,
journalist, novelist and screenwriter

TWENTY-ONE

1

THE TWO ADVOCATES HAD presented their closing arguments without fanfare or theatrics. Fact-based, brief and to the point, referencing the evidence or some witness's testimony as and when required. It was a gracious move. Some advocates claimed the closing arguments as their birthright to deliver hours of monologue that sent everyone in the courtroom to sleep.

Judge Anshuman Durve had patiently sat still, not letting his countenance give anything away. At the end of the two hours, when all had been said and done and the two opposing advocates were seated, he thanked everyone for their hard work and announced that he'd be ready to announce the court's decision after the weekend.

'Let's reconvene on Monday at 11 a.m. I expect the defence and prosecuting teams to be present, unless you have a more important reason to be elsewhere.'

'All rise – Judge Durve is leaving the courtroom.'

2

JUST LIKE THAT, MONDAY arrived.

Knots of people milled outside the courtroom since all the seats inside had been claimed and more people weren't being let in. Clutches of media personnel with cameras and microphones, each bigger and better than the last one, were in attendance. This was like the final over of a T-20 finale.

Ravi Nanda and Diya Albuquerque were the first to arrive along with Harsh Mehta. The sound of cameras clicking was overwhelming, the flashes blinding. Everyone was eager to take a picture before the advocates got into the courtroom and donned their robes. Cameras were still not permitted inside the courtroom as per Judge Durve's diktat. A high-profile trial like this would otherwise mean a short directorial venture for some news channels.

At precisely one minute past eleven, Amitabh 'no second name' announced the arrival of Judge Durve and requested everyone to raise their bottoms from chairs or benches, as the case may be.

Akash and Chavi sat behind Shilpa, who looked as if she hadn't slept at all. Anyone awaiting a court verdict in a homicide trial could hardly be at peace. Sleep would have been an enigma to her at this time.

'I thank all of you for your time and patience and labour,' Judge Durve started after settling into his chair. 'As you can all appreciate, this case wasn't a regular trial. If I am being honest, I wouldn't want to be part of such a trial ever again. But who knows? It's been tremendously nerve-racking for me this entire time. I wanted to be as impartial as possible, and hence I permitted a lot of requests from the State that I wouldn't have otherwise approved in my courtroom. In the bargain, I might have hurt some people who didn't deserve to be treated the way I had to treat them, chiefly Mr Akash Hingorani, who was the original choice of the defendant as her defence advocate on record. I had to respect and regard Mr Nanda's plea of striking him off from representing the defendant for reasons, which are all now well-known to all of you, and the rest of the world if they've been catching up on the news.

'To cut a long story short, I've spent the entire weekend deliberating the case, reading through all the evidence recorded and the testimonies provided, and the court has now come to its conclusion.'

'May the defendant rise for the verdict, please?' announced the court clerk.

Shilpa stood up, with both her advocates; the prosecution advocates stood up too.

'Based on all the evidence provided and considering the police investigation and witness testimonies, in the case of "State of Delhi vs Shilpa Singh", this court finds Judge Shilpa Singh "not guilty" on the charge of murder or manslaughter. This case is now over. Furthermore, I hereby order an inquiry into the conduct of Mr Kailash Prasad, MLA from East Delhi constituency. He needs to be investigated thoroughly by the police on two counts: one – for the threats he blatantly issued to Judge Shilpa Singh, a member of the law community, when she was presiding on the case of "State of Delhi vs Kailash Prasad". I have already urged the docket to be moved to my court for the hearing. Secondly, the court order needs to be collected by the relevant police officers to open the inquiry into the murder of Ashok Kumar. If Mr Kailash Prasad – absent from the court today – tries anything to interfere with or block the criminal investigation, I promise he will be punished to the full extent of the law.'

'I'm sorry, Judge Shilpa Singh,' he continued, 'that you had to go through this unceremonious trial, which now, after presiding over this hearing, I think wasn't necessary, but you of all people should know and respect the law as much as I do.' Durve's tone was very respectful now – like a king should treat a king.

Judge to judge.

'I thank Mr Ravi Nanda and Ms Diya Albuquerque for their selfless service to the State of Delhi by forsaking their caseload in Mumbai and helping us out during our time of need. Your sacrifice and work will not go unnoticed, and we will endeavour to help you in whatever way we can if ever you call upon us for help.

'This case is now closed. If the State wishes to appeal, they can do as per the normal procedure. Thank you all and Jai Hind.'

For a full minute after he stopped talking, as the courtroom went pin-drop silent, he made some notations on some papers in front of him, signed some documents, and then he stopped, abruptly got up, slid out from behind his desk and walked out without another word.

Sonia was the first to hug Shilpa, then Vansh. Akash resisted the temptation to jump over the short wooden barrier and pull her into an embrace. Not that anyone would have stopped him, but he knew the media eyes were glued on her. At him. It was a big victory and he didn't want to rain on her parade by giving the media some frivolous material to write up about their affair; he wanted them to focus on her, not him, not *them*. It was best to walk around the barrier along with Chavi and congratulate her. He did so. She had won the trial, but she was in tears.

Ravi Nanda, Diya Albuquerque and Harsh Mehta walked up to the defence table as professional courtesy and congratulated Judge Shilpa Singh.

'We can only apologize for anything untoward said or argued, but as you know we had to fight our corner, ma'am,' Diya spoke for all three of them.

'You had a job to do, and I must say you did it rather well,' Shilpa said, keeping her demeanour as regal and calm as she could. 'No hard feelings.'

'Thank you. And Mr Hingorani,' Ravi Nanda said, 'our honest apologies to you too.'

'No worries at all. When are you guys flying back to Mumbai?'

'We leave tomorrow morning.'

'Have a safe trip.'

3

AKASH WOKE UP WITH a massive hangover. The events of the previous night ran through his mind like a film missing shots. A night of unrestricted revelry can do that to you, especially if you've never been a big drinker. And as we know, Akash loved drinking but only cognac and champagne in small quantities. But the night before, he had treated himself to a mix of the two.

He had been elated after Shilpa was acquitted. He had never doubted for a moment that she was innocent and that she'd win but still, being a lawyer for two decades had taught him that anything could happen. Decisions could be swayed by the most insignificant developments if it caught the presiding judge's imagination. Despite being removed from the case for objectionable reasons – he had to give it to Ravi Nanda for so craftily shafting him without breaking any rules – he had forever stayed on top of the game with the help of his friend Vansh.

Last night's party had been hosted by none other than his best friends Priti and Vansh Diwan, in honour of Shilpa's victory against one of the worst smear campaigns against a sitting judge in recent history. Shilpa had left early, citing fatigue, and no one had raised an eyebrow. People could only imagine what she had just been through.

In the few solitary moments he had caught with her, she had told him that she had already heard from the panel of judges of the Saket district court, who had reinstated her back as a judge. It was all good, nothing was lost. She would be back in the courtroom and life would return to normal soon. As hard as he tried to, Akash couldn't bring himself to talk about their future together. The subject hadn't come up and it felt awkward to be confessing that he still had feelings for her.

After a while, he put a hat on his quixotic fantasy and told his brain to stop stressing about it and let time resolve the situation. If it were to happen, it would. Besides that, memories of his unashamed flirting with Chavi, after Shilpa had left the party, were rushing back to him with a fresh wave of embarrassment. Even with gaps in his memories, he could safely assume that he had made a fool of himself. He remembered that at one point, Vansh had come and put an arm around him and taken him away. God, what an ass he had made of himself. He could only wish Chavi hadn't taken offence and hoped she'd remain his friend.

Now, after gulping down a couple of analgesics and antacids with a bottle of water, he began looking for his mobile. He couldn't recollect where he had put it after his driver had brought him home. It took him twenty minutes to remember that – talk about slowing down one of the fastest brains in the country – his mobile was in the pocket of the trousers he had discarded somewhere in his legal studio yesterday, before walking naked into his bedroom. What an idiot!

The iPhone was dead when he extracted it from the pocket of his trousers. He connected it to a charger to bring it back to life. It was time for a hot cup of coffee. But he needed to put on his pyjamas first. The household help might have come in by now and would be shocked out of her wits if he just strolled into the kitchen without a cover.

4

I WILL BE OUT for a few days. I'm going to Mussoorie for a few days to see Raghuveer. Will be unreachable. Back soon. Love.

The latest message in his inbox was from Shilpa. And although it was understandable why she'd rushed to see her son, he was nevertheless disappointed. Why hadn't she asked him to join her this time around? Maybe she wanted to be alone with her son, which was reasonable, but still. They had driven up there before the trial, and she had introduced him to Raghuveer, who had seemed mature enough to appreciate that his mother was once in a relationship with Akash. But it was what it was.

He thought about keying a response but didn't. What would be the point? What would he say? It was her decision and she had not made him a party to the same. In fact, she hadn't even mentioned her travel the previous night at her victory party. Maybe it was an impromptu decision. Or maybe she had mentioned it, and he had been too drunk to pay attention.

How does the morning feel? read the second SMS. This was from Chavi Nair.

He felt stupid. He must have made a real ass of himself at the party for Chavi to be asking him about his morning. Oh God!

But it was a once-in-a-very-rare-while kind of thing and everyone was permitted to be the jester at a party sometimes, weren't they? He thought that his summary of his own behaviour would make him feel better, but it didn't.

He called Vansh.

'Good morning,' Vansh sounded hoarse and equally hungover. 'Woke up early or couldn't sleep?'

'Woke up early. How much of a fool did I make of myself last night?'

'What?'

'Pass the phone to Priti if she's around?' Akash knew that if one wanted the truth, Priti was the best person to speak to.

'Hi Akash, good morning.'

'Good morning, Priti, sorry if I woke you guys up …'

'Not at all, we were awake. How're you feeling now?'

The question of how he felt now affirmed his suspicion that he hadn't been too well the previous night. 'I'm good; sipping my second coffee. How did I embarrass myself last night? Did I end up making everyone uncomfortable?'

'Not at all. You were glued to Shilpa for most of the evening, and then, when she left you anchored yourself next to Ms Nair. You introduced her to me as the best thing on two long legs that happened to you – are you guys dating?'

'No … no … no! She's just a friend.'

'You sure?'

'Yes. Why do you ask, what did I say?'

'Well, you guys make a good pair, that's all. And by the way she does have very long legs,' Priti giggled.

'Hmm,' Akash was at a severe loss for words. 'I hope I didn't misbehave.'

'No.'

'Thank you, sweetie; please pass the phone back to Vansh.'

TWENTY-TWO

1

AKASH STAYED AWAY FROM work for a few days. He had nothing pressing to attend to at the office, and at any rate, he needed a short break. There was a lot going on in his mind, and in his life. And if he were to ever get back with Shilpa, he had made up his mind to wind up his practice as a defence advocate protecting the vile and the dirty and think of a new career. Maybe he'd join Diwan-e-Khaas and work alongside Vansh. He could specialize in cases other than criminal ones, which would take him away from things Shilpa considered dark. Maybe he could convince Vansh and take over the financial wing of his existing practice. He wouldn't be in it for the money – he had enough – but merely to find a place to work and manage and look forward to a life with the judge. Who knew how life would pan out once he decided to be someone else?

Chavi called and congratulated him once again although he didn't know for what. Did she know he had been one of the brains behind the entire trial? The non-playing captain as Vansh had put it? She wanted to go out for dinner with him again and after saying no a couple of times, he relented. What was the harm?

2

THE MUGHLAI FOOD AT Pindi on Pandara Road was awesome as always. The kebab platter, the rumali roti … they had a way with food. And Chavi looked gorgeous in a black dress with a deep neckline. Akash couldn't fathom how two such starkly different women could be so attractive to him. Shilpa Singh was as different from Chavi Nair as the night was from the day, but they had certain similarities, too. Both were independent, powerful women. His mind, despite appreciating Chavi as a friend, circled back to Shilpa, the love of his life. Where was she? Maybe she had, by now, updated Raghuveer, and was on her way back? Perhaps she was bringing Raghuveer to Delhi for a few days after the long battle she had fought and won? Maybe another round of golf with Raghuveer?

'You there? Hello?' he heard Chavi call out. And she was correct. He had been an awful date – if this was a date – he was still thinking of his old love, making plans in his head and ignoring the lovely friend sitting opposite him, who was simply trying to help him overcome the vacuum in his life.

'I'm listening.'

'Liar.'

'Guilty as charged, and I'm sorry. It's just that I'm preoccupied.'

'With?'

'You know what it is about.'

'Akash, my assessment was correct; you are still very much in love with the judge. As a friend, the best advice I can give you is to make peace with her. That's the only way you will ever be happy. Once you're with her, even a dinner with a boring journalist friend like me will seem interesting.'

'I hear you. I know what you mean; it's just that I cannot come to terms with everything at this moment.'

'What's bothering you?'

'Her silence. She's been away three days now and I've had no calls or messages from her.'

'She's busy, you must understand. She has just fought a difficult battle, which could have ended her career and reputation and destroyed the life she had built for herself. It's only natural she wants to spend some quality time with her child and explain things to him as they stand. She and you were here, watching the proceedings as they progressed, and the entire chapter was nerve-racking. Imagine how it must have been for her teenage son who wasn't privy to the proceedings. He lived in a hostel miles away, disconnected but not unaware of that dark episode in his mother's life, which could impact his life forever, too. The poor boy must have picked up morsels of information from news clippings and social media of what his mother – his only parent – was facing. Give them time. Give her time, is all I can say.'

'I never knew someone as young as you could be so mature, Chavi. Thank you.'

3

PRITI AND VANSH HAD similar advice for Akash. Give Shilpa a little time to get over all that had happened to her. Priti was more sensible than her husband though, 'But be aware that things might not return to the normal that you are used to, despite the favourable outcome at the trial. She may see you as a loyal friend, or maybe something more than that. But it depends on how she wants to move on from this terrible chapter of her life ...'

'What do you mean?' Vansh asked before Akash could.

'Well, she might look upon both of you as saviours who fought for her, but that does not mean she's bound to fall in love with Akash again. What I'm saying is that you should take it slowly. Akash, you need to let her know what you are willing to do to make your relationship work when the time is right. That you are willing to give up your practice as a defence advocate – the main bone of contention between the two of you – and then she might want to take a fresh look at the future.'

'Are you?' Vansh asked Akash.

'Am I what?'

'Are you willing to give up your practice for her?'

'Everything's fair in love—'

'It was a serious question, Guru Akash.'

'I am willing to give up anything for her, yes.'

'Lovelorn kitten, do you think Sonia Pahwa will come and work for me?'

'I can recommend your firm to her.'

'Are you interested in Sonia now?' Priti teased her husband.

'As an advocate—'

'And as a woman?'

'She's gorgeous, but nowhere close to you,' said Vansh, taking a sip of his drink.

'You're such a bad liar.'

'But he's telling the truth this time,' Akash added. 'However, Sonia may be a close second.'

'You guys are incorrigible.'

4

WHEN HE WOKE UP that morning, seven days after Shilpa was acquitted and six days after she had left for Mussoorie to meet Raghuveer, Akash Hingorani could not shake off the feeling that something was wrong. It wasn't due to his lack of sleep the previous night; in fact, the temporary insomnia was a consequence of the mental unease he was suffering from.

He had tried calling Shilpa after he didn't hear from her for two days after she had left the city. Each time it went directly to her voicemail. He left messages the first few times, but never received a call back, which was quite unlike her. Why had she switched off her phone, and why wasn't she calling him back? Or, at the very least, updating him via text about her plans? Why would she suddenly go incommunicado?

Something was amiss. But what?

He brewed himself some strong coffee and went into his legal studio to go through the files that had been sent across from his office. He hadn't yet been back to the office yet. There wasn't anything pressing, so there seemed little point in dressing up to go to work today either.

Still in his boxers and a t-shirt, he pressed the start button on his MacBook. While it booted, he switched on the television in front of him and sipped his brew.

There were umpteen emails from work – some expenses to sign off, some vacation requests. All routine emails and nothing consequential enough for him to write back immediately.

The television playing in the background at a really low volume did not bring up any meaningful news either. His eyes jumped from his MacBook and the television to catch the rolling script at the bottom of the screen. A politician had been accused of being involved in yet another corruption scandal, some film star had broken up with another film star, a cricketer had retired, the share market had been stable – all humdrum.

But then something caught his attention. He grabbed the remote and turned the volume up, but he had already missed the small snippet. He changed channels to check if the news bulletin was running on some other channel. Nope. It wasn't anything major, it appeared.

Realizing he'd have to wait another hour to catch the next bulletin on the same channel, he muted the television, opened his browser and searched for the latest news. He hadn't caught the name or anything important but the gist and hence, he didn't even know what exactly he was looking for.

He opened a Google page and typed 'Terrorist goes missing in Delhi', then pressed the NEWS tab on the top.

And there it was.

What he had never wanted to come across seemed to have happened:

> Infamous and much-wanted terrorist Ismail Khan, a faction leader of Pakistani terrorist circles, was last spotted in New Delhi in January. He had travelled from Jammu for a surreptitious rendezvous with the notorious ISI. According to intelligence reports, they were planning an attack on Indian soil. But he went missing soon after his arrival in Delhi before R&AW officials could nab him.
>
> An anonymous source within the ranks of the organization admitted that security officials had tailed him all the way to Delhi, but Ismail Khan gave them the slip somehow. This matter was not disclosed to the public because it would have been embarrassing for the agency to accept a blunder of this magnitude, which could have terrible consequences.
>
> Ismail Khan is a Pakistani resident, wanted in India for several crimes, most notably for attacks on Indian army personnel in the Valley. He came under R&AW's radar after evidence of his involvement in the murder of Major Rajendra Singh and three members of his team surfaced soon after the fatal attack on their jeep …

Akash was anything but dumb. Nanda might have stumped him in a court case, but that, in no way, had diminished his mental capacity. He drank his coffee in one go and poured himself another cup. The wheels in his mind had begun to move.

Ismail Khan went missing in Delhi at approximately the same time when Ashok Kumar had been killed.

Ismail Khan was responsible for the death of Major Rajendra Singh, the late husband of Judge Shilpa Singh and Raghuveer's father.

A strange coincidence? But nothing in life was ever a coincidence, was it?

The State's autopsy report, sent to him surreptitiously by Vansh, came to his mind. He opened the desk and pulled out the papers, and there it was:

Other: circumcised. Circumcision is practised in Judaism, Christianity (Old Testament) and Islam so the subject could be of any of the faiths. Most likely not a Hindu since the practice is not prevalent in Hinduism.

He re-read it, and then read it all over again until each word was embedded in his brain.

What if no one came to claim Ashok Kumar's body because he had no family in India? What if there was no record of him because he did not want there to be any? Could it be that …? The ISI agents would not have come forward to claim him if he was truly Ismail Khan. They weren't morons after all. In any case, a dead terrorist was of little value to anyone.

What was the probability of Judge Shilpa Singh being present at Lodhi Gardens in the middle of the day to recover evidence pertaining to a random case, to chance upon a dying man with a knife in his chest? Zero! Furthermore, that the said corpse the police had been unable to identify turns out to be a Muslim? Zero again, and only because mathematically, the probability of any outcome was never expressed as a negative.

He had never believed in coincidences.

While none of the websites he visited had a photograph of Ismail Khan, the description had a stark similarity with the corpse found in Lodhi Gardens. Anyone with an IQ of room temperature in Fahrenheit could figure it out. However, now that the trial was over, there was a-less-than-zero chance of someone exhuming Ashok Kumar to verify the same.

Akash opened the bottom drawer of his desk again and pulled out an envelope. The envelope that contained the gloves that his trusted soldier DK Pentium had found at Lodhi Gardens and sent across to him. The ones he was supposed to have submitted to the police. One reason he had packed these into his drawer since he had thought the discovery of gloves would only muddy the waters unnecessarily – especially since Vansh and he had already worked out the winning strategy for the trial already – and hence, he didn't tell Vansh that he hadn't sent them to the police. The second reason he had kept the discovery to himself was because of one of the possibilities Pentium had alluded to, and Akash had also noticed that the gloves either belonged to a man with rather thin and small hands or they belonged to a woman.

Now, as he pulled the gloves out and put them on his desk, he once again acknowledged that they were small. He picked one up and sized it with his own hands. Petite. Certainly a woman's. He knew the size; he could sense that he had held the hands that fitted these gloves several times.

Now he knew.

He thought about calling Pentium to send him on another search but gave up the idea. He wouldn't be doing anyone any favours. He wrestled with the idea of talking to Vansh about it. Vansh had been the advocate on record for Shilpa. And although he was a close friend, what if he decided to turn the evidence in? As her lawyer, he was legally obliged to inform the court of this discovery. And if Vansh didn't take it to court, why make him complicit in what had been Akash's decision?

Calling Chavi with the news could mean disaster, who knew? She was an investigative journalist, for God's sake. She might love him in a way, but he wasn't sure if he could trust her, or anyone for that matter, with this find. What if her moral compass suddenly swung north, and she decided that revealing the truth was the duty of a journalist or some such tripe?

There were some truths one took to the grave with oneself. Some stories needn't ever be told until the end of time. Amen.

Akash felt tears brimming his eyes. He tried reaching Shilpa for the next hour with no result. There was no voicemail, no recorded message at the end of it all. The call just wouldn't connect. All he could hear was an automated voice telling him that the subscriber was not reachable. Akash couldn't wrap his head around what was happening. He called for Mandeep.

'Janaab.'

'Mandeep, please go to Judge Shilpa Singh's place in Saket – you know where it is, right?'

'Yes.'

'Go now, ring the bell, bang the doors until she opens and make her call me immediately.'

'You got it.'

Even as Mandeep rushed out and Akash heard the Jaguar start, he realized it was an exercise in futility. She wouldn't have told him she was travelling to Mussoorie and then locked the door and stayed home and watched films until he came looking.

They'd been throwing shit at the windmill – not just a fan – all along. Yes, Kailash Prasad Yadav might have been a sanctimonious son of a bitch, dirty as sin, and yes, he benefited from her downfall, but it wasn't his doing. He hadn't thought of implicating Shilpa until after the event. The event she had orchestrated herself. While the answer to the *why* wasn't difficult to comprehend, the *how* still bothered him.

His phone rang. He realized he had dozed off despite two industrial-strength coffees. Maybe it was fatigue, maybe it was shock.

'Janaab, Mandeep here.'

'Tell me.'

'Judge-sahiba packed up her house and left around a week ago.'

'Any idea where she went?'

'I've checked with all the neighbours. She did not leave a forwarding address with anyone. Moreover, I spoke to a few people around and the transport truck was totally unmarked; it carried no logos or branding so no one knows which transport company it was …'

'Hmm …'

'What are my orders?'

Akash knew he was chasing a ghost. One part of his brain told him that he could call Pentium and ask him to find the name of the transport company that moved house from a particular address in Saket, and they'd know where it was headed for.

Then again, what would be the point?

'Come home, Mandeep. Thanks.'

5

Akash called up Woodstock, Raghuveer's boarding school in Mussoorie. After introducing himself as the guardian of Raghuveer Singh, he asked to be connected to the principal on an urgent matter concerning his ward.

'Mr Hingorani, how may I be of any assistance to you?' asked the principal in a high-pitched but polite tone.

'Sir, as I have explained to the person I spoke to before you, I am the guardian of a student at your school, Raghuveer Singh. I'd like to speak to him to make plans to see him at the earliest—'

'Just a minute, Mr Hingorani,' the principal interrupted his request, 'Raghuveer's mother, Judge Shilpa Singh, was here a few days ago. I'm sorry, but she's taken Raghuveer with her.'

'Taken Raghuveer with her where?'

'I'm terribly sorry, I'm not at liberty to tell you that. But Raghuveer is no longer a student at our school.'

'What?'

'You heard me right, Mr Hingorani, and like I said, I'm really sorry I cannot help you with your request.'

'Did she ... I mean did they leave a forwarding address with you?'

'No. However, if you have a message, I might check if I am able to pass it on to them, but I cannot guarantee it.' The principal was being cagey. It was probable that he had the forwarding address but had been instructed not to share it with anyone.

'Yes, could you please let them know I called, and it would be nice if they got in touch with me, too?'

'I shall endeavour to pass on your message, Mr Hingorani.'

'Thank you.' Akash knew it was useless. He could find her if he really wanted to, but if she didn't want to be found, what was the point? This wasn't some contest he had to win.

TWENTY-THREE

1

THE LETTER CAME IN the post a week after his call to the principal at Woodstock. It was with all the other marketing mailers and bank statements that came by in abundance every day. More than half of it was junk and a hand-addressed letter could have well gone into the bin along with them. But Akash realized that it was too bulky – like four or five pages – to be just spam mail. He wasn't familiar with the handwriting. In today's world, most people communicated electronically – when did one get to see anything hand-written? He opened the envelope.

The stationery said it was from Shilpa Singh.

Dear Akash,

I received a message from the office of the principal at Woodstock that you had called looking for Raghuveer. I'm glad you called, believe me. It confirms my confidence in you all over again. But it's my humble request that you stop looking for us, please.

The first few sentences chilled him to the bone. He read on:

I tendered my resignation the day after I was reinstated as a judge at the district court. It wasn't a spur-of-the-moment, irrational decision; I had deliberated over it for quite some time, and in the end, I knew this was the right decision. I have lost the moral ground to be a judge.

Before picking up Raghuveer from his school, I made arrangements to move out of my Saket residence. I didn't want to be in Delhi anymore. I am in another city now where no one knows me. I do not want us to be found by anyone I know. I wish he could have spent more time with you, but it wasn't meant to be.

Life is a mystery, one that you cannot always solve or interpret, Akash. But, knowing you, I have no doubt that by now you will have worked out what exactly took place at Lodhi Gardens that late afternoon in January.

When we were dating, I had made a huge issue out of our professional incongruence. I thought I led a more principled life as compared to you. Ironic, isn't it? I had to call upon you to save me when I was pulled down in life. We are all victims of circumstance; sometimes we are up on the ladder, sometimes we slip and fall. But whenever we are up, we pretend to be more virtuous and ethically superior to the people around us, don't we?

The true identity of the man christened Ashok Kumar by the police was Ismail Khan.

Ismail Khan was the head of the ISI insurgent unit that masterminded the ambush that killed Major Rajendra

Singh in Jammu and made me a widow, and my Raghuveer an orphan.

I was in my office when one of Major Rajendra's course-mates from Jammu called to inform me about Ismail's whereabouts. He was going to meet up with terrorists of another faction in Lodhi Gardens the same evening. That was it. They didn't expect me to do anything, although they expressed discontent about the fact that they had very little time to come up with a plan to capture or eliminate him.

They must have figured out what had happened to Ismail Khan, but none of them came forward to turn in the wife of one of their majors – such is the bond between the armed forces family. They wouldn't turn anyone in for the death of a terrorist who had killed one of their own.

It was pure luck that the call that had come in from Jammu on my mobile couldn't be traced – most calls from non-family military stations cannot be traced for national security reasons.

So when *you* told me – on your return from London – that the media had concocted a story around this 'unidentified call' I had received on my mobile, I decided to turn the narrative on its head by claiming that the call was about a piece of evidence that will bring down Kailash Prasad.

It's true that Kailash Prasad is dirty, and he did send death threats to me and Raghuveer, but the death of Ismail Khan has nothing to do with him.

I'm surprised the police never found the gloves.

I hadn't anticipated people turning up so quickly at the scene, so I was forced to throw them away. And to look the part of the saviour, I pulled out the knife, taking care to leave my prints in the opposite direction.

I knew my only defence would be the fingerprints which would indicate that I was holding the knife upside down. I couldn't tell you that directly, but I trusted you to find a way to save me.

Akash stood up, walked to the door of his legal studio and shut the door. Tears just wouldn't stop falling down his face. He couldn't understand what they were for. Was he unhappy that she got away? Was he unhappy that he could never again be with her?

You must think that I am being naive. How does getting rid of one terrorist change anything? Perhaps you have a point. But if everyone didn't do their bit for the world, it would continue to be full of bullies and terrorists. I had to fight back, and I did it my way. I hope you will understand. In any case, it's all done now.

I remember you had asked me right at the beginning: Who was turning the dials? Now you know. I didn't tell you the truth, not because I didn't trust you, but because I thought if I told you the truth, it'd be difficult for you to fight with the zeal you had shown. You might have decided to leave my case and me, too, and where would that have left me?

But deep in my heart I knew then as I know now that you would've never abandoned me.

The dam broke. Akash couldn't stop shaking, his vision was blurred and his heart on fire. He walked to the side stand, filled a glass with a spirit – he couldn't care less whether it was cognac or whisky or vodka – and drained it down his throat. The liquid burnt his insides as it travelled to his stomach.

> In the end I want you to know that it was not revenge. It was recompense. I wasn't dispensing justice. Who am I to do that?
>
> Writing this letter was a risk, but I am willing to face my fate if that's how it's meant to be. You have every right to turn me in with this letter, and I will never hold it against you. But you must remember your promise to me. You will have to take care of Raghuveer, which I'm sure you won't shy away from. Maybe you will take care of him better than I would.
>
> I hope you'll understand me some day, even forgive me, forget me and move on. I know you love me still. I love you, too, but I don't think we are meant to be together, not in this lifetime. *Agla janam bhi hota hoga,* Akash. I will pray to be with you in my next life, I promise you that.
>
> If you ever loved me, even for the little time we were together, please don't try to find Raghuveer or me.
>
> With best wishes,
> No longer a judge,
> Shilpa Singh

2

Priti, Vansh and Chavi were at Akash's place that evening. He didn't show them the letter earlier in the day, but told them that Shilpa had resigned, because she found it impossible to work in the same place in the same position after all that had happened, which wasn't an outlandish explanation.

'But she didn't have to move from Delhi, did she?' Vansh asked.

'I agree, but it is her decision. She thought it was the right thing to do,' Akash responded, 'at least for a while.' He added the last bit to soften the news that she had just upped sticks and left without saying goodbye to anyone.

'So where has she moved to?' Asked Priti.

'Dehradun, since it's close to Mussoorie where Raghuveer is,' he lied effortlessly.

'It kind of makes sense.'

'And what will she do there?'

'I don't know.'

'Will you be going up to Dehradun to see her?' asked Chavi.

'She's asked me to give her time with Raghuveer alone, exactly like you mentioned, so I'll give it a month or two before I go.'

'See,' Chavi was glad her advice had been useful, 'I told you so.'

Akash realized he was lying for nothing. He could have just as easily told his friends the truth – not about Ismail Khan, but about her moving away forever. It wasn't like they'd go after her to bring her back, but he didn't.

The evening progressed smoothly. Jazz was playing, and they had ordered Chinese from a nearby restaurant: a variety of noodles and rice with three kinds of chicken dishes. They drank a bit too – Akash more than the others. It was hard for him to keep up an optimistic appearance, but he tried his best.

Chavi left at midnight. She said she'd like to visit Shilpa with him whenever he drove to Dehradun, and he promised to check with the judge and take her along. He warned her it could take more than a couple of months at least for Shilpa to be ready to entertain visitors.

The Diwans were getting ready to leave, too. Vansh had one last drink before he walked to the door with his wife. Before they stepped out, Vansh announced that he needed to go to the toilet one last time.

'Best to empty the bladder here than having to stop on the way,' he smiled.

'Of course.'

As they stood at the door waiting for Vansh to return, Priti took Akash's hand in hers and told him, 'Good show, Akash. I admire you for keeping up this positive face the entire evening, but remember I've been your friend for over two decades, and I might not be as bright a practising lawyer like my husband and you, but I can read you a lot better. You were lying all evening, weren't you?'

Akash looked at her but didn't say anything.

'I don't want you to respond or admit anything. There must be a good reason, and you must keep it to yourself. But I think I can say one thing for sure – Judge Shilpa Singh is never coming back into your life.'

He just nodded and closed his eyes.

For once, the best defence lawyer in the country couldn't utter a single syllable in his own defence.

3

It was four in the morning. After everyone had left, Akash had settled down with a drink at his desk in his legal studio. And there he was still, wide awake like an owl. He had lost count of the number of drinks he had consumed over the course of the night.

He opened his drawer, pulled out Shilpa's letter and read it all over again. Tears filled his eyes again, then cascaded down his face. He opened the drawer once more, pulled out a matchbox, lit it and torched the letter. He held the burning pages in his hand until he could and then put it in the glass of whisky on his desk. He was a defence lawyer; he knew better than to keep any sort of evidence against the woman he loved.

'C'est la vie.'

He got up and walked towards his bedroom and whispered into the night, 'I'll always love you.'

AUTHOR'S NOTE AND ACKNOWLEDGEMENTS

The idea of bringing Akash Hingorani and Vansh Diwan together came to me long after the publication of *Unlawful Justice*. However, this time around I wanted Akash to play a central character and not the main defence advocate, otherwise the whole story would have been one-dimensional with him being the key focus. Also, to prevent the defence dominating the story, I brought in someone as brilliant as Ravi Nanda to represent the State and find a loophole in the law to eliminate Akash from the active trial. I think it balances the story, but that's just my opinion.

It took me three attempts and several months to write *Cold Justice*. The first two drafts I rejected halfway through, since I didn't find the narrative interesting enough to engage the reader. However, when my wife, Nidhi, read the first draft – which she usually does – she found some parts uninspiring, so I changed it yet again. I hope the readers appreciate the story as it now stands.

This is my fourth legal thriller. But as always, I would like to draw your attention to the fact that at any given point in time, there are over three crore (thirty million) cases pending in Indian courts. Which means, if I adhered to the true timetable on the hearings of this trial, this book could go on forever. So I've taken the liberty to fast-track the case to bring it to a quick conclusion.

In India, the terms 'lawyer' and 'vakil' are often colloquially used; the official term is 'advocate', as prescribed under the Advocates Act, 1961. I have used creative licence to use the words 'advocate', 'lawyer', 'attorney', 'solicitor' and 'vakil' in both their singular and plural forms to reduce repetitive use of any one of them. The quoted text on pages 120–121 has been borrowed verbatim from indiankanoon.org.

This book wouldn't have been complete without Nidhi, my wife and my partner in crime. A big thank you to Patrick Whittick, my friend, who was the first to edit it. I'm grateful to Mita Kapur and her team at Siyahi who helped me put the story in its current shape and form. Thank you, Sidharth Jain (of The Story Ink), for believing in my stories and always encouraging me to write more. I am indebted to a lot of my lawyer friends in India – it is they who help me write legal thrillers; without their help and advice, stories of this nature would lack authenticity. Also, this book wouldn't be in your hands if it weren't for the editorial team at Pan Macmillan India, specially Teesta Guha Sarkar. I sincerely thank all the wonderful people mentioned above for helping me grow as a writer.

Lastly, there would be no sense in writing if it were not for you, lovely readers. I hope you enjoyed *Cold Justice*.

Love, lots of it,

Vish Dhamija
Facebook: www.facebook.com/vishdhamija
Instagram: @vish_dhamija
Email: vishdhamija@gmail.com